DYING FOR A LIVING

Book 1

KORY M. SHRUM

This book is a work of fiction. Any references to historical events, real people, or real places have been used fictitiously. Other names, characters, places, and incidents are the product of the author's imagination. Any resemblance to actual persons, living or dead, business establishments, events, or locales is entirely coincidental.

No part of this book shall be reproduced or transmitted in any form or by any means without prior written permission of the publisher. Although every precaution has been taken in preparation of the book, the publisher and the author assume no responsibility for errors or omissions. Neither is any liability assumed for damages resulting from the use of information contained in this book or its misuse.

Dying for a Living (2nd edition)
ISBN 978-1-949577-18-1
Copyright © 2014 Kory M. Shrum
All rights reserved.

DYING FOR A LIVING

AN EXCLUSIVE OFFER FOR YOU

Connecting with my readers is the best part of my job as a writer. One way that I like to connect is by sending 2-3 newsletters a month with a subscribers-only giveaway, free stories from your favorite series, and personal updates (read: pictures of my dog).

When you first sign up for the mailing list, I send you at least three free stories right away.

If giveaways and free stories sound like something you're interested in, please look for the special offer in the back of this book.

Happy reading,
  Kory M. Shrum

For Kim

CHAPTER ONE

"Good morning, Mr. Reynolds." I used my best sing-song voice. "Are you ready to die today?"

"I don't think we should stand so close to him," Ally said, pulling me away from the bed. "And don't talk with your mouth full."

Mr. Reynolds still didn't respond when I turned on the bedside lamp, illuminating his bedroom in a butter-yellow glow. I nudged him. *"Good morning."*

His eyes flew open as he jolted upright and pressed his back against the wooden headboard. Crushing the comforter to his chest, he fumbled an earplug from each ear. His darting eyes searched our faces. "Who the hell are you?" he asked.

His graying brown hair was disheveled and thinning in front. His blue eyes squinted against the onslaught of light. He was an enormous man, six feet tall and nearly 300 pounds according to our profile.

I flashed Ally a look. Beside me, my personal assistant was taller by a few inches, making her 5'8" or so. We'd taken the stairs and Reynolds's apartment was warm. She unbuttoned her red A-line coat, revealing her off-white ruffled blouse and dress pants underneath. Her straightened blond hair, chocolate-eyes and tiny diamond nose stud, caught and held the soft light of Reynolds's lamp.

She flashed the photo attached to the front of the file folder at me, and then nodded twice. We were in the right place on the right day.

Of course, I could still have fun with this.

"Burglars," I said with my mouth full of muffin, chewing. "If you could just strip those pillowcases off and fill them with your valuables, we'll be on our way."

His eyes fixed on the half-devoured sugar bomb in my hand. "Is that mine?"

I slowed my chewing, thinking of how best to answer this inquiry. "Could be. It was on your kitchen counter."

"So you took it?" He pushed the comforter off his chest. The disorientation of sleep was wearing off.

"Mr. Reynolds." Ally leaned toward him, pushing her hair behind her ear as it fell forward. Her tone was professional and kind. She was good at dealing with clients. Me? Not so much. "We're here about your death-replacement."

His face remained pinched. One of the problems with letting hospitals orchestrate death-replacements was that clients didn't meet their agents until their actual death-day.

"At the hospital, remember? Your physician helped you schedule a replacement last April," Ally continued. "This is Ms. Jesse Sullivan. She'll be your agent today."

He turned his narrowing eyes to me. "She's the zombie?"

Was it my job to remind him "zombie" was a derogatory term? No, but I did it anyway.

"Necronite," I corrected. I tossed the muffin wrapper into the bedside trashcan. "I'm the necronite here to die so you can keep on a-*livin'*."

I said that last part in the twangy, country music tone our fair city of Nashville was known for. He looked me over head to toe. What did he expect a necronite to look like? Probably not this young or wearing nothing more than jeans and a T-shirt beneath my hoodie.

"How did you get in?"

"Doorman," I answered. "Look—"

Ally cut in, afraid to let my snark go unchecked. "It's important Jesse stays close to you until the incident occurs. As the doctor probably explained during your consultation, she needs to shadow you for the entire day."

Mr. Reynolds turned to the bedside clock. "It's only midnight."

"That's generally when the day starts," I said, stretching my cramped neck to one side. "Your death-day is September 18th and that's today, right?"

"Yes." He didn't sound so sure.

"Ta-da," I said, throwing my arms wide. "Here I am."

Startled, he leaned out of my reach.

Ally elbowed me and I jerked my arms in to protect my ribs. She forced another smile at Reynolds. "We called you earlier, but you didn't answer. We rang the doorbell and knocked, but you still didn't answer."

I folded my arms over my chest, tired of standing over him. "We thought you already died."

He uncurled a beefy fist to show his earplugs. "I wear these when I sleep. I guess I didn't hear you."

"We were concerned, that's all. It's our job to keep you safe," Ally added. Oh, her smile was really shining now. "We apologize for entering your home without permission."

She nudged me with her elbow again. "Yeah, sorry," I grumbled.

His shoulders slumped and he seemed more relaxed the longer Ally smiled at him. It was her gift, I guess, the ability to put people at ease. It certainly wasn't a trait I possessed.

"Sir, if you can just act normal today, follow your usual

routine, we'll be here and ready for anything," Ally grinned. Her weight shifted. She was tired of standing, too. "Please, go back to sleep. We'll remain close in case you need us."

I gave him credit. He did try to go back to sleep, though he left the earplugs out, probably suspicious of us. I guess I wouldn't be able to sleep with two weirdos leaning against my bedroom wall watching me, especially one as fidgety as myself.

Thirty minutes into this babysitting guard duty from which I derived an income, I was *so* bored. But waiting for death to show up was a normal part of the replacement process.

At 7:45 a.m. Reynolds was finally dressed and ready for work. He swore he usually walked to work, so walk we did. Franklin Street was busy, the honking horns conveying that not everyone was happy to be alive on this fine Monday. The morning air held a characteristically September chill to it, so I zipped my dark hoodie up to my chin and warmed my cold hands in my back pockets.

Ally could look as professional as she liked but my clothes would be destroyed by the end of the day—one way or another. Sure I had nicer clothes at home, but when I worked a replacement job, I couldn't wear those. Doctors really liked to cut my clothes off. I mean, they saw my dying body and it was like "Nurse! The scissors, *please*."

The time I was hit and killed by a bus, they cut my clothes off and I was wearing my favorite *Three Stiffs with Picks* T-shirt. The local band's members were necronites like me—which meant we had the same neurological disorder—but they weren't death-replacement agents and had no government employment contract like I did.

Man, *every* time I think about that shirt, I get pissed all over again. They'd signed it, for goodness sake. The hospital ruined it more than the bus did. I could've kept it, damn them. Blood on a rock T-shirt is cool.

Anyway, that was the last straw, so now I only own a plethora of dark jeans and hoodies. Sometimes Ally was able to intervene and save my clothes, but most body fluids stain, so I still went through an entire wardrobe quickly—shoes too. I didn't know how I lost my shoes when I died.

At home, I have a whole basket of shoes I only have one of and I refuse to buy more. They *work*. Like today, I was wearing one red Nike sneaker and one blue Reebok sneaker, each one tied with floppy laces. Maybe that's why Reynolds kept staring at my feet as we walked.

We'd only made it two blocks down the road, pushing through the swarming crowds, past opening shops and businesses, and then the conversation took an inevitable turn.

Mr. Reynolds turned to Ally and flashed what I suspected was a well-rehearsed smile. His voice shifted to a carefully inflected tone. "Are you a zombie too?"

"Necronite," I said, correcting him again. If I wanted to playfully call myself a zombie that was one thing. I was trying to reclaim the word. But people can't just go equating my lifestyle to mindless, brain-eating corpses. "The politically correct term is necronite. You don't call black people the n-word."

"Necronite, got it," he blurted, embarrassed by the fact that I was speaking at full volume. His eyes nervously scanned the passing crowd. He turned to Ally again. "Do you...reanimate also?"

"Ooo, *reanimate*. Breaking out the big words," I said. "No, Ally doesn't die. She is one hundred percent mortal."

I've seen the 'Let's get to know the cute assistant' bit. I don't blame him. Ally is gorgeous. I've made a play for her myself because gorgeous is *gorgeous*. I'm just lucky that Ally likes women or I probably would have looked as ridiculous as Mr. Reynolds here.

"I'm just the hired help," Ally said with a polite smile, which was a permanent fixture when mediating between me and my clients. Maybe it was her round cheeks or tiny cute nose that made people like her. She just looked like a nice person—unless you pissed her off, of course. "Jesse's schedule is hectic, and it's my job to keep her sane."

"You must have your work cut out for you," he said.

Did he just insult me?

I could play. "You're not her type. You need breasts, *bigger* ones."

His jaw set tight. "Is she always this... charming?"

I opened my mouth to show him how charming I could be. Ally shot me a pleading look behind his back. Brinkley, my government-assigned handler, popped into my head. *One more bad review, Jesse, and I'll kill you. A couple of times.* If Mr. Reynolds thought I was a challenge, he should try dealing with Brinkley.

I rolled my eyes at Ally and gave my rehearsed speech.

"Dear Sir or Madam, I am sorry for this inconvenience. In the light of your impending death, this must be a stressful time for you. Please accept my apologies for this situation and let me offer my reassurance that no matter what happens, you can count on me to save your *ass*."

Brinkley made me memorize this verbatim, and to be spiteful, I haven't changed a word. Not even the Sir or Madam part. Okay, maybe I changed *save you* to *save your ass*, but what's the difference really?

Reynolds blinked twice and stared. Appearing to reach some conclusion, he opened the door to his building and entered without saying another word.

The South Tower where Mr. Reynolds worked was huge, stretching far up into the overcast sky. The building looked like a cat to me, with a pointy radio antenna on each side of its roof. We followed him and his swinging briefcase through the revolving glass doors into the building, which smelled like women's perfume and floor polish. Once we had our plastic visitor badges attached, we took the elevator up to Reynolds's office on the fifteenth floor. His office was the coolest, strangest thing I'd ever seen.

It was laid out like a bi-level, encased in glass. The entrance was two glass doors that pushed open. The outer wall was a full window overlooking downtown Nashville. The floor was pale hardwood, shining in the slanted autumn light. A spiraling staircase with see-through steps coiled off to the right, very modern. The lower level held only his secretary's desk and a clear view of the city. Reynolds's desk was located on the upper, loft-like part suspended in the air.

Good thing he wasn't into dresses or the poor secretary would've had more than a downtown view through the clear floor suspended above her desk. Of course, it went both ways. I was sure that he spent his work days enjoying all the sunshine with a side of cleavage.

His desk and bookcase were as transparent as the window behind him. I gave Ally a weary look. She got it.

"We need your blood type," she said, as Reynolds put his briefcase on his desk.

"O-positive, why?"

"This is a lot of glass." I leaned over the metal rail encircling the loft area to see the secretary's desk and floor below. I know people dig the sleek, modern look, but all I saw was an accident waiting to happen. "We might have a problem."

Reynolds looked confused. "The doctor told me any type of death was replaceable."

No reputable doctor would tell him that. I can only do so much for a body. Most of my clients require post-replacement medical care. Point-blank gunshot wounds to the head, for example, are not replaceable. What did he expect me to do? Pick up his brain chunks and stuff his skull?

Ally sat her purse in one of the four bright red chairs opposite Reynolds's desk, the only splash of color in the whole place apart from the hanging fern with its greedy outstretched tendrils.

"Jesse can die for you, but she can't heal your body. If you get cut, you'll need blood."

I surveyed the titles on his bookcase and found not an ounce of pleasure reading, a real bore, this guy. I was looking for a personality, common interests, anything that would make me want to save Reynolds. Nada.

Ally pulled a survey packet and clipboard from her oversized purse, before fishing for a pen. Then she extended the ballpoint with a click, and settled into the chair. "While you set up your computer, I wonder if I can ask you a few questions about your replacement experience?"

Unraveling his laptop cord, Reynolds paused in his unpacking. "She hasn't done anything."

"No, not yet," Ally said, flashing her work-with-me grin. "You'll receive your post-replacement survey in the mail in a week or two. Hopefully, you'll fill it out and return it in the postage-paid envelope. These questions pertain to the enrollment process."

Reynolds bent down and plugged the cord into the surge protector under his desk. "All right, Ms. Gallagher, if it makes your job easier."

She tucked her hair behind her ear and tried to look sweet. "It does, thank you."

Ally might be a lesbian, but she knew how to charm the pants off any man. I rolled my eyes. The two were making me nauseous. She readied her pen. "Did you intentionally plan your death-screening or did your physician recommend it?"

He settled into his seat and turned on the computer. "I

went to get my blood-pressure checked and the doctor recommended it. He explained my insurance rates would drop if I pre-screened."

"How much time passed between the physician's referral and your meeting with the A.M.P.?"

"A.M.P.?"

"Analyst of necro-Magnetic Phenomenon."

"Oh, the psychic," he said, his eyes lighting with recognition. "I met her two days later."

"Psychic is another derogatory term, Mr. Reynolds," I said. Not to mention an inaccurate way to describe the ex-military, medically-altered analysts. My favorite A.M.P. was Gloria. She hated the term psychic and you've got to defend your friends when they aren't around to defend themselves. "We talked about derogatory terms, didn't we?"

The public wasn't supposed to think of them as psychics anyway. Somehow that dirty little secret leaked. PR tried to push A.M.P.s as nothing more than gifted statisticians, brainiacs who could take all the factors of a person's life and guess when they'd die within a twenty-four-hour window, up to one year in advance. Use the word "psychic", or "guess" for that matter, and no one would have invested in the replacement industry because the modern mind only believes in science and money. Of course Lane, my sometimes beau, argued that telling people A.M.P.s were guinea pig soldiers tortured into becoming drug-dependent psychics wouldn't incite much faith either. He had a point.

The Death-Management Industry, including the whole screening through replacement process had a 95 percent success rate. That's almost as good as birth control. No one wanted to be surprised by death and now they didn't have to be. People liked the security. The federal government liked the fact that every aspect of the process was taxable. *Hello*, revenue. And the military liked that they were putting a positive spin on their greatest screw-up of this decade.

Mainstreaming the Death-Management Industry created jobs, fattened pockets and basically pulled all our heads above the waters of a recession. Hell, even China and Japan have launched their own industries in the last few months. Death-screening commercials now outnumbered breast-cancer commercials two to one. However, not everyone accepted the industry.

The Church launched their anti-Death Management campaign not long after the industry was established. But it wasn't until lately, when the conservative party took office, that their power was really felt. Fewer people were screening. Those fat pockets were thinning. I was looking at the possibility of unemployment in a year or two. Frankly, I was okay with that—but for other reasons.

"Your A.M.P.'s name and how long it took for her to complete your evaluation?" Ally asked.

"Gildroy, Godfrey, or...," his voice trailed. His eyes glanced down, unfocused. "I can't remember. The doctor called early the following week and asked me to come back in to discuss my options."

"How did you feel when you first learned the news?"

He leaned back in his chair, running his thick fingers through his hair. "You mean, when the doctor told me some psychic—sorry, A.M.P.—said I was going to die? It's not the conversation one professional has with another. I didn't believe it at first."

Ally kept scrawling on the page, nodding. "When the doctor informed you of the analyst's results, did he make your options clear?"

He scratched his chin. "Either I took my chances and hoped the day passed without incident or I took precautions."

"Was it a difficult decision?" Ally asked, looking up from the page.

"Not really," he answered. "I get the money back if nothing happens. I'd say my life is worth more than a mere fifty grand."

"That's right," Ally said.

I'd also have to return the fee if I screwed up and he died. I could die myself and wouldn't even get to keep my 20% cut. Since he'd be dead, I guess that didn't matter to him.

"Last question. Would you recommend death-replacement to a family member or friend?"

"Ask me that one at the end of the day," he said. "Once I see what happens."

Behind one of the books I found a little panda, the kind you squeeze and its eyes bulge out of its head. When you squeezed the panda, it squeaked. I pointed it at Reynolds and gave it a squeeze. "What do you *do* here?"

He came around the desk and took the panda from me the way one might seize their mother's urn from a child's grubby and unreliable fingers.

"I'm a marketing and media consultant," he said. "We do advertising for local businesses, night clubs, and popular consumer products."

I'd bet he was one of our very own PR guys. Otherwise, I wasn't quite sure why Brinkley put his file in my bin. Not that Brinkley would tell me if I asked. Boss Brinkley was pretty tight-lipped unless he was giving direct orders.

The secretary went home at 5:00 p.m. and I'd been working seventeen hours straight, so I decided to dig through her desk to ward off sleepiness.

In addition to an impressive array of writing utensils, her desk had several pictures of her kids and a coffee cup that said, "Procrastinate and you tempt fate!" A real go-getter. I played with her label maker, placing labels that read "Zombie touched this. Eek!" on everything: her chair, her cup, her computer. I spared the kids' pictures.

Ready to surf the internet, I pressed the power button and was startled by a loud *pop*. Deep inside the computer tower something fizzled and a wisp of smoke wafted through the vent holes.

Shit.

I thunked my forehead against the desktop. Second computer this week. It was like I short-circuited electronics by my touch alone.

I didn't even have time to come up with an excuse for exploding the secretary's computer when a familiar sinking sensation washed over me. My grip tightened on the edge of the desk.

"Ally," I said, calling her name as loud as I could manage as my throat tightened around the words.

Mr. Reynolds froze in mid-motion. Ally spoke to him, but too softly for me to hear.

Reynolds hesitated. Clients often freeze up when I start to react. No one wants to die. To the clients, in this moment before it happens, it seems as if any movement could be the wrong one. He stared at me through the glass floor.

Sensing death was like a panic attack. I tried to breathe against the pressure in my chest. Nothing was actually wrong with me, except that some part of me knew what was coming, and that part of me panicked. My body flooded with adrenaline and was ready for anything. Here in this bright office, it seemed unlikely I was going to get hit by a bus, stabbed, crushed or shot, right?

Wrong.

I closed my eyes and tried to quell this sick feeling. Before I opened them again, something heavy came crashing right through the desk, knocking me backwards out of the chair. I hit the back of my head on the window-wall with a thump and my ears rang on impact. Shards of glass from the secretary's desk sprayed my face like water. I tried to shield myself with my open hand and swore like crazy.

"Who designs this shit." I pulled a large sliver of glass out of my left forearm. It had gone straight through my arm. Blood spurted out of the wound, ruining my jeans. *Again*.

Ally came down the stairs, taking the steps one at a time, carefully holding onto the rail. Good girl. Death-replacement was a one-on-one exchange. I couldn't die for two people at once.

"Mr. Reynolds?" It was his body that had fallen on top of me, lying now in the mess of the secretary's shattered desk. I kicked a chunk of desk off of me and I pulled myself out from under him, dragging my burning arm through broken glass.

"Mr. Reynolds, can you hear me?" I checked his pulse and it was faint, slowing.

I opened his suit jacket and pressed my hands to his chest as Ally's voice echoed through the room. She gave the address and situation to the emergency operators on the phone. The tiny glass chunks in my arms and legs burned like hell as they worked their way in deeper into my skin. I saved the freaking out until after she hung up.

"What the hell did you say to him? We don't do suicides." I was talking too fast. Okay, so having a body drop on me unexpectedly caught me off guard. At least I couldn't be blamed for the broken computer now. "And what the hell is it with fat men falling on me? That's two this week. I'm like one hundred twenty pounds, assholes."

It became a race to see who could speak the fastest with the widest eyes.

"I didn't make him jump, *thank you*. I told him when you get pale like this it means it's about to happen. So instead of paying attention to his own two feet, he watched you. He tripped on the laptop cord and rolled right over that damn rail." She pointed up, looking freaked too.

"You have to stop telling them they're about to die," I said. I leaned close to his ear and shouted, "And you have to get *wooden* desks."

As if reacting to the thunder of my own voice, my vision gave over completely, switching from dizzying spottiness to full-blown waves of color.

The room was a shifting aurora borealis of heat and light. Even weird shit can be comforting, when you expect it.

I really wished Ally could see it.

"Jesse, he isn't looking so good."

I focused on the man still partially in my lap. Reynolds was no longer a warm red-orange tinged with yellow like Ally. He was green, edging his way into the dormant blue-gray of the floor, the desk, and the walls. It was my job to keep the blue from overtaking him.

I couldn't explain what I do exactly.

Death was the transformation of energy. I admit I was guessing. When someone was about to die, a tiny black hole was created inside them. Like a black hole in space, it looked like an empty swirling vortex. This vortex was what sucked all the warm, living colors out of a person, leaving nothing behind that could survive.

My job as a replacement agent was to convince the fleeting red of Mr. Reynolds, so ready to burn up its little flame and become a dormant blue, it really didn't want to go into that swirling drain after all. Somehow I did this by *willing* it.

My colors have never matched Ally's, Brinkley's, or anyone who'd accompanied me in the room during a replacement. Lane too, I imagine, would be a more vibrant hue if I ever got a good look at him. The point was I seemed a welcome home for blue flame since I was *always* blue flame.

Not the cold blue of furniture or buildings, more like a sparkly blue. Electric blue.

With Reynolds's flame drawn into my own, it gave his red-warm fire room enough to burn. But there was a special spark I was looking for, and I had to find it inside him and keep it from being washed away.

The elevator opening and Ally shouting to the paramedics seemed like sounds underwater, as I focused harder on Reynolds.

"Hurry, Jesse," she whispered.

A hot-cold chill settled into the muscles in my back and coiled around my navel like an invisible snake as I pushed my own flame further into Reynolds.

There—a spark where our flames danced around each other. Reynolds's chest rose suddenly, jerking as he gasped, like gasoline thrown on the blaze.

But even though I scooped Reynolds's precious spark out of danger's way, the vortex didn't simply close. Somebody had to go through that death drain. Unfortunately, that somebody had to be me.

So I exhaled one last breath and gave myself completely to the waiting darkness.

CHAPTER TWO

The ornate tile above Kirk's head came into focus. Soft, creamy swirls and the smell of carnations welcomed me to the land of the living. I tried to sit up but stiff pain shot through my shoulders and back.

"Be still," Kirk commanded, pushing me back down. It was the warning tone a grandfather gives his unruly grandchild.

My mortician Kirk loomed over me. He was well over six feet tall, bald, his skin the color of cocoa beans. His square frame cast a long dark shadow as I lay stretched out on his work table.

I hated *everything*.

The color of the walls, those damn stinky flowers, Kirk's face. I was sore and wanted to walk it off, not lie here in pain.

Kirk's face was a mask of concentration as a thin applicator brush jutted at my eye from one hand. He was an artist with a canvas.

"Smells good," I said, trying to say something nice. It was a tip from Ally. *If you feel hateful, just say something nice about the person.*

"Organic Rosemary Tint," he said.

Real dead people don't care about their cosmetics. However, with developing necronite-mortician relationships, a whole line of organic cosmetics for customers like me had spawned. No amount of Maybelline would make me look okay after a replacement. I have a super-fast metabolism and some regenerative healing skills, but I need help putting parts of me back together. Which is why I needed Kirk.

Morticians were used to working with stiffs, so I could trust him to fix me up at any stage of decomposition. The hospital was responsible for making sure all my organs and appendages were accounted for and Kirk made sure I didn't scare small children when I ambled home.

"Did you notice anything strange?" I asked.

He paused, the brush hovering over my bottom lip. "Your heart beating in my hands is strange."

"No, I mean anything unusual," I said. "Anything you don't usually see?"

He considered my question. The he returned to painting my face. "No. Why?"

I thought about the strange electrical problems I'd had lately: coffee makers, light bulbs and the secretary's computer, all exploding on their own. That wasn't normal for me and it scared me a little—the way missing my period or losing a wallet scared me—not the mishap itself so much as the possibility of greater mayhem.

Kirk grinned and pulled off his glove with a snap. "All finished."

He packed up his black case, arranging the box of gloves, varied brushes and cosmetics. He pulled off the other glove with a second snap and threw it in the waste bin. The fact that I could turn my head at all said I wasn't "zombie-shuffle" sore.

"When did I reboot?" I asked.

He turned his wrist over and read his watch. "Four hours ago."

That explained why the rigor mortis wasn't so bad. My cells would've had time to push some of the calcium out and lessen the muscle contraction, but the only cure for rigor mortis was a hot bath, massage, lots of gentle stretching and most importantly, time.

"What was my D.T.?" I meant "down-time" or "death-time." Necronites stay dead—no heartbeats, no breathing, actual decomposition and all that—until our brains reboot. Then we experience the coma state, in this case, the four-hour stint Kirk mentioned, while our bodies heal enough to support themselves and regain consciousness. Scientific minds are politely calling this whole process NRD, or Necronitic Regenerative Disorder. No hocus pocus here, folks.

Kirk looked at the ceiling as if calculating in his head. "About fifteen hours. We're coming up on 9:00 a.m."

"Tuesday?"

"That's the one."

I loved it when I slept through the night and woke up at a normal hour. It made the death-life transition easier.

"Where's Ally?"

He wiped the bristles of a dirty makeup brush clean with a towel. "Gone since she delivered your body last night. Brinkley's here to take you home."

On cue, Kirk reached over and touched a sensor, letting Brinkley know he could come into the room now.

As soon as I saw my boss, I fell against the bed and faked a coma.

"That shit won't work on me," a familiar voice said and I didn't feel the least bit compelled to quit playing dead. I'd rather be dead than deal with Brinkley any day.

"Get up," he said, hands on his hips.

I groaned and dragged myself from Kirk's table. My legs instantly stiffened as my feet connected with the floor. Groaning, I stretched each limb before rolling my eyes up to meet Brinkley's.

"Have I ever told you how much fun you are?" I asked.

"More than once."

Brinkley was a tad shorter than Kirk with the same wide shoulders and early signs of a beer gut. I thought they knew each other from the past. I knew Brinkley was in the military at some point before joining the FBRD, the Federal Bureau of Regenerative Deaths. Maybe he knew Kirk back then, and that's why Brinkley set him up as my mortician when we relocated from St. Louis.

Whatever his past, Brinkley was more like a cop than a soldier now, given his work with FBRD. But his graying hair and sour face said it all. He'd seen some things in the world that he hadn't liked and he'd been dealing with them ever since.

I often felt like I was one of those things.

"I got another batch of your reviews," Brinkley said.

Brinkley waved a thin stack of post-replacement survey cards at me before tossing them for me to catch. They were held together by a rubber band. Each sported a different color ink and handwriting.

I groaned. I could already feel the lecture coming.

"My personal favorite, and I quote," he said, through tight lips. "Ms. Sullivan is like a human Chihuahua who barks at anything that moves."

"I don't bark." I flipped through the cards.

"I believe it's a comment on your constant sarcasm," Brinkley said. He slipped his hands into his pockets. "Not that any of us have had the pleasure of experiencing said sarcasm."

"My commentary is not constant," I argued. I flicked the

card. "That woman was mad because I called her a hoarder. She had, like, two million creepy dolls."

Kirk grunted, suppressing a laugh. "What kind?"

"Porcelain—and some of them were clowns," I answered, stretching my neck long, left then right. My neck muscles ached like I'd spent the night head-banging. "If I really was a mean person I would've teased you about that stain on your pants."

All of our eyes went to Brinkley's crotch and the dark stain about four inches below his gun.

I arched an eyebrow. "I could say—"

Brinkley stopped me, ears bright red. "That—" He refused to look at his crotch, which resulted in his pointing at it. "—is your fault."

"I'd remember making you piss blood."

His tone turned dangerously even. "The doctors missed a piece of glass. When I pulled it out, you squirted on me," he said, jaw tight. "It would seem even your corpse is a sarcastic little shit."

Kirk, whose eyes had merely gone back and forth between us as we argued, gave a polite cough.

"If you'll excuse me," Kirk said, squeezing my shoulder. Kirk and Brinkley did a male nod thing. Brinkley and I were left standing in the back room.

We've worked together for the last seven years, yet I found being alone with him awkward. Maybe awkward wasn't the right word—uncomfortable.

"I'm scared to even ask how it went with Mr. Reynolds," he asked, relaxing his shoulders a little. "I hope you gave him a nice impression of necronites. We pay him to make you look good."

"I saved his life," I said. "If that even counts."

"That's only part of the job."

"The hard part," I mumbled. "The part I don't even get thanked for."

"You have to comfort them. People need to feel safe," he said, as if he hadn't said this a bazillion times.

"They aren't safe." I thought of all the ungrateful jerks I've had to deal with. How many lives had I saved? Sixty-seven. Sixty-seven, yet I could count on one hand the people who'd actually thanked me for it. "If they were safe they wouldn't need me to begin with." I made a big show of flipping through the survey cards without actually looking at them.

"Are you trying to get fired?" he asked.

Yes, I thought. I dreamed about quitting my job twenty times a day, about the clever things I'd say to Brinkley at the moment of regaining my freedom.

"It's not like it's raining zombies or anything."

"Don't use that word." His anger was back, unfurling as fast as mine.

"Fine. *Necronites* are like 2 in 100 people. You've managed to convince less than half of us saps to be death-replacement agents. Act like you can call up an old friend to do my job. *Puh*-lease."

Silence filled the room, amplified by the whirl of air seeping through the overhead vents. I'm not so good with silence so I kept talking.

"I just wish you wouldn't work me twice as much as the other agents."

His eyes narrowed. "What's that supposed to mean?"

"I mean that I have to do twice as many replacements as Cindy. And Cooper weasels his way out of a replacement every five minutes."

"I'm not their boss. I'm your boss."

Too late to turn back now. "The point is I work harder and I get yelled at more. That's the definition of unfair."

Brinkley's face went from white to red. "You don't know how good you've got it."

"Clearly," I huffed.

"Cooper is on a military contract," Brinkley said. "He goes where they want, when they want. He doesn't get a say about where he eats or sleeps. You and Cindy were both hired on as personal consultants. You should appreciate that."

I clucked, indignant. "Why?"

"Cindy and Cooper have clocked five times as many hours as you in community seminars, hospitals, police stations," he continued, waving his hand. "They do that to protect you. All of you. A necronite's rights are void upon death in Utah and Alabama. They amended their state constitutions saying that once you die the first time, you don't deserve rights anymore. You are no longer a person. What if they do that here in Tennessee? The bill is already drafted. And I can't even trust you to behave in a five-minute interview."

"Because you think I'm a social cripple. I don't know why," I said. I pointed at the feedback card on top. "This person gave me a three."

"Out of ten."

"Isn't one the best?" I asked.

"Ten is best," he said. "And you promised me ten years."

The temperature shifted. An imaginary cube of ice slid down my spine and Brinkley's eyes grew dangerously steady. When he went real still and quiet like this, it freaked me out. If he were a cat, his tail would be flicking, signaling that he was about to pounce.

He took a step closer.

His large body blocked the light from the hallway, making the room darker and smaller. I was trapped.

He placed his hands on his hips making himself look even bigger. His voice dropped. "After what I did for you, Sullivan, you owe me."

I looked up into his black eyes. "Do you enjoy blackmailing your slaves?"

"Slavery is a life sentence," he said. "Which is what you'd be serving in the Illinois State Penitentiary if it wasn't for me."

He was right of course.

The suffocating smell of smoke and the sounds of sirens in the distance came back clear and sharp. Wooden rafters crashed down around me as the flesh of a man, charred and black, roasted in front of my very eyes. My very first death had been a barn fire—and not an accident.

I only remembered vague bits and pieces of my life before that death. I didn't even remember Ally though she told me we've been friends since childhood. What few early memories I had were not of birthday parties or the prom.

But I remember killing a man.

I pushed against the memory until I was dizzy, grabbing the edge of the table.

Brinkley knew he'd won. "And don't talk to me about your emotional suffering. What if I added a year to your contract for every ounce of grief you give me?"

I bit my lip until the room and Brinkley came into focus, but I couldn't get the smell of burning flesh out of my nose.

"I can't help it." I shrugged. I had to do this to lessen the horrible tightness between my shoulder blades. "It's what I do."

"Here's what else you're going to do." He took another step toward me and I stepped back. So much for standing my ground. "You're going to do your job. Smile until your lips bleed. Bend over backwards to make your clients happy. Become the poster child for death replacement until every last one of those extremists believe necronites have souls. Saving lives is only a small part of what we need to accomplish here. We have to change the world."

"Gawd, you don't want much, do you?"

"I mean it, Sullivan," he said. "You might not take your job seriously, but it is serious. This is a war between us and them and I want you front and center. You think I make your life hard but believe me, I know plenty of people who want to make it harder."

"Very motivational, chief."

He turned to leave. "If your next review is anything less than a seven, I'm pulling the plug and you can spend the rest of your life wearing an orange jumper."

"That's it? End of discussion?" Someone needed to teach Brinkley how to communicate.

"Just wait until the prison inmates hear about your talents," he added, finally moving toward the door. "They'll enjoy discovering all the ways you can die."

CHAPTER THREE

Greenbrook was a cute suburb of Nashville, enterable by two roads that intersected on either side. Fifty or so houses sat on six blocks. The houses weren't uniform, which I liked, although each unit had a certain similarity. For instance, like mine, most were two stories high with an attached garage. The exteriors varied in their brick, stone, or siding combinations, but the garage doors were usually white, windowless slats.

Lots of trees and flowerbeds and a running trail wove in and out of the woods to form a two-mile loop. Each house had an acre or more of grass and trees surrounding it. I walked up my driveway, past the burgundy Japanese maples with their starfish shaped leaves. Ally planted those last year. They complemented my house's white-gray marbled brick exterior and black shutters nicely.

I padded across the tiles to the sliding glass door, throwing my jacket on a chair and my keys on the counter on my way to greet Winston. The pug was a heap of wrinkles in his doggie bed, legs spread wide, and his face pressed desperately into an empty food dish.

"I know Ally already fed you."

Drool oozed from the side of his mouth and he batted his sad brown eyes at me.

"You're disgusting," I said, lifting him from the bowl and snuggling him. "But I love your squish face so *much*."

"Hello," a voice called from the living room.

I carried Winston in my arms to the edge of the couch where I found Lane. He was tall, but to me everyone was tall, packing a good deal of muscle in his slender frame. Lucky for him, I had one of those large sectional couches. He'd never have been able to stretch out as he was now, one arm behind his head like a makeshift pillow and other hand lying across his stomach, if I had anything smaller.

He smiled that mischievous, knee-buckling smile. He wore pressed, black jeans and a short-sleeved button up dress shirt the same ocean blue as his eyes. If he was dressed so nice, and smelling so nice—he was either here for sex, or he'd come from his mother's house. If it was from his mother's no doubt she lectured him about his dark hair being a month overdue for a cut. Though I'd never had said a word, loving the way it curled at the ends around his ears, chin and brow.

He also wore a smiley face button pin above his left breast, near the collar. I'd given it to him on our first and only date to a carnival where I'd won it. I was trying to win a goldfish, but twenty dollars and forty terrified fish later, the carney gave me the button and politely told me to go the-F away.

Ok, yes, so Lane and I went on one date. One. Why only one date? Carnival games, gut-twisting rides, and cotton candy beneath the swirl of an artificial lightshow had somehow turned into mind-blowing sex—in my bed no less. Mind-blowing anything was bad for a zombie. Let me say I reacted as any sensible person would. I promptly locked him out, leaving him on my front porch, clutching his remaining clothes. I'd tricked him by saying I'd left my phone in the car and of course he volunteered to get it. Mean, I know, but how else could I get him to leave? He's twice my size.

To my credit, I've since learned that asking works just fine and no longer resort to such trickery. But in the beginning, I hadn't known that.

"And you're here for—?" I already knew why he was here.

"I was hoping it was one of those days," he smiled—a small but hopeful smile.

One of those days—a sex with no strings attached day. Because even though I didn't want to be someone's girlfriend, Lane and I were fan-TAS-tic, so I had a hard time keeping the boy out of my bed.

"Perhaps," I said and scratched the pug behind his ears. "But I'm awfully sore."

"I can be gentle," he said.

I grinned and Lane was on me. Poor Winston was flopped onto the couch like an unwanted remote and I was lifted up and carried to my bedroom.

"Okay, not too gentle," I said and bit his neck, leaving a small crescent moon of teeth marks. "Don't treat me like I've got a broken hip."

"Do you?" he asked with a quirk of his lips.

"Not this time," I said. To make my point, as soon as he set me on the bed I started to tear off his clothes. But when it was my turn, I always thought a little too much about my autopsy scar. Lane made a point of kissing it just to prove it didn't bother him, and while I found this gesture sweet, it didn't completely erase that moment of panic I got when I removed my shirt in front of anyone.

I pushed my insecurities aside and gave in.

He stayed true to his word and was careful with me—except for where it mattered. I had to change positions a few times when a muscle seized up, but overall it was just *wham, bam, thank you man*.

I felt a million times better when I woke up in the gray shadow of my room. Brinkley's lecture and Mr. Reynolds's snide remarks had faded into the background as night grew thicker around us. Sunset fell in orange ribbons across the bed sheets and through my open bedroom window a soft breeze cooled the sweat on my skin.

Lane was a dark lump beside me. He was stretched long and the curve of his neck, shoulder and chest muscles collected the pooling darkness. I watched his chest rise and fall.

My phone vibrated on the nightstand. Ally's name and picture showed up on the little square screen. "Did you make it home okay?"

"Yeah."

"Good," she said and then sighed. "But I think we have a problem."

Of course.

"I checked the appointment book and we have a replacement scheduled. At midnight, we're supposed to meet"—the sound of a page flipping crackled through the phone. "—Eve Hildebrand."

"Brinkley's an asshole," I grumbled and Lane curled up to me. I threw his heavy arm off of my shoulder and pushed him away. He seemed to have forgotten that we don't cuddle. "I haven't even healed."

"That's the thing," Ally said. "I don't believe Brinkley filed it."

"Who else could have?" Brinkley was the only one with access to my office and the only one who signed off on replacements. There was a bin on my desk and even if Ally and I did a million consultations, I only replaced the clients whose folders were in my bin. And Brinkley was the only one who put names in that bin. He was like God in this way, deciding who deserved a second chance.

"I don't know, but it's strange. The profile is for a hooker," Ally said.

"Since when did you care about non-traditional occupations," I asked, honestly surprised.

Ally was one of those tree-hugging, I-love-everyone types. In her senior photo, she had dreadlocks and hemp jewelry, though you'd never know it for all her professionalism now.

"I don't care what she does for money. I mean, I care because it's sad, but she doesn't exactly fit our typical client profile," she said. "There's barely any information on her, like no address, no medical history, no anything. It's only her name and a phone number."

Lane stirred and I switched the phone to the other ear. "Did you ask Brinkley?"

"I can't get ahold of him," she said. "Can you call him?"

That unhappy feeling crept into my gut again. I was hoping to avoid Brinkley for a week if I could get away with it. "I think he's tired of me questioning his methods."

"Yes, but something about this is wrong," she said.

"Does it have Brinkley's signature?" I asked. "Is the money present and accounted for and the paperwork filed?"

"Yeah, but—"

"Then we have to do it," I said. Or run the chance of going to prison.

Ally exhaled slowly. She didn't like it, but she wasn't going to fight me. "Do you want me to pick you up at eleven?"

"Please. And can you bring me a coffee. Triple shot. I'm already exhausted."

"Why wouldn't you be?" Lane purred.

I hadn't realized he was awake. The dead silence in the phone said Ally had certainly heard him. She hung up without even saying goodbye.

Lane propped himself up on one elbow, watching me watch the phone.

"I thought you told her we were dating."

"First of all," I said, angry now because I half-believed Lane had said something on purpose just to upset Ally—some kind of territorial male bullshit. "You and I aren't dating. We're fucking and there's a difference. Secondly, she does know, but I don't feel like I have to shove it in her face every five seconds."

He got out of bed and pulled on his pants.

I didn't want to be the only one naked here, so I pulled on my clothes too, shirt first.

"You are very considerate," he said. He ran his hand through his hair but wouldn't look at me. I didn't know what else to say, so I picked up a fallen pillow from the floor, tossed it onto the bed and stormed past him.

"I'm going to check the mail."

"You do that," he fired back. "I'm leaving anyway."

I could be just as stubborn. "*Bye.*"

If he said bye, I didn't hear it. I ran down the steps and out the front door.

Why were people so hard to deal with? Why did they have to be so emotional? God, my job came with so many risks, so many complications, that I wanted something easy. Something that wasn't so serious. Hell, tomorrow I could start hallucinating big-eyed aliens come to probe my ass because my brain suddenly decides it has had enough of death-replacing and rips itself in two. It happens. My old mentor Rachel—the ex-agent who trained me—was already locked up for losing her shit. What if I spent the rest of my life in a loony bin, eating mashed bananas? That's my possible future, so why the hell would I want to think beyond today?

Why didn't Lane understand that?

At the end of the driveway, the first few yellow, orange

and red leaves rolled down the paved street, a flurry of them, guided by the light breeze. I tried to let the air relax the tension between my shoulders as I listened to the dried leaves scratch along the concrete. I closed my eyes and took a breath but when I opened my eyes I saw a bird.

A big black crow hopped at my side and cawed loudly. I yelped in surprise, catching my hand on the mailbox's metal red flag. After shaking the pain out and sucking at a red gash, I retrieved the mail slowly. I was afraid the bird might peck my eyes out if I made any sudden movements. His sleek, black body was such a contrast to the gray concrete, that he looked wet.

I scanned what was visible of the block. The orange-pink sunset was settling between the houses and cars, giving their edges a soft glow. The bird continued to do that side-to-side wobble of a creature unaccustomed to using its tiny legs. He defaulted to a sort of flap, hop, shuffle, like he was trying to get my attention with this little dance.

"Go on. Shoo," I said, irritated. "You're creeping me out."

He cawed loudly, spread his black wings out on either side of him, and looked as if he would fly right at my face. Maybe I screamed once because Lane appeared out of nowhere. He was dressed now, but hadn't done a thing about his mess of hair.

"What's wrong?"

"That crazy bird," I said, pointing my mail in that direction, but the bird was gone. There wasn't even a single speck of black in the sky.

"I don't see any bird," he said. He pulled his keys out of his pocket and unlocked his truck.

"I guess you scared it off."

"That's what I'm good for," he grumbled and got into his truck.

"Are you really going to pout?" I grabbed his door. "When did you become such a girl?"

He put his keys in the ignition like he was going to leave me without even saying goodnight. He just got laid like a million times and he wanted to be mad about it? Seriously?

"Fine. See you around, I guess." I would, of course, since my office and his comic bookstore were in the same building. It's how we met. He owns the building, some inheritance from a dead family member, and I rent one of the offices. Brinkley chose the location, so it wasn't like I chose my office space for the hottie landlord. Though that sounded like something I'd totally do.

"Jesse, wait." He stopped me when I was halfway to the front door.

I slowly walked back to the truck and propped my elbows on his open window frame.

"I'm not mad," he said.

"You sure seem mad."

"I'm not mad at you anyway." His voice was soft and sincere.

"Who are you mad at?" I asked. "I hope it's not Ally and that's why you shove our—whatever—in her face."

"Relationship."

"Arrangement," I corrected.

"I can't—" he made a gesture to imply the word he couldn't even say.

"Don't I make it easy?" I asked.

He gripped the steering wheel until his knuckles went white. "Men actually do have feelings. And if you haven't noticed, I care about you, enough that I can't—" he sucked air and when he spoke again, his voice was so much softer. "I can't just *fuck* you without wanting more."

"Then maybe we shouldn't have sex," I said.

He didn't say anything right away and my heart skipped a beat.

"Yeah, maybe," he said finally and the pounding grew louder.

He was going to *agree* with me? Don't people believe in idle threats anymore?

"Okay." I had no idea what else to say. I was choking on this horrible lump in my throat. That's twice someone had said this to me. *I want more.*

First Ally, now Lane.

Lane leaned out of the window and kissed me goodbye—a very soft, very sweet, brush of the lips. Then he turned the ignition over and was gone.

CHAPTER FOUR

When midnight rolled around neither Eve nor Brinkley answered their phones. A very bad feeling told me to walk away from this replacement. But Brinkley's threats just kept coming back and the more I thought about it, the more I suspected this was some kind of test. I had to do it—no matter what. When Eve finally called us back at 6:30 a.m. I refrained from screaming, "What kind of hooker doesn't work nights?"

She insisted we meet her at the Vanguard Hotel downtown at 8:00 a.m. and gave us the room number. She wasn't getting the "I have to shadow you for the full twenty-four hours. Who knows when you'll die?" explanation. Obviously, she didn't realize how serious this was.

Brinkley remained M.I.A. so I had to call Lane in to help us. I *really* didn't want to but we needed someone else to carry my body out. The paramedics would give Eve priority, so the extra muscle would help, depending on what kind of replacement this turned out to be. With surprising enthusiasm, Lane agreed, though I'd been certain I wouldn't see him for days. Despite the freshness of our argument, I was relieved to have him. Ally, on the other hand, was not.

In the car, Lane made me swear not to use the word hooker. She was to be called a "sex worker." The clarification didn't tell me why the hell Brinkley put a sex worker's file in my bin. A personal favor? That humored me.

Eve entered her tenth floor suite, and threw her purse and oversized black bag on the floor with an air of irritation that suggested she regarded this whole situation as a total pain in the ass. The idea that she and Brinkley had a past seemed less likely.

The room was gorgeous, with a view of downtown, the park, and river below. The wind-caught river shimmered like iridescent fish scales. Opposite one wall was a floor-to-ceiling mirror. It made the room feel bigger. The king-sized mattress sat between two end tables. A desk made of dark cherry wood matched the armoire, and drawers for clothes underneath. I'd have found the room more impressive, if I hadn't been distracted by why I was here in the first place.

"We should put the camera here," Lane said.

"I don't want to be taped," Eve said. Her bleached hair was pulled up high in a bun and her button-up gray jacket heightened her naughty-but-nice persona.

"This isn't a pornographic video, it is a security camera," Lane said. "And it wouldn't be necessary if you'd let us stay in the room."

Eve removed mascara, a compact and lipstick from her purse. "Want to watch, do you, sweetie?"

"I need to know the second she dies so we can carry her out," Lane said.

Ally snorted and my back muscles tensed. Lane's did too, his shoulders rolling up toward his ears, but he didn't look away from Eve. As she touched up her makeup, Eve stole glances at Lane's tattoo as if confronted by a rough-tongued rogue for the first time. But surely she'd met tougher men in her line of work.

"No," Eve repeated.

Gritting his teeth he said, "It's for your safety."

"No."

Ally's arms crossed. I rocked back and forth on my heels waiting for this to get crazier, but Lane didn't say anything. Defeated, he bent down beside the bed to pack up the camera. Legally, he couldn't install the camera without her consent. But legally, Eve wasn't even allowed to do whatever —whomever—she meant to do in this room. I crossed my fingers and called Brinkley again, only to have it go straight to his voicemail.

This is a test, Jess. To see how high you're willing to jump. What'll it be? The moon or prison?

To combat the heat of the crowded room, I opened the window. Broadway Avenue below was infected with chanting anti-necronite protesters and honking horns, none of which made me feel better. Ally hadn't even removed her red coat. Irritated by Lane's presence, she sighed, grumbled and muttered under her breath as she shuffled the paperwork for the fourth or fifth time.

Ally's job was to make sure there weren't any physical obstacles to prevent the swift removal of my corpse. She had put down blankets in the car so I wouldn't dirty the seats, in case an ambulance wasn't called. Her big brown eyes were focused, her dark lashes reflecting light from the high windows. She slipped her hair behind her ears, revealing her furrowed brow and angry mouth.

"You'll want to take this stairway." Ally said to Lane, pointing at the map with her index finger. "It leads right to the parking lot."

"Why can't I take these stairs to the lobby?" Lane asked.

"Because—" Ally huffed. "Those stairs are marked off for

the housekeeping staff. You don't want to start down them just to find yourself blocked by a towel cart."

"We don't know what time the replacement will happen," Lane countered. His voice mirrored her irritation. "There might not even be a towel cart. How would they even get a towel cart into a stairwell, anyway?"

"Look, the desk person told me this was the best way in the event of a fire." She jabbed the map with her finger. "But even though this is your first replacement job, you're the expert now."

"I don't need practice to be good at something."

Ally's face started to match the red shade of her coat. "No wonder Jesse keeps you around."

"She doesn't keep me around for my learning curve."

"Whoa," I jumped in, signing time-out with my hands. "A bit of professionalism, please?"

I noticed Eve had paused in applying her makeup to stare at us like we were a circus. Damn, I knew I was going to get a big, fat ZERO on that survey card.

"Y'all about done?" Eve asked and arched a perfectly penciled eyebrow. "We've only got about five minutes until showtime."

This argument ended with Ally fussing over the paperwork she'd already organized and Lane huffing over the hotel map he'd already memorized. Oh, what fun we were having.

I wondered if all the bickering made Ally forget about the prereplacement survey or if she just didn't think Eve would be open to the questions.

At least she remembered my paperwork. It proved my occupation, in the event the authorities wanted to know what the hell we were doing up here. If someone had walked in right now, do the math: the three of us, a prostitute, one bed and a video camera. Throw in a corpse, a.k.a. me, and the authorities might be more than curious. All of this on top of the fact that my handler was MIA, the need to defend myself felt more immediate.

Eve forced Lane and Ally from the room at 8:25 a.m., wanting them gone before her first patron—or whatever the hell you call such a connoisseur—showed up. I was more nervous about the two of them alone together in the hallway than what the hell I might expect once left alone with a sex worker. I watched Lane close the door behind them with a feeling of dread that left my limbs heavy and heart racing.

"How will you explain why I'm here?" I asked Eve once we were alone. Still by the window, I glanced at the tiny people below, pulsing like blood platelets through the clotted streets.

She had her hands in the front of her shirt again, lifting one breast and then the other. "I'll think of something."

I was scared to ask what "something" might be.

"What are they screaming about down there?" she asked, now satisfied with her breasts inches higher on each side.

"The Vanguard agreed to hold the first ever NRD conference next month. The Church isn't so happy about it," I answered. I only knew this because Ally told me.

"I wish they'd shut up," she said. Her cheeks flushed. "It's worse than the abortion clinic."

I assumed she meant the women's health clinic on 4th and State. "They do more there than abortions. I'm sure people appreciate the free yearly exams and birth control too."

Eve smirked. "You ever even been to that place?"

I shifted my weight. "No."

Let's just say I wasn't afraid of dying of cervical cancer.

She shrugged. "It's a nice place."

"You say it like you go there a lot."

"Free STD testing," she said.

I must have made a face. "You use protection." It didn't come out like a question.

She folded her arms over her chest. "I do what I need to do to keep my baby in a good school."

I was at a loss as to what to say. Then she handed me a picture: brunette pigtails, her mother's big eyes and pretty smile, dimples for goodness sake. I muttered some sort of compliment, feeling the heat rise in my face at the realization that Eve had a beautiful little girl.

"She goes to St. Mary's," she said. I recognized the name of the prestigious private elementary school on West End Avenue.

"Don't you have to test into that school?"

"And my baby passed easy," she said, returning the picture to her leather wallet. "She's smart like her daddy." Her face went red and eyes wet. "She's the reason I'm doing this," she whispered, and I didn't think she meant for me to hear that last part.

I wondered if one of her patrons was her kid's daddy. Not like it mattered. I couldn't remember mine, and my mother's replacement husband Eddie—ugh.

I turned to the protesters again. Around and around they went, marching in a circle, their signs bobbing over their heads. Given my condition, I try not to judge someone just because society says they're different, not normal. What could I say to Eve by way of an apology?

Someone knocked on the door before I could come up with anything good.

"This is Charlie," she said, escorting the young man into the room. Her face brightened with his smile. Charlie had bright orange hair and so many freckles that it looked like a skin condition. He emptied his pockets on the vanity table like a kid offering his lunch money, but in the vanity's light, I saw at least two hundred dollar bills.

"Who is she?" Charlie asked. He put his shifty hands into his pockets.

"A voyeur, honey," Eve said. "Just what you need."

I opened my mouth to protest but Eve cut me off. "Don't be shy, sugar. Charlie likes an audience." He blushed deeper. "Humiliation is his thing."

Then she smacked him. The air was static with its echo. My hand instinctively reached out but I retracted once I saw his face. His eyes glazed into an expression that I could only describe as calm ecstasy.

"Ain't that right, baby?" Eve asked him and ruffled his hair. He smiled and gave a soft nod. She hit him again and he was in heaven.

Turned out, all of Eve's clients had their own thing. The few I thought most interesting:

"It needs to be about ten inches longer. See? Like in this picture."

"Put on this hat. I'll be the boat."

"Just take a deep breath and we'll try to fold it the other way."

"Meow. Purr." (Yes, like a cat. Repeated in accompaniment with only cat-related noises for about 45 minutes.)

No matter how many toys she pulled from the mysterious black bag—gels, handcuffs, nipple clamps, ball gags, collars, whips, harnesses, butt plugs, dildos, CDs for the black radio in the corner armoire—there seemed an unending reservoir of more. Like a clown car. She didn't always have sex. Interestingly enough, it was rare. Once she did, I took to distracting myself. I'd stare out the window, use the bathroom or try to fix the crooked bedside lamp. It wouldn't sit right for some reason.

Things in the hotel room got real interesting when Eve's last client showed up. Just before 2:00 p.m., Mr. Brad Cestrum walked through the door. I have to say, Eve looked upset to see him.

Though she'd introduced me, she didn't make up a story

this time. This was a surprise given the fact that in the last six hours I'd been a voyeur, a sex worker in training, a social psychologist, and her parole officer.

He was disturbingly average. I couldn't identify one distinguishing feature that would make him noticeable in a crowd.

Eve had her shirt undone and hair down and Mr. Cestrum wasted no time in bending her over the bed. Her skirt flipped up, resting on her back. From what I'd discerned from infrequent peeks this morning, this was about as average as sex got for Eve. Vanilla as it was, I blushed when my eyes caught a glimpse of the long curve of her hip and exposed thigh.

In the awkwardness of the situation, it occurred to me she might not even die in this room. She could get attacked on the street or hit by a car or anything, and I would've had to watch all this for nothing. Who has sex all day anyway? Okay, most of this wasn't about sex, but wasn't she hungry? Didn't she want a cupcake or Frappuccino? I wanted food. And I wasn't even the one getting the workout.

I checked the clock at 2:28 p.m., my head felt swimmy. Anxiety slid over my chest like a second skin. A draft of cold air swept the room, which to a replacement agent, meant that Death, knocking the door wide, had entered and announced itself.

I turned around to check on my charge and found Brad choking her. Her face was already a red-purple-blue color, so I had a decision to make. I tried to pull Brad off of her but she croaked, "Don't."

"You want him to do this to you?" I couldn't believe it.

She sort of nodded despite the hands on her throat, and reached out for my hand.

This is a test. To see how far you'll go.

Every bit of training that Brinkley gave me over the years pulled itself into play. It's important to understand that death was, by nature, precarious. Death-replacing was not the same as preventing an accident and a good agent was required to keep this in mind.

This is why I was forced to let Brad choke Eve instead of choking him to see how he liked it. The only choice I had, according to Brinkley's rules, was to give Eve my hand and replace her when the time came, if this is what was going to kill her. But to jump in and change the situation, changed the A.M.P. prediction. After all, I'd never been part of Eve's life before this. And if I changed it, I changed her reading.

I even had an FBRD contract saying I couldn't do anything to change the circumstances of a replacement.

So I offered Eve my hand.

Brad reached out as if it were myself I offered. It had not been the first time today I'd had such offers. I told Brad—as I told the others—that I was here for her, not him. I slipped my hand into hers and let her squeeze the hell out of it.

But this seemed so wrong. Being choked in a hotel room was too easy, so preventable. I've had to catch people falling off buildings. Wrap my arms around people as the sound of metal crunched around us in brutal car wrecks. I even had to replace a baby that would have died in childbirth while it was inside the mother. But this?

Surely this wasn't how Eve would die.

It didn't feel right. Why hadn't my eyes changed to their weird zombie vision? Infrared, x-ray, or whatever all that sparky electric stuff that happens to me when I replaced someone—the weird shit that makes me sound much more like a freak than an unfortunate person with a neurological disorder.

I thought of Lane and Ally. They were nice and comfy out in the hall, while I was in here struggling against the burning pain in my chest. I gagged, but no air came in or out of my lungs. At least I recognized this as sympathetic damage, something my body experienced because Eve experienced it. I was certain that if I'd held a mirror to my face, I'd see every little vein in it bulging at the surface. I didn't let go of her hand, though I wanted to clutch my own throat and try to pull free whatever was suffocating me.

The pulse in my ears drowned out their noises, the furious slap and squish of their bodies colliding, faster now and in time with the protests of the groaning bed. The pounding in my chest was so hard that either my heart was going to smash through its bone casing or my lungs wouldn't survive this thrashing. It'd be a tossup as to what organ would survive.

I was losing consciousness. The room reduced itself to spots, the usual lack of oxygen kind, not zombie vision, as I crumpled to the floor. When my face hit the carpet, I wasn't sure if I still held Eve's hand or not.

Instead, I paid attention to the one physical sensation I associated most with death: the stomach tug. Every time I died this happened. There'd be a tug through my abdomen as if a string were tied around my waist and through my belly button.

I focused on the tug and the growing sense of separation, fascinated and lulled by it. The ceiling above me went in and out of focus, but there was no vortex, no black hole of death, no—

Eve climbed on top of my dying body, and I was forced to accept that something was *definitely* wrong with this replacement, and I was in big trouble.

Her hair was down and in disarray. Her shirt had been left unbuttoned and the white lace of her bra peeked through either side. At least her skirt was back to where it should be.

But she settled her weight against my chest, reached under the bed, between the mattress and box spring and pulled out a large kitchen knife—the kind Ally used to chop zucchini.

You've got to be kidding me, I thought. Followed closely by, *God I hope you're wearing your underwear*.

She pinned me to the floor with her knees as if I could actually go anywhere even if I tried. I barely kept my eyes open despite the desperate urge to see what the hell she was going to do.

My eyes were closed when the knife first pressed to my throat and I tried my damnedest to open them. They fluttered enough to see her crying. For a moment, her hands relaxed as if she wouldn't do it. A deep voice spoke somewhere out of sight, in a tone used to issue a command or a threat. "If you don't we will kill her."

Her resolve returned.

"I'm so sorry," she said and broke the skin with a burning slice. "I have to."

Before I could really freak out about what was happening, or even consider I couldn't resurrect if decapitated, the tug through my abdomen gave a final jerk.

Then I felt nothing at all.

CHAPTER FIVE

I was somewhere quiet and clean. Clean because of the strong smell of antiseptics and lemons. Warm hands were on me, adjusting me, molding my body against a mound of pillowy softness. Someone kept saying my name.

Brinkley stood in the doorway, a stark contrast to the interior of the simple room: one bed, one lamp, and a curtain-drawn window for the sake of my burning eyes. I'd woken up at the funeral home before, waiting for Brinkley to pick me up, so why did this feel different?

"I'm cold," I told Brinkley, feeling again the warm hands on me though he remained in the doorway, me in the bed. "I hurt *everywhere*."

"Walk with me," he said. Just like that we were in a cemetery as old as Nashville itself. He was forced to angle his body and squeeze between the close set of the headstones. The ancient monuments leaned toward one another confidingly as we approached.

"I worry what he'll do to you, once he realizes what you are."

"Who?" I asked. I scanned the headstones and the cemetery. We were alone and it was strange to see so much stationary space. There was always someone here, at Mount Olivet's, black knee-length coats, flowers wrapped in cellophane or tissue paper. Now, there was only us, the headstones, and the trees, which stretched their bony branches down over us, protecting us. The landscape was too still, too silent. Except for *da dum da dum da dum* pulsating, where was that coming from?

Stone angels and hollowed trees bent easily in the wind, everything was so cold. *Da dum da dum da dum*. I put my hands in my pockets. Had I been wearing this jacket before? Where did this sudden press of heavy fabric come from? The wind in my hair moved like warm hands.

Brinkley wavered as if made of water. "Do you remember him?"

"Who?" I asked. I watched horrified as his face began to melt.

He wasn't Brinkley anymore. Not really. "Know thy enemy. Know thyself."

"Who are you?" I asked and took a step back, but I didn't really move. I couldn't.

"I'm your friend," he said, as if it was true. But he wasn't Brinkley. Brinkley didn't have green eyes or a wide-set, full mouth like that. Whoever this was wore Brinkley like a suit.

Still my body refused to move. "Where is Brinkley?"

Jesse. Can you hear me? Don't you give up on us, damn it.

I turned around at the sound of my name but didn't see anyone, only the little black bird from before perched on a tombstone in the distance.

"Listen to me." Brinkley's voice echoed through the cemetery. When I looked back, I didn't see him anywhere. He'd disappeared, leaving me alone in the chilly cemetery with that bird, his voice carrying on the wind.

"Listen, listen," the bird said. Opening and closing its beak like a crude puppet. "Listen."

The one bird became three. Three became nine until a multitude of birds filled the cemetery. They screamed and flapped from narrow branches, cold stones, cawing from the wings of poised angels, to drown out the echo of Brinkley's voice. A horde of them like black blisters bubbled on the surface of the cemetery's dying lawn.

"Brinkley," I yelled, scared. "Brinkley, where are you?"

The birds melded together into a single black wall that drew itself up, higher than the tallest oaks. It cast a shadow over the cemetery, over Nashville's cityscape behind me, and washed out the last bit of sunlight. The skyscrapers too, with their eyes of glittering glass, watched from the distance until the shadow obscured their windowpanes, the glass filling up as if with smoke.

For just a moment I saw a face in the black mass. Like a face from a half-recalled memory, soft around the edges.

I stumbled backwards away from the dark wall of birds, but caught my ankle on something. I tripped. The sinking sensation in my guts rose and I jerked, scared to be falling.

"Brinkley!" I screamed, hoping he'd come to my rescue. My throat vibrated for the first time, giving weight to his name. It burned like hell. There was too much light suddenly and the echoing *da dum da dum* I'd been hearing became my wailing heartbeat amplified through the monitor attached to my finger by a tiny cuff. "Brinkley?"

"Shhh, shhh, it's okay," Ally squeezed my hand. "We're at the hospital."

Eve—on my chest with the knife—right. The world shifted, coming into focus, yet Brinkley lingered. The smell of him, like cinnamon and aftershave, tied me to the dream. "She was crying."

I tried to sit up. Ally repositioned the pillows, propping

me up. She spoke a mile a minute, but I was still half-lost in the cemetery—trying to remember that face I saw, bubbling up in the blackness. "Wait. What?"

"Lane hid the camera inside the lamp," she repeated. "It's a good thing too because if he hadn't we wouldn't have seen her try to cut off your head."

She gave some brief explanation about using the hotel's wireless signal through his laptop, that these cameras were like the ones he'd installed at work, *blah, blah blah*.

"How long was I out?"

"Two whole days," she said. "The database doesn't have any entries for decapitation, but you weren't completely decapitated. You lost too much blood."

I lost blood all the time, so my AB+ blood type came in handy.

Replacement agents started an online database where we could log in and input what kind of death we experienced and how long it lasted and what sort of recovery time it took. With new entries coming in all the time, we can crosscheck a whole bunch at once, which keeps the estimations pretty accurate.

If Eve's replacement had been normal, asphyxiation typically cost four hours. Decapitation or any kind of brain damage isn't listed since necronites don't usually survive.

"Let me see." I took the compact mirror Ally offered. I pulled the gauze down enough to see underneath. My skin was purple and bulging through little black stitches along my throat. Blood crusted and flaked between the black strings.

"Damn, I'm like Frankenstein's monster," I said, pouting.

She made a half-hearted gesture toward my chest. "It won't scar like your autopsy."

"Why would she try to cut off my head? Who cuts off people's heads?" I asked. What was this growing void in my mind? Shock?

"Maybe she'll confess," Ally said. "Lane knocked her out with one punch. She's in custody."

I was genuinely surprised. "He hit a girl?"

"He said he believes in gender equality," she answered, her voice cold. Clearly, they'd not become friends during their joint hall duty or in their efforts to save me.

I tried not to picture myself bleeding to death and failed. I imagined what it might look like with my body in Lane's arms, blood trailing all over the hotel's cream-colored carpet. In my imagination, my head flopped all over the place, barely attached, as Lane stepped through the sparkly glass doors onto the sunny street.

"What about the guy?" I asked.

"He got away. It wasn't until Lane replayed the tape that we saw him duck into the bathroom as soon as he heard us at the door. We ran right past him and he slipped out."

"I want to see that tape," I said.

"Too bad, the cops took it," she said, wiping my sweaty bangs off my forehead. "I'm glad Lane installed the camera and stole Eve's key card."

"What, why?" I took a sip of water that she offered.

A rough knock rattled the door and a man entered with quick, purposeful steps. He wore a suit and his hair was slicked in a good-boy part across his forehead. His face was shaved. I suspected he was older than he looked, which couldn't be more than forty. Maybe because I looked like a Girl Scout on most days, I was always suspicious of a person's "real age."

"Ms. Sullivan, I need to speak with you."

"I'm heavily medicated." No one had actually told me I was medicated, but I'd have guessed from the thick paste feeling in my mouth and how my eyes felt a bit too wide and slightly off-centered.

"I'll be brief." He came to stand at the foot of my bed,

staring at Ally with a stare that certainly said *get the hell out of here*. "Can we have a moment alone, Ms. Gallagher?"

Ally didn't look the least bit intimidated by this guy. She stood up from her chair and I saw she was half a foot taller than him.

"I'll be outside if you need me, okay?" All the tenderness had returned to her voice. Eve's attack must've really scared her if she'd already forgiven me for screwing Lane.

The suit took Ally's seat by the bed, scraping back the chair to a less intimate distance.

"Agent Garrison," he said, extending his hand. "Ms. Sullivan, if you can answer a few questions, the bureau would appreciate it."

"Which bureau?" I asked, shaking his hand.

"Your bureau," he said. He said *your* as if to imply ownership, like we were in the same club. "FBRD."

"Where's Brinkley?" I asked.

Something dark danced behind his eyes. "Let's come back to that. Can you tell me what happened today?"

"I just watched," I said, heat flooding my face. Or at least I thought I was blushing. I certainly felt the heat rise in my face. "I don't have any fetishes, if you're asking about that. Most of my jobs have nothing whatsoever to do with sex, only death. This is the first sex job I've ever taken."

His brow furrowed.

"Okay, that came out wrong. I wasn't having any kind of sex. Actually she didn't even have much sex—I think she was one of those dominators."

"A dominatrix?" he asked.

"I was trying to do a replacement. I did not pay her for sex if that's what you're wondering."

"Let me be specific." Clearly, he wanted me to focus. "Why did Eve Hildebrand try to kill you?"

"I don't know why. I think I'm a pretty okay person. Will

her review count? Since she tried to kill me, I don't think her review should count."

He shifted in his seat. "Did anything strange happen in that room?"

I arched my eyebrows. "Everything strange happened in that room."

He touched the bridge of his nose as if I were stressing him out. Hello? I was the one who'd been attacked here.

"Look," I began. "One minute I was holding her hand to replace her, the next minute she's on my chest with a machete."

"An actual machete?"

"Well, no, but a really big knife." I made a chopping motion with my hand.

"Have you ever met Eve before?"

"No."

"Would you consider yourself suicidal?"

"What? No." I frowned. I didn't see any connection between those two statements. Maybe I was higher than I thought. "Not at all."

In case he thought I was of low moral fiber I added, "And I didn't even want her to be choked, but I let it happen because that's what I was taught."

"Yes, we don't challenge fate," he said. "But you see, you didn't tell me anything about her being choked, only that she was having sex."

I backed up and told him the whole story from the beginning. I finished my statement by asking, "Why would she do that? If she wanted to kill me, couldn't she put a bullet in my brain?"

"Not if she wanted it to look like a replacement gone wrong," he said.

"It was definitely a replacement gone wrong."

"Ms. Sullivan, remind me how you came to be an agent," Garrison said. He leaned his weight into the armrest.

And I wasn't on enough painkillers to overlook this out-of-nowhere question. The smell of smoke and burning flesh threatened to overtake me again. Why was Eddie's death so horribly vivid for me? Thinking about it around this agent made my teeth ache. How much did Garrison know? Surely Brinkley hadn't ratted me out, right?

I decided a half-truth was safest. "I died in a barn fire. When I woke up two days later, Brinkley was there to recruit me. He brought me a cherry coke."

Garrison nodded like he already knew this. "And your autopsy scar?"

"The jerk coroner freaked out and made a phone call. What he should've done was close me up."

"Why did you accept his offer to be a death-replacement agent?"

"I love cherry coke." And because I didn't want to go to prison. "I had medical bills and no job prospects. I needed to do something with myself." The taste of ash flooded my mouth.

"Did he tell you why he chose you?"

"I'm rare," I said. Duh. "We aren't Cabbage Patch kids. You can't grow us." The military tried that with A.M.P.s and failed horribly.

"Didn't you want to go home?" he asked.

I chose another half-truth. "I thought it would've been too hard for my mom to look at me without thinking about what happened."

Garrison leaned forward. "Because her husband Eddie died in that fire too?"

It wasn't really a question. I traced the cross-stitch pattern of my blanket with my eyes.

"Yeah, her husband died too."

I didn't dare say anything else. Brinkley had taught me to keep my mouth shut. This happened to be one of the first times I'd felt the pressing need to execute that right.

Garrison must've sensed my imminent shutdown.

"I have a couple more questions. Why did you leave St. Louis?"

"What does this have to do with Eve?"

"What happened in St. Louis?"

I didn't answer and he shook me.

"Did Agent Brinkley have a reason to relocate you?" he asked.

"A few agents died and Rachel got sick," I said. The room looked funny and dis-proportioned. Was the morphine kicking in? "Rachel got sick and Brinkley said—"

"Said?" He was on the edge of his seat.

"He said we needed to leave St. Louis before I got sick too."

"Rachel Wright?" he asked.

"I don't want to talk about that."

"You realize you've broken the law, don't you? If you don't cooperate, I can make this much harder for you," he warned.

"If I had a dollar for every agent who threatened to make my life miserable," I muttered. The heat of my anger made my face hot and pushed the dulling effects of the drugs back a bit. "I was told to do a job and I did it. I can't help it if the client was a prostitute. I didn't break the law by being in the room with her. I didn't pay her for sex or anything illegal."

"When you agreed to become a death-replacement agent, you signed a contract agreeing to abide by our laws. You broke the law when you performed an unauthorized replacement," he said. "The rules we've established regarding death-replacing are specific and necessary. Disregarding them carries steep consequences."

"We have the paperwork, and I know my contract," I said. "In no way did I violate it."

"There was no paperwork," he said. "That's $100,000 and a year in jail. At least."

"Yeah-*huh*," I said. "Brinkley wouldn't break the rules like that. I know because he's been shoving them down my throat for the last seven years. Eve was the one who tried to cut off my head," I said. I tugged at the gauze, but accidentally scratched the wound with a fingernail and cried out against the pain shooting all the way to my toes.

"Our division is working very hard to repair our image. We can't have any replacements that would compromise our efforts, Ms. Sullivan."

$100,000. Where would I get that money? "I told you, there is paperwork. Ask Ally. She'll have it. And you shouldn't doubt Brinkley."

"Don't you?" he asked.

I hesitated, which I'm sure was real convincing.

"No."

"When was the last time you spoke to your handler?"

"We tried to call him before Eve's replacement, but he didn't answer." Because this is a test. This whole big mess is a test.

"I find it interesting that you don't doubt him," Garrison said. He gestured at the length of me stretched in bed. "Here you lie in a hospital bed, wounded. You almost died and yet your handler isn't even here to check on you. Don't you find that strange?"

Please let this be a test. "He isn't here?"

"Did you think he was?" he asked, curious.

"I thought he was in the hall." I really did.

Garrison pulled a business card from his back pocket and shoved it in my hand. I could barely lift my arm to take it.

"Until we clear this up, you are suspended. You are no

longer authorized to perform replacements, but you may continue your other duties. You are not to leave the area and you are strongly advised to contact us the moment you hear from Agent Brinkley."

"What? Why?" The heart monitor beside me wailed again. I had to talk to Brinkley if these guys were going to investigate me. We needed to get our stories straight about Eddie and Rachel.

"If you're telling the truth," he began and he stood to announce his departure. "If he really gave you this replacement and he isn't here to verify your safety, you should assume he's the one who wants you dead."

CHAPTER SIX

Dr. Stanley York removed the stethoscope buds from his ears. I liked Dr. York with his snow-white hair, bright eyes and thin smile. Unlike other doctors, he made me feel like a person, not a test subject.

The blood pressure cuff's Velcro made a ripping noise as he pulled it free. "The blood we've drawn shows no abnormalities. It's been properly re-oxygenated and is flowing fine. The calcium in your muscles has stabilized, but you can expect the usual soreness. Your body temp and blood pressure are a little low, but they'll come up."

Ally entered my ICU with one of those paper cups from the cafeteria.

"Does that mean I can leave?" I asked. After a restless night, I was so done with this hospital. I wanted to be at home, in pajamas, remote in hand, sweet and salty snacks before me in assorted bowls. I wanted Winston too, curled up and warm in my lap.

"Yes, you're free to go, but you'll need to return for the psychiatric evaluation," he reminded me, placing a butterscotch candy in my hand. "And I am serious about getting some rest."

Ally helped me into some scrubs because my clothes had been destroyed in the Eve fiasco. The red Nike sneaker I'd been favoring lately was gone, so I had only one shoe. Over the scrubs, I fastened my black wool coat and eased into the wheelchair Ally offered. Ally wore her usual red, A-Line coat and pushed her hair behind her ears, taking hold of my chair.

"I hope you're ready for this."

"Ready for what?" I tried to make myself comfortable in the chair but it wasn't happening with the rigor mortis.

No explanations could have prepared me for what I saw when I went through those automated doors leading to the parking lot. Camera flashes and microphones were everywhere. I mean, someone actually hit me. They thrust their device into my face.

"Oww." I rubbed my cheek gingerly. "Watch it."

"Ms. Sullivan—" a reporter interjected. "Is it true a woman by the name of Eve Hildebrand tried to murder you?" She was older, maybe fifty, with teased hair piled on top of her head and a rasp to her voice as if she smoked two packs a day.

"Yes," I said.

Ally pinched my shoulders and I squeaked. "I don't think you should answer questions until you talk to a lawyer." Convenient since Ally's older brother was a lawyer.

The reporter leaned closer, followed by another round of blinking flashes. Her henchman's camera lens zoomed open like an insectile eye beside her, inspecting me.

"Was she working alone or did she have accomplices?" someone shouted.

"Well, there was this guy—" I began but Ally pinched me again. "Oww."

"Can you describe the man?" The reporters' questions

didn't stop. They were shouting at me from so many directions that I had no idea who was saying what. "Were they working for an organization? Is this attack connected to the Church's campaign against NRD?"

"Shit," Ally said as my wheelchair jerked to a halt. "Your wheelchair is stuck."

"Is this connected to the Atlanta murders?" someone shouted.

"What Atlanta murders?" Ally asked, unable to help herself.

I couldn't hear the reporters' answer over the sudden wail of police sirens. They weren't in the distance either. They were practically on top of us. Then I glimpsed them through the shifting bodies of the crowd. Two police cars pulled up behind Ally's and blocked her in. The press seemed unfazed by sudden police involvement, whereas I was totally freaked out by it. After Garrison's you've broken the law speech I was certain they'd pulled up to arrest me.

Worse, I wasn't getting out of the wheelchair. Oh, I wanted to get up and run at the sight of a big cop barreling toward me, parting the crowd like a modern day Moses, but that wasn't going to happen. I understood this as I stared at his broad chest stretched under his tight uniform.

"Are you here to arrest her? On what charges?" The woman with the microphone asked.

The cop extended his massive hand toward me and pulled me from the wheelchair as if I weighed but twenty pounds.

"Oww, oww, oww. I'm really sore," I pleaded.

He said nothing.

"I can't go to jail," I said, now hanging over his shoulder. "I'm too cute. They'll kill me."

Ass in the air, I was happy I traded the flimsy hospital gown for scrub pants.

He shouldered through the mass of reporters, while Ally,

hot on our heels, protested my abduction like a banshee. His partner opened the door to the cop car for him as he shoved me into the backseat.

"You didn't read her her rights," Ally said. She grabbed the top of the car door with one hand and refused to let him shut it. "You haven't produced a warrant or a badge or anything that tells me what you're doing is legal."

"Get in," he said to her. Ally didn't hesitate to jump in.

With Ally and me in the car, the reporters flooded the windows.

"Gee-*zus*," I muttered. Some reporters ran from the crowd toward news vans or parked sedans. "They don't give up do they?"

As we pulled away, the tall black officer said something into the small walkie-talkie attached to his shoulder. Ally was back to business, her authorial voice in full swing. "Gentlemen, I expect you to explain how this isn't kidnapping."

The white cop in the passenger seat turned around toward us. "I'm Officer Jeffers and this is Officer Gaul. We've been assigned to protect you."

"By whom?"

"FBRD." The officer's lips tightened as if he wasn't too happy about it.

"Protect me or arrest me?" Because medicated stupor or no, I definitely remembered Garrison telling me he'd arrest me.

"It's okay." Ally touched my arm lightly. "They'd have read you your rights by now."

"Why couldn't you explain instead of hefting me out of the chair like a barbarian?"

Gaul huffed under his breath. His eyes remained on the road. "It's not my job to explain myself to you. My job is to make sure you don't get your head blown off or chopped off or in any way damaged or severed from your body."

Wow. This guy was charming.

Ally's phone rang. "It's Lane." She flipped it open. "Hey. No, she's fine. They're escorting us home—" She huffed. "I said she's fine. Whatever."

"What'd he say?"

"Your *boyfriend*," she grumbled. I knew better than to show any emotion in the 'pleased' spectrum. "Said he'd come over as soon as he could."

"How long will you be, uh, escorting me?" I asked the police.

"Until the second assailant is apprehended," Jeffers said. He lifted his cap. He smiled enough to show crooked teeth and accentuate a pointy nose.

I assumed he meant the man from the hotel room. Okay, I could deal with some official stalkers if that meant no more attempted decapitations.

"Call Brinkley," I told Ally. Both of the officers cut their eyes at each other. If Ally noticed their ears perk up, she pretended not to. "Never mind, I'll do it."

I took her phone and dialed. It might've been a risk talking to him in front of the cops, but I wanted to know where the hell he was. But I got a recorded message repeating Brinkley's number back to me. Irritated, I tossed the phone back to her.

I realized I didn't recognize any of these side streets.

"Are either of you members of the Church?" I asked. Ally looked up from the digital planner she'd been rearranging with furious taps on the touch screen.

Officer Jeffers smiled. "Don't worry, Ms. Sullivan. The FBRD screened us for any conflicts of interest that would put your safety at risk."

"That doesn't answer my question," I said.

"Just because the Church is united, don't go lumping us all in one basket, okay?"

"Fair enough," Ally said on my behalf before I could bitch about being reprimanded like a child. I was pretty sure I had every right to be cautious at this point.

Gaul caught me staring at the back of his head and glared at me through the rearview mirror. "Maybe you'd prefer I lead the press straight to your house?"

Eventually, I did recognize the roads once we crossed Harding Place. We passed a Waffle House smelling of sweet syrup and fried goodness. My stomach growled. It hurt now to swallow my own spit. They'd given me a prescription for painkillers that I was going to need—no question.

Just before the locked backseat and the scent of leather drove me into a claustrophobic mania, we were home. The cops got out of the car slowly, looking around the neighborhood. Once it was deemed clear, they let us out of the backseat.

"I'll get the door." Ally moved ahead of us. "Then we'll get you into the bath." Every moment that I wasn't in hot water or on a massage table added to my misery.

Ally's keys jangled against the door as it creaked open and then our little group filed into the foyer. My one salvaged sneaker hit the floor with a thud.

Officer Jeffers stopped me on the stairs. "I'd prefer you wait here until we search the house."

"I'm cold," I said, shivering. Now that I was finally home and felt kind of safe, my adrenaline dropped.

"Check the bathroom," Ally told Gaul.

"It can wait," he said.

"No," Ally said, flatly. "She needs hot water."

He stared at us as if he might refuse the request, but Officer Jeffers followed Ally, taking the lead at the top of the stairs. "Which way?"

Ally nodded toward the master bedroom on the right. I lingered in the doorway, looking for Winston.

"He's at my apartment," Ally told me. "I wasn't sure how long you'd be unconscious so I picked him up last night."

Jeffers reappeared in the doorway. "Go ahead," he said. "But don't leave her alone."

By the time the bathroom door closed behind me, I could barely move.

"Do you need help getting in?" she said, rolling up her sleeves.

I nodded.

I had a hard time pulling the shirt over my head. My back and shoulder muscles didn't want to flex that way. I hesitated to let Ally help me. When I didn't move, her hands went to her hips and she tilted her head sympathetically to one side.

"I promise I won't look at the scar," she said, because I'd already cradled my chest bashfully. Ally's seen it all, sure, but seeing it in full daylight was different than seeing at night under my covers.

I nodded and she helped pull the shirt over my head. Then she slipped her arms under mine and helped me into the water. I slid down into the water and immediately felt a hundred times better. My muscles, thirsty for the heat, drank it down.

She flinched at the sight of my bruises. "Before you even ask, no, you're not a freak. Yes, I think you're beautiful. It just upsets me that she hurt you."

"We do this a lot, huh?" I asked.

Her smile was patient as she checked the water temperature, trailing her fingers over the surface. She added bubble bath and let the faucet run until the bubbles foamed up, white and frothy.

Even after each of my muscles relaxed, one-by-one, I couldn't stop frowning.

Ally put a clump of bubbles on my nose. "Don't worry, okay. It'll work out."

"Yeah, I'll work it out. In jail. Or in an asylum." I exhaled and a fluff of bubbles flew up and away from my face.

She arched an eyebrow. "Why an asylum?"

"They use us up and throw us in the nuthouse. Isn't that how this goes?" And with good reason, because something was wrong with me.

She lathered up a wash cloth. "I gave Garrison the paperwork we had. There's nothing else we can do except hope that he's smart enough to figure out what went wrong."

"If he doesn't, I'll have to pay $100,000. I don't have that kind of money unless I sell the house, and if I do, where will we live? Winston is too spoiled to rough it on the street."

Ally found my hand under the water. "Listen to me. Everything will be okay. If the worst happens, you'll sell your house and pay your fines. You can buy another house. You can survive jail. Neither of these cases are the end of the world or your life. And you know I'd never let anything happen to Winston."

I was having a hard time focusing on any subject for very long with the pulsing pain in my neck. I stared at the speckled white ceiling and heating vent. My mind wandered over the last few days without focusing on anything specific.

"What I want to know is what is going on," she said, and scrubbed at the dried blood from under my fingernails with a little brush. "The paperwork is real, even if we don't know where it came from."

"And why is Garrison interested in Rachel?" I asked.

"You never mentioned Rachel."

I let out a long, dramatic breath. I hated talking about Rachel but since it was important to the FBRD, then it must be related to my situation, right? Ally was smarter than me. Maybe she'd make some connection I'd missed.

"When I first paired up with Brinkley, we worked in St.

Louis. Rachel was my mentor, another one of Brinkley's charges."

"What happened to her?"

"After a replacement, I went to her house to bring her this huge bag of jellybeans. I knocked on her door like fifty times and she didn't answer, so I got worried. I went in and found her in the living room, sitting in a circle of her own blood."

Ally gasped. "She killed herself?"

"No," I said. "She'd just cut up her arms and hands. Then she used her blood to draw a circle around herself, calling it a protection circle."

"Did you get the knife away from her?"

"I tried. I asked her what was wrong, tried to get her to talk to me, but she kept going on about angels telling her what to do and that she had to protect herself from the bad angels."

"So wait, what happened with the knife?" Ally asked, and poured shampoo onto my hair.

"She was sitting on her living room floor and sort of mumbling all this craziness. Then she looked up at me and her eyes got really big—as if she didn't look crazy enough already, covered in her own blood. And she started screaming, 'It's you. *You*.'"

"What did you do?" Ally asked, her hands were still in my hair.

"I screamed too because this naked, bloody girl was waving a knife around and trying to tackle me. I was ready to get the hell out of there but I dropped the jellybeans and the bag busted open. Now, I'm slipping and sliding all over the floor like a cartoon character or something. Then Brinkley shows up and saves the day."

Ally let out a breath. "How did he know you were in trouble?"

"He was in the car. He heard me scream and came

running. When he pulled her off of me, she kept screaming, "She came from him. She came from him."

"Bizarre," Ally said.

"They blamed the number of death replacements she'd done, saying that 200 was bound to make her crazy. After she was institutionalized, Brinkley said we needed to leave St. Louis. The city was too dangerous. Most of my replacements were gun violence. Not like here where choking on a fried chicken bone is more common than finding a muzzle pressed to your head."

My thoughts had wandered and Ally brought me back with a gentle squeeze. "That won't happen to you."

I looked up into her face.

"You won't go crazy, Jess," she said. "We're being careful."

"Yeah, we're being careful and someone almost cut off my head." The burning loss of Rachel intensified in my chest. I redirected the conversation so I could bear it. "We almost moved to Atlanta, actually. He'd already rented my office space and signed a lease for my apartment, but then Brinkley chose Nashville at the last minute."

"Did he say why?" she asked.

"Too hot and too much traffic." Talking about him made the burn climb higher into my throat—*Brinkley where are you?*

Ally's eyes lit up with recognition. "I looked up Atlanta in the car. Eight death-replacement agents were murdered in there."

"What?" I asked. Eight agents killed? Why the hell didn't Brinkley say something? Why didn't he warn me to be careful, that we have some kind of NRD serial killer on the loose?

"The internet says an anonymous caller was the one who broke the story to the Atlanta press," she said. "But that's all it says."

I slid farther into the tub so Ally could rinse the shampoo out of my hair and let the gauze get wet. Dried gauze stuck to a wound was hell to peel off. Once it soaked, Ally removed it with tender fingers.

"Why would the bureau hide the fact that death-replacement agents were murdered?" I asked. And why would my handler leave me alone—defenseless—if it was still happening?

"Clearly this isn't a random isolated event," Ally said and turned to throw the wad of wet, pink gauze into the trash can. "Something else is happening."

CHAPTER SEVEN

"How are you today, Jesse?" Herwin asked. Because of the angle of the overhead light, Herwin was nothing more than a shadow in the corner, a disembodied voice speaking from beyond.

"In pain," I said. I was sluggish from medication and desperate for another pill, which Ally wouldn't let me have until after therapy. She said my appointment wouldn't go well if I was doped up. I reminded her that Herwin has seen me in worse shape. I'd completed my mandatory psychiatric evaluation as soon as I had woken from death before, with a contorted, bloody body and looking like a zombie in the old-fashioned sense. Still, she wouldn't budge, giving me some crap about being especially good, since I was under investigation.

Herwin wore the only suit I'd ever seen him in, brown tweed that matched his brown office. Brown, brown, brown everything except the walls and floor, which were the same as the rest of the hospital with its cinder-block walls and speckled white floor tiles. It gave me the impression of a bomb shelter or a bunker, equally submerged and depressing.

I settled into an overstuffed chair that made me feel tiny—another trick to get to my neglected inner child? Big chairs just made me want to cry. Not that I didn't have plenty to cry about—one court date away from becoming somebody's bitch, for example.

"Is there anything I can do to make you more comfortable?" he asked.

Yes, I thought. Make Brinkley call me. How hard is it to return a phone call?

I let my head fall back against the cushion. "Just get on with it, please."

He nodded, pulling a stack of cards from his desk. "Look at these and tell me what you see."

"Yeah, yeah." I waved a hand to hurry him. "A black bird."

"And this one?"

"A black dog," I said.

"And this?"

"Two seals having sex on a rocky beach."

"Good," he said.

Only a million cards to go.

"My dog Winston, but he's missing a leg."

"And this one?"

I didn't see anything, but you can't say nothing, at least not when pretending to be sane. So I went with the next best thing—feigned realism. "A puddle of oil left by a clunky old car."

He put the cards in an even stack by tapping them against the table.

"How'd I do?" I asked.

"Just fine," he said. He motioned to the couch. "If you'll stretch out, please."

I dragged my body out of the chair with much difficulty and stretched myself long on the couch. I got as comfortable as possible, despite the scratchy brown tweed upholstery and the sticky gauze clinging to my neck wound. Once I settled, Herwin moved his chair closer and pulled out the pointer light and shined it down into my eyes. The lights in the warm room softened, making the pointer light look like a searchlight, pouring into my skull.

"Follow the light, Jesse."

The longer I stared at the light the more relaxed I became. I drifted off and before I knew it, Herwin was out of his chair, exchanging the pointer light for the soft glow of the lamps. He offered me a tissue and I had to sit up to wipe the water out of my eyes.

"How do you feel now?" he asked.

"Tired and sore." I pinched my eyes shut beneath the tissue. They always watered like hell after the light test. I never really understood what the light test was for. The other therapist, Jen, said it was a kind of hypnosis used to see if we remembered anything from beyond the grave—figuratively speaking.

"Sit tight while I check on your blood work."

The door clicked shut behind him. I opened my eyes and blinked, trying to focus. I felt dizzy and leaned my head against the couch, hoping it would cease its incessant pounding. No help. And when my spotty vision cleared, I knew for certain that something was terribly, *terribly* wrong.

Against the opposite wall of Herwin's office, stood a man. He was tall with dark features and a wide brow. His eyes were light, intense, and his mouth larger than most men's. And he had wings.

He looked nonchalant, his arms folded over his chest and black feathers draped over each shoulder. He'd made a mess of feathers on the floor, a few downy strands sticking to his pressed black suit. I blinked several times, but he didn't disappear. In fact, his big green eyes held mine with a placid expression, as if he had all the time in the world.

"Hel-*lo*," I said. My voice caught in my throat and I sort of choked on the word. I cleared my pipes and tried again. "Hello. Who are you?"

"You can see me?" he asked.

"Uh, *yeah*." I let out a high, nervous burst of laughter. "How could I not see you?"

"I tried to reach you before," he said. "It would seem, however, that you agree with my current form."

Before I could respond, the door opened and Herwin entered. The therapist never took his eyes from the manila folder he held an inch from his button nose. "Which news do you want first?"

"Uh," I said and gestured to wings over there, leaning against the wall. Herwin looked up from his file folder and blinked. I jabbed my finger at the guy again. "Is this some kind of joke?"

Herwin looked at the wall but not at him. The angle of his gaze was all wrong. "You don't like the painting?"

"The painting is fine," I said an octave too high. "What about—*him*?"

Herwin's eyes searched that side of the room for an alternative. He settled for a photograph that wasn't really near the painting at all. "In the picture? It's my son, Trevor."

"He cannot see me," the winged guy said, inspecting his fingernails in the soft light of the lamp. "If you have not noticed."

And Herwin did appear completely oblivious to the guy in his office or the feathers he kicked up with his feet as he crossed the room to lift the picture from the table. How could he not see the little storm cloud of swirling feathers sticking to his pleated pants?

Then it hit me this wasn't just some joke, just some guy with fake wings messing with me. I was actually hallucinating. "*Shit*."

"Excuse me?" Herwin asked.

"I—uh—" I searched for sane words but it was hard to grab ahold of anything with the world falling away. "Your son?"

"Yes," he said and set the picture down. "I have a son and a daughter."

Herwin shifted his weight and stared at me as if he was completely aware that I was unraveling in front of his eyes.

"Let's hear those test results," I said. "Good news first, please." I had a feeling the bad news was "you're crazy."

"All your blood tests are clean and Dr. York thinks your neck will heal fine."

"Any brain damage?" I asked, staring at those abnormally green eyes and black wings.

"Nothing unusual," he said. "Do you feel ill? Headaches or nausea?"

I stared at the wall behind Herwin and it blurred. "Yeah, I have a hellacious headache building right behind my eyes."

"The pain medication has probably worn off." Herwin closed the file and took his seat again. "The part that concerns me is the alkaloid levels in your blood. They're above normal now."

My mouth felt sticky. "Will you have to commit me for that?"

"No," he said. He patronized me with a smile.

"You told me that my levels were great last time."

"Yes, they were. Better than average for agents." Herwin laced his fingers and sat back in his chair. "I'm sure you're aware the average mind folds around ninety-five deaths. Replacement agents often retire once their alkaloid levels are too high because it signifies toxicity in the blood. You've kept your levels low but this last replacement must have changed something."

I met those green eyes. *Hell yeah* it changed something.

And I wasn't fooled. *Retire* was code for institutionalized. I wet my lips. "So I shouldn't do anymore replacements?"

"It would be wise to slow down. But you've got another year or so at this rate."

"Listen to him," he said with a twitch of his wing.

"Don't tell me what to do," I said. My hands clasped my mouth in surprise.

"I'm sorry, Ms. Sullivan. You're right. I'm not here to give you career advice. And you must be under a good deal of stress now. Would you like to talk about what happened in the hotel room?"

No way in hell I was going to explain to Herwin that I hadn't been talking to him. That I was talking to a hallucination. And about what happened at the hotel room—where to start? What was more traumatic—the smorgasbord of prostitution? Partial decapitation? Being straddled by a pantyless sex worker?

I forced a tight smile. "I'm tired. I should go lie down, or something."

"It's difficult living in a highly political climate with passionate people whose views differ from your own. That being said, you should know you deserve all the same rights to life, liberty, and happiness as everyone else."

I waved a disinterested hand and thought of pills. Not pain pills. What did hallucinating people take? Some kind of anti-psychotic, right? I could manage this. I needed the right pill—but how to get Herwin to prescribe an anti-psychotic without arousing his suspicion? Maybe an anti-anxiety med would hold me? I could ask for that right? Later. Yeah, later.

"I've got to go," I said. "That headache is getting worse."

Herwin offered his apologies but I'd already stumbled out of the office. The hallway whirled on its side. I hit something solid with my hip and saw a nurse run past me down the hall, chasing after her medication cart.

How the hell was I going to keep a six-foot invisible guy with wings a secret? How does someone pretend not to hallucinate?

"You start by not talking to yourself," he said.

I whirled on him, processing what he'd said. The dark smudge of his body against all that sterile white was startling enough. The strange expressions from the nursing staff and the man at the vending machine retrieving his Coke suggested, indeed, I had narrated my concerns aloud.

I flashed a few tight smiles and laughed. Nothing to worry about here. But under my breath I muttered. "Not another word."

I found Ally where I'd left her. Dr. Stanley York stood beside her in his lab coat. Both of them looked really grave about whatever it was they were speaking about. Ally bobbed her head up and down slowly, regretfully, like she hated to agree with what Dr. York was saying. They were talking about putting me away forever.

"Not hospitalization, no, but they are talking about you," he said. I jumped at his voice in my ear.

"Did they lie about me passing my exams? Did they want me to voluntarily come out to the waiting room so they could get me here?" Why was I whispering? Hell, why was I asking him?

"They didn't lie," he said.

I didn't see any cops or staff on hand to sedate me. The only cop I saw wasn't even dressed properly. His shirt was all wrinkled and untucked as he leaned over the nurses' station to kiss a nurse.

"It's his wife," he said, as if he'd been watching the pair too.

I whirled on him. "I thought I told you to quit talking to me."

"Jess?" Ally said. Great, she'd probably heard me yelling at myself.

"Congratulations, Jesse," Dr. York said. He extended his hands to envelop mine as I crept toward the pair. "I hear you passed your tests with flying colors."

"Except that I've got high alkaloid levels," I said, suspicious of his well-wishing. Ally forced me into my jacket.

I tried to pay attention to Dr. York but *wings* over there made me nervous. He was eying Ally.

"You're not in a hurry, are you?" Dr. York asked. I refocused.

"No, not necessarily." This was it. They were going to keep me here. Ally scratched her cheek as a feather brushed it but she never acknowledged the cause. I turned farther away, using my back as a shield against the weirdness. At the very least, I didn't have to look at him.

"What do you need?" I asked. *Don't turn around. Don't turn around.*

"I heard about the FBRD suspending your replacement license, but I hope you will still do the seminar. I spoke to Special Agent Garrison and he is perfectly fine with that."

The back of my neck crawled. Don't look around. Just answer him. "I don't feel well. Can't someone else do it?"

"Cindy was scheduled to, but she took one of Cooper's replacements. I understand you are very busy. Really, your work load is already quite impressive. If only all the agents serving our community were as fine as you."

Flattery. My one true weakness. "When is the seminar?"

"Friday." He let his pleading eyes seal the deal. Damn it.

"I don't know why more NRD-positives aren't dying to become replacement agents," I said. Because sarcasm makes everything better.

"Exactly," he beamed. "See you Friday. Get some rest."

Rest? My hallucination was picking at his under-feathers.

The good doctor rounded the corner and called out to the nurse behind the station. "Stacy, tell your husband to wait until your break."

Blushing, the nurse stepped away from her cop and pulled at the hem of her scrub shirt.

Her husband. It really was her husband. Had I known that before the illusion told me?

"Turn that up," Ally said as she came to stand beside me. I turned my attention in the same direction and saw a familiar face on the television hanging above the nurse's head.

"Ms. Sullivan, is it true a woman by the name of Eve Hildebrand tried to kill you?"

"Yes. Ouch." A strung out looking zombie with rat nest hair bulging from one side of her head, answered with a raspy voice.

"I look like shit," I said. Ally took my hand to reassure.

I should've been mad. My first time on television and I looked horrible. But I wasn't mad because I couldn't quit thinking about my newest problem—and what the hell I was going to do about him.

"My name is Gabriel," he said, as if reading my thoughts.

"No," I said. "No, no, no."

"You don't look so bad, honest," Ally said, misunderstanding my panic.

No names, I thought. No names.

After all, if hallucinations were anything like puppies, naming them meant trouble. A name meant it would stick around.

CHAPTER EIGHT

I sat cross-legged on my bed with two white 800mg painkillers on the comforter in front of me. Ally had given me the pills and the glass of water on the bedside table before disappearing downstairs to work in the home office. Although she'd already given our paperwork to Garrison, she wanted to get all our papers in order in the event this investigation got uglier. Clearly, she'd been talking to her brother the lawyer.

Of course, no amount of paperwork would undo the fact that I'd murdered my stepdad. Gabriel sat in my desk chair, his massive wings stretched all over the desk itself. He'd knocked my pencil cup to the floor without as much as an apology. I couldn't chastise him louder than a whisper because I was supposed to be asleep.

I pointed at the growing pile of feathers at his feet. "Do you shed like that wherever you go? It's screwing with my OCD." I couldn't get the picture out of my head—his wings out the window as Ally drove, little black feathers swirling up to the sky at fifty-five miles per hour.

"You're the only one who sees them." He didn't bother to whisper like I did.

"How do you do that?" I asked. "How can you be both real and not real? I mean, none of you is real, but—" My voice faltered.

He didn't answer, only blinking those large green cat-eyes at me. I resorted to gesturing wildly. "Like in the car you were sitting in the seat, but your wings went right through the door and out the back like the car wasn't there. But you were there enough to sit in the seat. And you're doing it again now with my desk."

He shrugged. "I do not know."

"What *do* you know?" Again he said nothing. "How am I supposed to figure out what you are if you won't talk to me?"

He tilted his head. "Why must you understand what I am?"

"Because something is wrong with me." I took a breath. "I'm trying to figure out if I'm having a psychotic episode. Help me out here."

He sat up straighter in his seat, losing that casual air of his for a moment. Instantly, I realized the ridiculous nature of asking my hallucination to help me distinguish itself as a spiritual being or a psychotic episode. His tie changed colors, from black to the green of his eyes.

Dazzled, I pinched my eyes shut. "I'm under too much stress. Maybe you're a psychological device to keep my mind from completely ripping itself in half?"

"If you take your pain medication, your judgment will be impaired."

"Ah, so you're like a voice of reason?" I bounced the two pain pills in my hand. "Does this mean I'm not having a psychotic episode? My judgment is irrelevant if I am crazy."

"You must make an important decision soon. If you take those, you may make the wrong decision."

"Ok, you seem judgment-oriented. That's progress," I said. "Insanity couldn't care less about judgment, right? Besides have you ever tried to sleep with a neck wound? Dr. York told me Eve's knife scratched my spinal column. Think about that for a second."

He watched me with quiet amusement, like I might be a puppy tumbling all over my big floppy ears.

"And have you considered that my decision-making abilities will amount to squat if I don't take this pill and get some sleep?" I added.

He lifted an object from my desk and turned it in his hands. It was a snow globe that Ally sent me from London last winter while vacationing with her older brother. Gabriel kept turning it over and righting it as if he'd never seen one.

"You can't see the city," he said.

"You're supposed to look at the snow not the city."

"But it is not snow," he said.

"It's not a city either." I set the pills down again. If I held them for too long they'd start melting in my hand and leave that disgusting taste in my mouth on the way down.

He dropped the globe to the floor and it rolled across the carpet, stopping when it hit the leg of the desk. Tidiness meant nothing to this guy.

What the hell was I going to do with him? He acted as if he'd follow me forever. Just picture me at the grocery store, pretending not to notice a man with black wings fondling and dropping produce like that damned snow globe.

"You know the problem with insanity? I can't tell anyone I'm am crazy. Maybe I could work through this if I could talk to someone—but no. That's not an option, is it? So you know what I'm left with? You. I can only talk to you. And that I'm even willing to talk to you, the hallucination in question, is proof that I'm crazy."

"She sees that which is unseen. She will understand."

"Rachel? And she was locked up."

"Not Rachel," he said and blinked those big cat-eyes of his.

The only other person I knew who "sees that which is unseen" was Gloria. I didn't even know how to begin that conversation.

"Back to our little game of 'What the Fuck Are You?'" I said. "If I touched you, would I feel anything?"

He was out of his chair and across the room so quick I missed it in a blink. I gasped, face to face with a red tie. It had changed color again.

"What are you doing?" I choked.

He touched my cheek and my breath caught in my throat. His hand hovered for a moment, and then it moved right through me. I felt the strangest sensation, a warm tickle from head to toe, like each hair and nerve stood on its end. He returned his hand to his pocket, leaving my heart palpitating strangely. But he didn't move away. He waited.

"Why are you standing here?" I asked and tried to breathe my heart into a more comfortable rhythm.

"You want to touch me," he said in a matter-of-fact tone. "Touch me."

My hand was half-raised to his face before I realized what I was doing. I jerked back, alarmed. He caught my hand. His touch was as tangible as any I'd ever touched, and equally as real as the chest he placed it against. He guided my fingertips under the soft satin-silk of his suit jacket's lapel. But his chest was, silent. No heartbeat.

"So—" I stammered. "Am I imagining what your hand feels like or do you really have a hand?"

My pulse had become a raging, monstrous thing in my ears. The swollen size of my heart made it difficult to get any air down my throat.

"I am more real than this life you live." His tie turned

dark blue, the color of midnight. The look in his eyes made me shiver. They weren't green. They matched the tie, and the longer I stared into those dark pools the more I felt I was falling forward into water. Not just any water, nighttime waters, fathoms-deep, and holding the starry sky's reflection from above, a perfect replica of the heavens.

I bit my lip for focus. "I'm so totally fucked."

And he moved through me to the windows on the other side of my bed. His hands sought his pockets. His wings stretched and then folded against his back until they disappeared completely. He'd become a man with long dark hair staring out my windows. A strange man in my bedroom.

"When you're upset your heart beats much faster," he said. He turned toward me and, as he did, his tie changed to the red shade I'd seen before.

"Quit doing that thing with the tie, please. It's making me nauseous."

"It alarms me when you are upset," he said, quietly. The seriousness of his tight-set mouth made me believe him.

"It alarms me that I'm having conversations with a winged guy that no one else can see, that a guy I've trusted with my life for the last seven years might have conspired to kill me, and that I was this close to having my head chopped off. On top of all of that, I might have to go to jail and be somebody's bitch."

"Explain trust," he said. Gabriel was looking out the windows again, which were orange now with the light of the sunset closest to the earth. Long shadows stretched along the world as if to make the most of themselves before their moment was gone. He was very beautiful in this light. The whole scene, his back to me, edges of his body soft from all the light pushing past him, was like a dream.

"I'm not the one to ask about trust," I answered. "I'm

terrible at it. What little trust I have is easily broken." I sighed. "And it shouldn't be."

"How can it be broken if it is not tangible?"

I fell backwards onto the bed with tears in my eyes. "Because it's so fucking fragile."

"Fragile," he said, as if he liked the sound of the word against his teeth.

I placed one pillow under my head and squished the other against my chest. I curled into a ball and let the exhaustion settle into my bones. "You may not be able to touch or see trust, but you sure feel it when it's gone."

"For all your questions, you never asked why I am here," he said.

I nuzzled into my pillows. "Because I know why you are here."

My thoughts went to Rachel sitting in her dark living room with bloody fingerprints on her face and a circle of smeared blood drying on the carpet around her.

"You are stronger than that," he whispered as if he'd plucked those thoughts right out of my mind. I felt the soft press of a hand on my forehead. It was comforting, like something Ally would do.

"Are you a good angel or a bad one?" I asked.

"I am here to serve you," he said, his fingertips touching my cheek. "And I am determined not to fail."

I WASN'T SURE WHEN I FELL ASLEEP. ONE MINUTE I WAS listening to the soft caress of Gabriel's voice and the next I was jarred awake by the sound of something hitting my bedroom window. I came to a sitting position in one fluid movement.

Gabriel was gone and I had mixed feelings about that.

I listened hard for the sound that had woken me, thinking

it might be him—or God help me, some other psychological development—but I didn't hear the noise again.

Then I saw it. Across the room, one of my bedroom windows was partially open. I thought I had left all the windows closed, but this one was open a crack.

As I crossed the room I saw something was wedged into the corner of the sill. I opened the window enough to retrieve the small folded paper. It was a business card for Jade Palace, the tiny Chinese food joint off of 22nd avenue. On the back of the card, scrawled in black ink, was a message.

House bugged. Meet me off the trail.

It didn't have a name but I didn't need one. I'd spent the last seven years reading this crappy handwriting.

I crossed to the other side of the bedroom so I could see the street. A black car was parked near the house but I couldn't see who was in the vehicle from here. More cops or perhaps even Garrison himself—was I really considering sneaking out to meet my fugitive handler? If it meant some freaking answers, hell yes.

The creak of someone coming up the stairs made my heart leap.

It was Ally who appeared in the doorway. "You're awake. How do you feel?"

"I feel groggy," I said. I gave Ally my note from Brinkley. "I think I might want to take a walk to wake up. Do you want to come with me?"

Ally read the card. "Sure. Are you hungry? I can make you a sandwich."

"Yeah, a PB and J, please."

I dug a green and a yellow sneaker out of the basket in my closet. Of course, it didn't have a match so I paired it with a pink and white one. "And bring the bug spray so we don't get beat up."

Ally's eyes widened.

"I mean eaten up. Man, see how loopy I am?" Clearly I was not made for secret missions.

Covered in bug spray, a PB and J in my hand, we exited out the back door. Ally had Winston on a leash but he wasn't acting very interested in taking a walk. I kept an eye out for Gabriel, waiting for him to pop up at any moment.

My backyard was lined with trees, and as I pushed past them, it was only a few feet until we hit the dirt trail that made a two-mile loop around the entire suburb, cutting near the road at one point further down. I opened my mouth but Ally shook her head. It wasn't until we'd been walking almost five minutes that she finally spoke.

"There are zero ways this can go wrong," she said, sarcastically.

I followed her lead and kept my voice low too. "I want answers."

"And hopefully that's all we get," she added, her jacket's sash lightly slapping her legs as she walked.

Garrison had gotten to me. What if Brinkley did mean me harm? What if he was tired of working with me, of my attitude or something else?

I glanced over my shoulder again but still didn't see Gabriel, only the damp stretch of the narrow trail and the surrounding woods that pressed in on us. "If you really thought we might get attacked, why did you bring him?" I asked her, pointing at Winston whose belly dragged along the trail. He wouldn't so much as bark at an attacker.

"He needs more exercise," she said. Her breath sped up from the walking. Mine too. Winston was practically wheezing.

"Yeah, but we can't exactly run away dragging forty pounds of pug behind us," I argued.

"We'll have to carry him," she said. "Wait, *shhhhh*."

Ally's hand flew up and stopped me in my tracks. She

moved closer to the edge of the trees and peered into the spaces between their trunks. "Do you see it?"

Yes. I saw them.

The dark outlines of man-shaped bodies shifted through the trees. And not just one man, which I took as a very bad sign.

"Can you make out their faces?" I whispered.

"Not Brinkley," she answered. "There's at least two of them."

"Three," I said, doing a headcount of moving shadows myself.

Ally picked Winston up off the ground and positioned him in her arms. I took that to mean we were going to run for it. *Shit*. I would've laced my sneakers better if I'd known we'd have to run. Too late now.

"Ready when you are," she whispered.

I took off, leaving Ally in the dust. I wasn't really worried because Ally could outrun me any day, carrying forty pounds of pug or not. Not because she is inches taller than me with a longer stride, but between the two of us, she was certainly healthier.

She went to the gym. She ate vegetables. The only exercise I got was from death-replacing and sex. The only vegetables I ever ate were potato chips, French fries and the occasional spinach dip.

Ally passed me on the trail like I knew she would, velvet black pug ears flopping in the wind. But Ally passing me wasn't the problem.

The problem was the person coming up behind me. Someone*s* actually—sounding like a herd of rhinoceroses tearing down trees as they thrashed through the woods after us.

"Faster," I yelled after Ally. No point in playing it cool now.

She increased her pace but I had a hard time catching up. Again I made one last furtive search for Gabriel. Nada. *Protect and serve, my ass.*

"Gotcha," I heard someone say. A pair of large hands emerged from the trees and snatched Ally by the back of her red coat.

She disappeared into the trees. I froze on the trail, stunned. A hand clasped hard over my mouth and I was pulled kicking into the surrounding darkness.

CHAPTER NINE

I fought hard. Not just for Ally and Winston, but for me. I did not want to be that girl on the six o'clock news: *body of a young woman found dead in Greenbrook woods today, wounds from extensive head trauma*—or decapitation, or whatever my attackers decided to do to my brain to keep me *dead* dead. I managed a couple of decent shots: an elbow strike to the sternum, a hard bite to the forearm and couple of kicks to the shins—all of which elicited swears from my attacker.

"Fuck this, Brinkley. Wrangle your own wild cat." I was dropped like a hot iron and my knees hit the dirt. My attacker was very tall and very blond. The kind of pale that made me think he was from somewhere frigid and altogether unaccustomed to sunlight: Sweden or Finland maybe. Just a shade shy of albino. No accent though, so maybe it was more like Canada or just pasty genetics.

"Language," a familiar voice said, a voice I'd know anywhere. "There are ladies present."

"She isn't behaving like a lady."

I pushed off the ground and turned toward the voice but

didn't see the face covered in shadow. The pale man stepped away from me, cradling his forearm where I'd bitten him. The man bringing Ally and Winston into our circle was also a stranger.

"This one isn't a lady either," the second man said in a cocky accent. He was from somewhere east—Philadelphia or Boston.

He stood 5'10 or so with hair the same color as mine. He was probably a couple of years older than me with sharp features: a pointy jaw, hooked nose, jutting cheek bones, and pit marks from acne. He had a lean body, no fat and was dressed in black from head to toe, cotton T-shirt to leather boots. I couldn't tell his eye color in the shadow of the trees, but his brow was dark and bushy.

"Are you okay?" I asked her.

"I'm fine," she mumbled, but I could tell by the blush of her cheeks she was not happy.

Brinkley stepped from the shadow of a tree into the light. Relief washed over me. He was alive. Brinkley was alive. I hadn't realized how worried I was about him until that moment. But my relief was quickly replaced with confusion.

"How are you, Sullivan. Are you okay?" Brinkley asked. Concern. Actual concern. My mouth dropped open. When Brinkley saw my shocked expression his lips twitched to one side. "You're fine."

"How old is she?" Boston asked.

"Old enough," Brinkley said.

"No," he began.

"It's the regeneration," Brinkley told him.

"She doesn't age?" Swede asked.

Brinkley was visibly annoyed. "I needed you to come outside, because your house is bugged. I cleared it but I may have missed one in the kitchen. It is safer to talk out here."

"You disappeared on me," I said. The anger and fear rose

to replace the confusion. "If you'd have answered my call to begin with, I wouldn't be in this mess."

Brinkley flicked his gaze toward his companions. "Patrol the area. Make sure we are clear."

The men hesitated. Then Boston spoke. "Whatever you say, boss."

I didn't like the way Boston said "boss." It seemed much more sinister than it should have.

Brinkley watched the men go while Ally patiently stood with the pug at her feet. She might have been able to wait all day for answers, but not me. "Where the hell have you been?"

"I didn't disappear on you," he began.

"It sure—" I started, feeling the heat of my anger on my face as I pulled myself up to standing.

"Shut up," Brinkley said, before I could really get going. "For once."

I closed my mouth and watched Brinkley run a hand through his thick hair. "My superior called me in after I dropped you off and held me all night for questioning. I wasn't released until Eve's replacement. Conveniently."

"Why would they do that?" Ally asked.

"To make me look guilty and to leave me without an alibi." Brinkley punctuated his words with little jabs of his index finger.

"You could have at least checked on me." I watched the trees move around us until all the hairs on my skin stood on end. This dark little patch of woods, completely out of sight of the trail and houses beyond was creepy to begin with, but as the sunlight faded around us and the sound of crickets and bugs rose to an overbearing cacophony. It was more than creepy.

"You're tough, Jesse." Brinkley grabbed my shoulders and forced me to look at him. "But if they arrest me, we'll never be able to prove the truth."

"Why do I even have to prove my innocence?" I demanded. I deflected his show of concern. "I was the one who almost got my head cut off."

Brinkley shuffled in place. I knew this dance. He did this dance when Rachel got sick.

"Just say it," I demanded. "What the hell is going on?"

"The man in the hotel room with you was one of our own men. Another agent from FBRD. Replacement agents are dying," he said.

"Yeah, I know," I told him and he looked surprised. "We know about Atlanta."

Brinkley's sad smile said a lot of things. "Not just Atlanta. Everywhere. Someone is setting up fake replacements and killing as many death replacement agents as they can."

My knees shook but didn't give. "Who? And why?"

"I don't know," Brinkley said and I saw his own frustration etched in his face. "At first I thought it was the Church. They aren't exactly secret in their rejection of replacement agents and it isn't like religion doesn't have a habit of killing in the name of God. But our own man—that changes everything."

Winston snorted at our feet.

"Tell us what you know," Ally said. "Don't leave us in the dark here."

Brinkley considered her for a moment. "FBRD has a log of all active agents and their work assignments. They have the information and means to stage these attacks. They made me unavailable at a critical time. I wasn't supposed to be debriefed for weeks. The time change, the abruptness of the request, all of it is suspicious. And then seeing our own guy on the footage—"

"How did you see the footage?" Ally asked.

"Busy boy," I muttered. "No wonder you haven't called."

Ally's forehead pinched in tight furrow. "But the bureau

was established to manage the death replacement industry. Without agents, it'll be shut down."

"Not everyone wants to make death replacement a permanent fixture of American culture."

"What does that even mean?" I had a massive headache. Knowing the whole world wants you dead did that to you.

"The military never wanted replacement agents mainstreamed. The only reason they released them from protective custody was because the human rights activists raised hell and they felt pressure from the President come reelection time. And the military wants all of you back in custody. That's hardly a secret."

"But that means FBRD and the military would have to be working together," Ally said.

Brinkley gave her an unkind look. "Alliance: the union of two thieves who have their hands so deeply inserted into each others' pockets that they cannot separately plunder a third."

"Are you quoting someone?" I asked. I'd never heard Brinkley talk bad about the FBRD.

Protective custody was before my time, thirty years back, after NRD became a noticeable condition. History speculated that cases existed as far back as ancient times, and could be responsible for vampire and Christian mythologies involving resurrection. But it wasn't until the 1990s that the numbers grew exponentially.

People started dying, but didn't stay dead. The public didn't react so well. The military's solution was to take necronites into protective custody. Only protective custody turned out to be a cross between a science experiment and a torturous detainment camp.

"They could use these attacks as an excuse to reinstate protective custody," Brinkley said.

"Or?" Ally asked. She was never happy with one explanation.

"Or the FBRD might have another motive. This is why I have to see how deep the rabbit hole goes. If the agency considers you a threat, they'll terminate you. That's always been protocol; if it can't be fixed, kill it."

"Who are the most likely suspects?" Ally asked. I saw the questions racing in her mind. She formed her own beliefs and theories quicker than Brinkley could get the information out from between his lips. It's one of the things I loved about her, that she was quick.

I caught myself staring at the curve of her neck and the pout of her lips. She was terribly beautiful in the dim light. I wondered if I could convince her to make out with me a little. That wouldn't be emotionally confusing, right?

Brinkley barreled on unaware of my distraction. "The Deputy Director, who answers to the FBRD director, donates large sums of money to the Church. The Executive Assistant Director of our division must know because he is the only one who issues orders unless individual agents are being paid or coerced by outside forces. Many FBRD agents are ex-military. Maybe that is where their true loyalty lies. It is also possible that our division's EAD is taking orders from the dirty-handed Deputy and not the Director himself. I hope so because I thought the Director was a good man. A man Hoover would be proud of."

I did not want Brinkley to start talking about Hoover again. Talk about hero worship. "So EAD and the agents who order our handlers around probably know. But you're a Supervisory Special Field Agent and you didn't know."

"Given how closely we work with the replacement agents, I don't think we were to ever supposed to find out. They'd expect us to become attached to our charges," he said. Again, blood flooded my face. "The bottom line is FBRD is like a three tiered cake—top to bottom: directors, branches, divisions. We're on the bottom, so we don't know anything. Most likely it's the guys on top who know and they're the ones I'm going after."

"Is it possible that Special Agents like Garrison might not know either?" Ally asked.

Brinkley shrugged. "It's possible, but for now everyone is a suspect. There are too many connections to the Church and the military both professional and personal. We have to be on our guard until we can identify the hand in the glove."

"Suddenly, I feel so damn lucky to be me," I groaned. I pushed myself away from Ally and squeezed my temples.

"Stay tough and keep your eyes open," Brinkley said. Someone tried to kill me and I didn't know why. All the possible explanations for "why" weren't making me feel better. My eyes were *wide* open.

"Why not just close the program?" Ally asked. "What's to be accomplished by launching all out genocide against NRD?"

No one offered theories. We didn't have any.

"The bottom line is they failed to kill her," Ally said. "And you know what they say about failure."

"Try, try again," Brinkley answered. He turned to me and squeezed my shoulders. "You can't give them the opportunity. They'll bait you, manipulate you, and try to get you alone."

Winston snorted again as if these decaying leaves were fresh bouquets.

"You need to head back," Brinkley said and released me. "They're about to come looking for you."

"How do you know?" I asked.

"I've been following FBRD protocol since before you were born," Brinkley said. I couldn't see his face clearly in the darkness anymore, but I sensed that sarcastic smile and had seen it enough over the last seven years to picture it perfectly. "Off you go."

Ally scooped Winston out of the underbrush around her

feet and turned back toward the house. We'd made it to the edge of the trees when I looked back.

"Brinkley, hey, Brinkley," I yelled in a hoarse whisper.

"Don't worry, kid. We'll be close by." It was Boston's voice. So not comforting considering I couldn't even see where the creepy bastard was hiding.

"No, seriously, Brinkley, I need to talk to you," I demanded.

First there was silence. Then the silence grew so long and thick that I thought they'd slipped out of the woods like ghosts and I'd never get an answer to the question I'd meant to ask in the first place.

"What?" Brinkley groaned.

I jumped again. I hadn't seen or heard him approach through the darkness of the trees. Good to know he still had some moves. We might need those.

I clutched my chest. "Give me a freaking heart attack."

"What?" he asked again, this time with less patience.

"What's our story?" I asked him, heart racing. I panted the question. "About—the fire?"

Brinkley was quiet for a moment. "Tell them you don't remember."

"But—"

"Listen," Brinkley said. "You're different and Garrison will figure it out. He'll be curious and he'll poke around, but he won't find much because I've made sure there isn't much to find. No matter what they say or do, no matter how they try to intimidate you, don't confess. As long as you don't, they have nothing."

I looked down the trail to see Ally, a red outline in the distance, Winston waddling at her feet.

"No confessions. Got it," I said. Then I caught what he said. "Wait—what do you mean by different?"

He didn't answer.

"How am I—" I started again, but Brinkley was already gone.

CHAPTER TEN

In all the excitement of the woods, I didn't get a chance to tell Brinkley about Gabriel. And did I really want to tell Brinkley that another one of his agents was losing her shit? Not really.

I didn't mention it to Dr. York either when I showed up to help with the sensitivity seminar.

I walked into the spacious white room on the main level of the hospital and sat down at a table, without any attempt at conversation. The room was set up like a conference room, except instead of one long table there were several smaller, movable tables for people to cluster around in groups of four or five.

Gloria walked in and took the chair beside me, even closer to the door, as if she too intended to flee the moment this was over. I didn't do so well with crowds and already two dozen people had taken their chairs. Their various uniforms suggested they'd only gotten a few hours off of work to complete this training.

Gloria's face washed with relief as soon as she saw me and a small smile dimpled her cheeks. Her eyes were bright amber, lips full and hair cropped close to her head, a leftover preference from her former life as a soldier. "You're still alive."

"Please tell me you didn't see that coming," I said.

Gloria's face pinched and I feared maybe she hadn't realized I was joking. Of course she hadn't seen Eve cutting off my head. It wasn't her job to view me. And if it was, it wasn't like I'd blame her for something like that.

She opened her sketchbook and picked a page in the middle. She'd already half-filled this thousand-page monstrosity since her birthday in February. Clearly, she worked too much. What she showed me was an astonishing charcoal rendering of a man. This disturbingly lifelike headshot featured long shaggy hair, prominent eyes, a wide mouth and sharp jaw. She'd drawn Gabriel, both strikingly beautiful and with wings.

"I've been drawing him for days," she explained and held her hand above the picture as if she could feel the heat radiating off of it. She repositioned the sketchbook turned back a few pages. "Every time I try to view you, he's all I get. I wanted to know if the danger has passed, but he's all around you." She gestured toward the picture.

It was my understanding that remote-viewing was like clairvoyance—viewers saw pictures of stuff in their heads, but remote-viewers could do more than see. Somehow they could keep "entering" into a vision or asking the question differently to get several pictures.

Gloria used her skills to find missing kids, and sometimes she'd remote-view the same child a dozen times. Every time she'd get something new: a house, a landmark, a suggestive sound like water or trains. All of these clues were used to pinpoint a location. This was why it usually took time, sometimes a week or more, to do a full reading and get all the pieces into place.

She kept track of the info by sketching it down in the spiral bound pad I gave her for her birthday. Before that, she did the creepy pictures-all-over-the walls-like-a-psycho thing.

"Weird." I said, trying to steer clear of any angel talk.

A few pages of her sketchbook fell forward and a drawing caught my eye. I snatched the book from her in order to get a better look at the pines encircling a small clearing. In this picture, I stood on the clearing's edge, half-hidden in the pines as if afraid to go farther. I knew that place.

"When did you draw this?"

"Months ago," she said, as she reached into my lap and flipped the page. The next one was an unfinished door centered above a porch.

So this was the future, not the past.

I burst out laughing. Not like *ha ha funny*, but hysterically, like a crazy person. A few heads turned my way.

"What is it?" Gloria asked.

"That's my mother's house," I said. "You couldn't pay me to go back."

"Why don't you want to go?" She leaned forward in her chair.

"It's complicated," I muttered and looked down at my mismatched shoes.

Gloria's eyes glazed again, giving them that I'm-communicating-with-the-universe-leave-a-message look. "But he—"

"You could be wrong," I said and hoped she'd take the hint and drop it. I didn't like to talk about my family.

Gloria wasn't as good at reading necronites, especially agents. I guess because the flow of time was choppier around us given the die-rise-die cycle we operate on. It makes it harder for her to follow the "threads" as she calls them because we're always upsetting the magnetic fields.

"He's all I see." She pointed at Gabriel's picture again, but there was something else in her expression that I couldn't quite peg. Insecurity, maybe, though I've never known Gloria to be insecure about anything. She was an amazing A.M.P., so she had no reason to doubt her abilities—even if I was a hard read.

Dr. York clapped his hands to get our attention and then slipped them into the front pockets of his lab coat. "I want to welcome everyone. I know most of you are here because your employer requires it. Regardless, I hope you find the information interesting and helpful. Our program is divided into two parts: a short orientation video about twenty minutes long, followed by a Q&A with an actual death-replacement agent and an Analyst of necro-Magnetic Phenomenon."

Everyone sat up in their seats glancing eagerly around. It was like a game of *Who's the Zombie?* Slowly, all eyes settled on me. Me. I started to panic. How did they know it was me? No one ever guessed me—then I remembered. The freaking newscast following Eve's attack. *One* partial decapitation and suddenly everyone knew who I was.

Dr. York killed half of the lights, ending the painful staring contest. Slowly the eyes turned toward the video flashing an opening montage of healthcare professionals, law enforcement, and school teachers before moving into the testimonies.

Ally rushed into the room, mouthing 'Sorry' to Dr. York and handing me a Starbucks cup. Dr. York graced her with a patient smile and motioned for her to sit. I pulled out the chair on the opposite side of me, furthest from the door.

"Death-replacement is the greatest scientific discovery of the twenty-first century," a doctor with coke bottle glasses said as the video rolled on. His eyes were magnified by those thick lenses and looked twice the average size. He had this habit of flicking his tongue over his lips between words. "NRD opened a Pandora's box for neurologists."

I huffed. "Yes, please equate us with the legend of how all suffering entered the world."

The announcer continued, "...not all of those with NRD choose to be death-replacement agents. Most fear announcing their condition to their communities because of discrimination, possible violence..."

I was dozing off. Ally nudged me. I reluctantly sat up straighter and focused my attention on the TV. A pretty blond schoolteacher appeared. The camera panned over her classroom, zooming in on her as she wrote on the board, explaining the lesson. The children sat rapt in their seats, hands neatly folded. Clearly, this was staged.

The following clip was her again, post-mortem and racked with rigor mortis. She moved with the shuffle-step most replacement agents have before a good rub down and steam.

"I know this might be frightening," the teacher said. Her neck was twisted oddly to the side, looking pale and bloody. "But I'm perfectly harmless."

"Oh, come on, this isn't muscular dystrophy," I said. "She just needs a bath." That woman didn't have to look like that, which is why her pulling the sympathy card irritated me.

Ally pinched my leg as several people glanced my way. Dr. York was one of them.

A social worker spoke now. A child stood beside him. "Most of their families turn them away. They can't handle the adjustment of raising a special-needs child."

Ally leaned toward me, keeping her voice low. "How are necronite children special-needs? As long as you don't kill them, they're no different."

I smiled at her, but my mind had begun to wander at the idea of necronite children and their families.

"And sometimes the children must be removed from the home for safety reasons. A child who can be tortured to death, and then resurrect, attracts the wrong kind of foster parent."

The video gave a parting shot of a mother who'd discovered her six-year-old daughter, thought dead after drowning in a river, was NRD-positive. "I'm so happy she's alive," she cried. "It's a miracle."

That's not how my mother took the news, let me tell you. Yes, when I woke up from my very first death to find Brinkley recruiter extraordinaire, I did make one last call to my mother. I'm not sure why. I think a part of me wished that, since her child-molester husband was dead, maybe I could repair my relationship with her. Maybe she'd even thank me for rescuing her from a perverted husband, because maybe she'd been too scared to kick him to the curb herself. I was willing to forgive her for everything, if only I could come home to her and Danny.

My daughter is dead.

I even thought maybe she was confused, grief-stricken and thought I was some jerk pranking her. So I laid it all out for her: NRD, my regeneration, and that I didn't have to become an agent right away. I could come home and finish school if I wanted. Brinkley threatened to expose me as an arsonist and murderer if I didn't work for him soon, but I had time.

My mother wasn't confused.

"Don't call here again, Jesse."

The lights came on as the film's credits rolled on the black screen. A few people clapped, so I did too, to get Ally to quit elbowing me in the ribs. Dr. York resumed his position in front. My stomach flopped, knowing it'd be my time to talk soon. I shifted in my seat, suddenly unable to get comfortable.

Dr. York broke the silence. "Before we turn it over to our guests, does anyone have any questions about the video?" Dr.

York capitalized on this pause. "Allow me to introduce Ms. Jesse Sullivan and Captain Gloria Jackson." Dr. York gestured for us to join him at the front of the room.

Ally had to push me from my seat. I walked as smoothly as possible to Dr. York's side, careful to not look like one of those shuffling weirdoes on that horrible video despite the fact I was sore. I couldn't do anything about my gauze wrapped neck though. I was sure that gave them ideas.

"Ms. Sullivan is a resident here in Nashville and one of the three death-replacement agents serving the Davidson County area." People clapped. I think Ally started it. "Captain Gloria Jackson also works in Nashville. She collaborates with several Federal Bureaus, as well as with the local authorities to solve cases."

I said the line Dr. York taught me to say. I tried not to sound too robotic. "We're here to answer any questions you might have about replacement agents or death-management in general."

Almost every hand shot up. Just great. Gloria looked like she was pulling herself together, so I took the initiative. "Uh, you." I'd pointed at the person closest to me, a black woman with beautiful coiled braids piled on top of her head, but scary neon green nails, curling like freakish talons.

"How do you decide who lives and dies?"

"I don't," I said. "I get told who to save. The FBRD issues us handlers to ensure all our replacements are federally compliant. I show up for work like everyone else."

I picked another hand. "What about people in a burning building? Wouldn't you save them?"

"I don't randomly walk past burning buildings," I said. Ally made a face suggesting I'd missed the point so I tried to answer him again. "If I came across someone who happened to be dying, yes I would save them, if that's what you meant."

An Asian man with glasses on the end of his nose went

next. "My wife is sick with cancer and I was told she can't be saved. Why can't you save her?"

I tried to avoid the personalization of the question. If I didn't, this could get ugly real quick.

"Unfortunately, replacement agents can't heal people. If I were to sit with your wife until she died and replace her, it'd keep her from going—wherever—but she'd still be stuck in a body that'll kill her. She'll die again almost as soon as she's replaced."

He wet his lips. "I understand it would only buy more time, but—"

"Which is why health replacements aren't allowed," I said. "It's a waste of time."

That came out wrong. I knew it as soon as I said it. The air burned hot around my face.

"I mean, because I lose a day or two also, you know, being dead. In that time, I could miss the opportunity to save someone else." I wet my lips and chose the woman who'd cried during the video. I was counting on her to be nice. "Yes?"

"I don't understand how A.M.P.s work," she said.

Several hands went down, suggesting this was a hot topic, though not an easy one to explain.

I gestured to Gloria whose first reaction was to force an awkward smile. "Once the government ruled out NRD as a contagious disease, or biological warfare, those with NRD were taken into protective custody. While in custody, military scientists conducted numerous tests, and death-replacement is one of the talents they discovered. Some researchers believe an electrical transference between the magnetic fields surrounding humans occurs. Their magnetic fields reverse, and it prevents the clients from dying, but takes the life of the death replacement agent instead."

Everyone leaned forward now, and I felt like we should

have flashlights and toasty marshmallows for this story. "In the light of this discovery, the government saw limitless possibilities in military development, but with so few cases of NRD, they sought to replicate the phenomenon. This is how A.M.P.s were made."

I turned to Gloria and tried to remember all the things she'd told me about her experience as a soldier turned A.M.P. —which wasn't much—only enough to suggest how horrific the ordeal had been. Of course, if you'd asked me, anything with needles and medical testing was torture.

Gloria hadn't quite erased the pained expression on her face, so Dr. York decided to step in and help with the medical aspect. "The most significant difference in a brain with NRD and a brain without is magnetite. They have a significant quantity of magnetite in their cerebral cortexes."

"What is magnetite?" a man asked.

"It's a ferromagnetic mineral that some animals have in their bodies. It helps them sense magnetic fields. Birds have it in their beaks and use it to fly between the north and south magnetic poles in the winter. It's basically a natural magnet."

The military got the bright idea to shove a huge wad of magnetite into their soldiers' brains. Mostly it killed people or left them severely brain damaged. Survivors became A.M.P.s. They can't resurrect or anything because they don't really have NRD, but the magnetic material helps them read magnetic fields and make predictions. This skill is further enhanced with a little trick called remote-viewing. This seems to be the only real outcome of the experiments, their ability to read patterns in the world and know what will happen based on where things are going.

Dr. York gestured with his hands. "We believe A.M.P.s read the Earth's magnetic field and the magnetic fields surrounding people, and that's how they help the replacement agents target deaths. Death is a measurable disturbance in the magnetic field."

"But how do you read the fields?" a woman insisted, smacking the gum in her mouth like a cow with a wad of grass.

Gloria didn't look up from her polished shoes. *Oh, G. Why does she agree to do this if she hates it so much?* "In the nineties, the military conducted ESP research to see if they could develop psychic warfare. A.M.P.s like myself were taught to use remote-viewing, a skill established during that research. I personally use drawing as a medium to transfer the images."

Dr. York said my name softly as if to steer the attention away from Gloria. "Can you explain to them how your NRD wakes you up?"

"Sure." I inhaled trying to shift the growing pain out of my muscles. I hated standing in one place. "Have any of you ever jerked awake when you were almost asleep? You know, like you're dreaming that you miss a step, and then you jerk and wake up?"

Several heads bobbed in unison with the soft murmurs.

"That's called a myoclonic jerk. Your body jerks because your brain, mistaking your slowed breathing for dying, sends an electro-impulse through your body to cause your muscles, including your heart, to contract. That jolt is meant to wake you up. With NRD it's like that. Once we've died, our brain starts sending a bombardment of electro-impulses through the body to wake us up. It's why we need our brains to resurrect. No brain equals no pulsing. Neurologists aren't sure why our brains do this, but that didn't stop them from naming it Necronitic Regenerative Disorder."

"How long do you stay dead?" The green-nailed woman asked.

"It depends. The amount of damage the body suffered

during death determines how long we'll stay dead before our systems—circulatory, respiratory and so on—respond to the pulses."

"Why does the Church hate you?" someone asked.

Off-topic, much?

I grinned. "I think they're jealous Jesus isn't the only one coming back from the dead these days."

This got some laughs. Too bad it didn't last.

A man in the back who reclined in his chair, arms resting on his lap spoke with an accent. He had the puffed up chest of a cop. "Last night, two kids were gunned down near 11th and Vine. Three days before that, a woman was raped and stabbed to death over on Chester Ave. I find it hard to believe that replacement agents are doing the world such a service. Incidents like this keep happening."

"There are only three of us," I said. "And I can't be everywhere at once. Not to mention that when I die, I lose a few days of my life. So even if I stayed dead every possible moment, I could only make about a hundred replacements a year and I'd be completely fried out of my mind."

The cop looked like he couldn't care less about my mental stability. He grabbed the edge of his table. "You make up 2% of the world population. That figures out to like 120 million people. Together, you could save millions, maybe a billion people a year."

"It doesn't work that way."

"Why?" he said. "Because you don't feel like being a stiff for a few days?"

My voice got louder. "No, because your math is shitty."

His mouth opened to say another dumb thing but I cut him off.

"I don't have 2% of the population backing me, giving me this valiant life purpose. It's not like some glorious police force where we trade battle scar stories. I've had conversations with maybe six replacement agents in my whole seven years of death-replacing. You're basing your numbers on the world population, but that's inaccurate. In most Middle Eastern and African countries, your head is cut off as soon as they find out you've got NRD."

I took a breath.

"Japan and China are the only other countries that have a death-replacement system comparable to ours. So you need to cut your numbers down to just those populations. Then cut your number smaller because most NRD-positives don't know they have NRD and of the ones that do, even fewer of them become agents. You want to know why?"

I'd define rhetorical question for him later.

"Jesse," Dr. York raised his hands toward me as if to calm a crazed animal. Okay, maybe I was foaming at the mouth a little, but I wasn't about to pull my punches now.

"Do you even know what sacrifice is?" I asked him. "You're a white American guy. I bet no one has ever treated you like you're different."

"I've been shot protecting someone."

"Whoopty fucking doo, how noble of you. I got shot because someone thought I was a freak and I was trying to save his life."

I stormed out of the room. Good thing too because the air around me had become static. Like really static. I felt like if I didn't leave, I was going to blow up.

I was in the hall pacing back and forth, trying to slow my breathing when Ally caught up to me. Gabriel appeared.

"Not now," I yelled at him.

Ally stopped mid-stride.

"No, not you," I said and realized what I'd done.

"Are you okay?" Ally asked. "What was that?"

"An asshole stepping out of line," I said. Gabriel's tie was red. What did red mean?

"No, I mean, you got mad, the room sort of crackled—" she shook her head. "You want to go back and jump him? With Gloria, I bet we can take him."

I gave her a warning look. "Don't tempt me."

Again I caught myself looking at her. I wanted to pull her into my arms. I wanted to bury my face in her neck, let her kiss my cheeks and tell me everything was going to be okay. I felt myself leaning toward her, knowing she'd accept me if I tried, but the damn door burst open.

Dr. York came trotting out. "Jesse, I'm sorry, but—"

"Don't lecture me," I told him. "That guy was being a jerk. Sensitivity training my ass."

"I can ask him to leave, give the others a chance to ask more questions," he said. He looked willing to do anything I asked. He also looked terrified to get very close to me. Why? Had I really been that scary in there?

I looked through the little window to see that Gloria was taking questions again. "She's got this," I said, pointing at her.

Ally's purse vibrated and played a silly little tune. She rummaged for my phone while Dr. York continued to beg. I thought about it but couldn't bring myself to go back in. Call it pride, but I couldn't. Ally finally managed to get the phone out. I didn't recognize the number, but the area code was familiar. I didn't care who it was. I'd take any call if it ended this horrible seminar duty.

"You better go check on her," I said, gesturing to Gloria. "She gets a little weird around people." Before he could object, I took the call. "Hello?"

"Jesse?" A small sheepish voice asked.

"This is she," I said, wondering what the hell a kid was doing calling me.

"Um," he said, stuttering. "Um, I—"

"Oh, Jesus, kid," I said, hot with irritation. "Start with your name."

"My name is Danny Phelps," he choked on the words. "Daniel, actually. Do you remember me?"

"Yeah, Danny, of course," I said, gently this time. And it was the truth because not even I could forget my little brother.

CHAPTER ELEVEN

"Your mother is dead?" Lane asked and sat down on the steps beside me.

"Word travels fast," I said. I'd been sitting on my porch steps ever since the seminar, watching Winston play in the grass beneath the Japanese maple.

"Do you want to talk about it?" he asked and bumped his knees against mine.

"Daniel said she died in a car wreck yesterday and that the funeral is the day after tomorrow. End of story."

"How did he know how to get ahold of you?"

"My mother had my number," I said. "Not that she'd ever used it."

Why bother tracking me through the years—city to city—if she never intended to call.

"Are you going to go?" He nudged the pug with his foot until he offered up his soft belly.

"I'm not allowed to leave town," I said. "Garrison will hang me."

"I'm sure you can petition for special circumstances," he said. "Your mother did die."

"Showing up with a police escort might send the wrong message."

And that wasn't all of course. How much did Daniel know? How much did any of the family or her friends know? My mom might have told everyone about what happened. The last thing I needed was some grief-stricken friend or family member yelling "Did you kill Eddie? Did you really kill the poor bastard?" loud enough for Garrison to hear.

No. I couldn't risk that if I intended to stay out of prison. Then again, I did want to go to my mother's. I wanted to see that Danny was okay. How could I possibly explain to a tween that he's an orphan because his father was a sick rapist? Even if I could somehow make it up there to Danny without Garrison knowing, someone still wanted me dead.

A brilliant image of my mother sprang to mind. She was in our backyard, dress sparkling in the sunlight as she looked out over the pond behind our house. The barn was up—the barn my father built—his last remaining relic and the one I'd sacrificed in order to take out Eddie. I didn't remember why we were standing there, how old I was, or even what we'd been doing, but I remembered her face awash in sunlight.

Tears stung the corners of my eyes and spilled over when I squeezed them shut.

"Are you okay?" Lane's warm hand clasped my shoulder.

I don't know why I didn't want to share the memory with him, but I curled around it like a closed fist.

"My pain pill is wearing off," I lied. I brushed the gauze for show.

I remained quiet, contemplating the amazing sensation of seeing my mother alight in watery sunshine, Lane spoke again. "Do you want me to leave?"

My chest clenched and the memory faded. "Isn't that what we decided?" I asked.

"I could make dinner," he said.

"I don't need you to. I'm perfectly capable of whipping up something snazzy," I said, a little angry. I didn't understand the change in his stance and it was irritating.

He grinned. "Not gingersnaps, I hope?"

Ok, so maybe I'd remodeled the kitchen because I set a batch of cookies on fire. So I have a short attention span. Sue me. "Sweet potato soufflé, thank you very much."

"Do you even know what that is?" he asked.

I considered lying. I'd gotten quite a bit of practice today after all. "Sweet potatoes...souffléd."

"Do you even know what a sweet potato looks like? Could you describe it to me?"

"Hey, I can cook."

His smile tucked itself into a corner of his mouth. "Let me make dinner."

"Thanks, but no thanks."

He wet his lips. "If you turn me down, you'll be alone."

"I should get used to being alone," I said. "Isn't that what you were saying?"

He didn't take my bait. "But you just got bad news on top of bad news."

"Why do you care? I could die tomorrow and you'd probably think I had it coming," I said. I felt a twinge in my gut as if I were inviting fate to step in and annihilate me. I glanced nervously at the sky and added, "Though I hope that doesn't happen."

"I do care," he said. "That's the point. I'm not here for sex."

His cheeks were smooth from a fresh shave and line of dark hair made his neck and ears look kissable. It was enough to make me pause.

"I thought you needed time to think?" I asked.

"I know how I feel about you," he said. He leaned so close

I could feel the heat of his lips radiating against my face. "I only need to think about how to—not—"

He wrapped his hand over mine and everything in the lower half of my body tightened.

"Yeah?" I said and my voice was definitely higher.

But instead of kissing me, he grinned and walked into my house.

I clamored after him, Winston at my heels. "Tease."

The deadbolt clanked shut as I flipped the foyer's main light switch and all five bulbs it controlled blew simultaneously. I gasped as the sparks rained down on us and grabbed my hair, running it through my hand, hoping it wasn't singed.

"Got it," Lane offered. "Where do you keep the spares?"

"Laundry room," I said. "First I break a computer. Now, I explode light bulbs. This is becoming a problem."

"You're challenged," he said. "It's why you can't match a pair of shoes."

"I'm a tightwad. That's why I can't match a pair of shoes," I said, feeling a tad insulted. My mind was doing the math—all the appliances I'd wrecked in the last week or so. I couldn't connect the dots—but something was wrong with me. Gabriel. The electronics.

Lane ducked into the kitchen with the step ladder in one hand and a collection of busted bulbs in the other as I gave up and went upstairs. He found me in the bathroom, pill bottle in hand as I manipulated the childproof lid and dug out two honking horse pills. They were white with a deep crease dividing each. I stacked them together on the sink, and filled an old glass with tap water.

"You planning on sleeping through the whole night?"

"If I take these now I should," I said. "And that'll certainly help you figure out how to—not—" I impersonated his dramatic pauses from earlier.

The doorbell rang.

"No. Whatever it is, no." My voice echoed inside the glass. "Who is it?"

Lane went to the window and looked down to the front porch. "The cops are getting out of their car."

"That can't be good." I finished off the water and left the empty glass on the sink.

The doorbell rang twice.

"I'm coming." I yelled as loud as possible with my sore throat. I glanced back to make sure Lane was close.

He insisted on opening the door. If he wanted to be some sword-wielding knight, whatever. I tapped my foot impatiently, waving for him to hurry up as he inspected the guests through the glass panel beside the door. He looked confused. Once he opened the door, I was alarmed by the number of people crowded on my porch, four altogether.

"Are you cops?" I said and pointed at the strangers.

"Ms. Sullivan, do you know this woman?" the tall maybe-cop asked.

"Yes. This is Cindy, another death-replacement agent. Friend, not foe."

The one who held Cindy under her upper arm like a naughty child released her. I didn't bother to introduce the other woman. They probably knew Gloria if they were local cops. She worked with them often enough on various cases. And neither of them had been stupid enough to grab her. Once both Gloria and Cindy were beyond the threshold, I gave the cops a polite nod and shut the door in their faces.

"What's going on?" I asked.

Cindy's face was bright red. No doubt she'd been crying for hours. "I need to talk to you." Her eyes cut to Lane, her voice thick with snot. "Alone—if that's okay."

"Of course," he said. "I'm going to put some food together for Jess."

"Thanks," I told him. I squeezed his arm and he softened.

"I'll help you," Gloria said and followed Lane into the kitchen. Winston was also interested. He'd always been particularly fond of the sound of clanking pots and pans.

I led Cindy into my office. I offered her my desk chair with a gesture. She shook her head, seemingly happier to pace. So I slid into the chair myself and watched her march back and forth in my office, her arms crossed over her chest, hands tucked under her armpits.

Cindy's hair was blonder than Ally's, more of a white blond than a honey, but not full on platinum like Eve's. It was also shorter, cut near her chin, and her big blue eyes were like glass marbles. Cindy had a little mole on her cheek and pretty white teeth to match her pretty French-tipped nails. How often did she have to redo those nails? They must get trashed during replacements. With her knee-high boots, thigh length coat and overlapping necklaces, she looked like she had walked right out of a fashion magazine. She looked like an exotic bird in the neutral landscape of my office, amongst the beige walls and white furniture. And here I was in torn jeans, a zippered hoodie and my dirty, mismatched sneakers propped on a wreck of a desk.

"I need a minute," she said.

"Let's try to make this a quick minute," I said. "I took some pain pills so before they kick in would be good. Not sure what kind of sympathetic ear I'll be once I am high out of my mind."

"I had a problem and Gloria told me to come and see you."

I was surprised that Gloria would refer Cindy to me for anything. There was nothing I could do that Cindy couldn't. She was a necronite too, after all.

"She thought if I talked to you, I'd feel better. Or that if I talked to you, we might be able to figure this out, and that would make me feel better."

Eve popped into my head. "Did someone attack you?"

She shook her head. "No, not exactly."

I thought she'd elaborate, but she sort of paused, falling into a neutral pose. I wanted to shake her. "What? Just tell me."

"Would you think I was crazy if I told you—" she swallowed. "If I told you I'd seen something really, really, *really* weird."

"Midget clown porn weird or Ripley's Believe-It-or-Not weird?"

"Like a guy with wings weird," she said.

My throat twitched as if my larynx might have a seizure. I took a deep breath. "You've seen him, too?"

She exhaled as if she'd held all the air in the room in her lungs. "Thank God. I thought I was losing my mind. Not that I feel any better of course."

"When was your last death?" I asked. God, I didn't want this to turn into another Rachel incident. Then I remembered all the strange questions Garrison had asked me about Rachel and wondered if this was connected somehow.

"Nine days ago," she said. "But I've got one tomorrow."

"Why did Gloria bring you here?" I asked.

"Maybe she wants us to think we aren't crazy," she said. "But we totally are."

"Definitely. And shocked," I said, thinking of the first time I saw Gabriel against the wall. "I mean, who sees— Gabriel, right?" I bit off the words *'the archangel'*, suddenly feeling weird about giving Gabriel such a formal title.

Cindy's ecstatic relief vanished. "Gabriel?"

"Tall guy, black hair and wings, crazy green eyes, stupidly gorgeous—"

"—No. That's not who I see." Cindy's fear crept into her eyes.

"Who do you see?" I asked. I couldn't get Rachel out of

my head, the sight of her covered in her own blood. I tried to imagine finding Cindy the same way and my blood turned cold.

"Tall guy, red hair, brown eyes. He's got white wings and says his name's Raphael."

"You're seeing someone else?" I desperately tried to remember exactly what Rachel had said about the angels, but that was years ago. All I could recall was good angels and bad angels. "But—" I kicked up proverbial gravel, the wheels were spinning so fast. "What'd he say to you?"

"He wants me to go to Church," she said. "He wants me to go confess all of my sins."

I bit my lip, but that didn't work. I couldn't contain my laughter. "You're kidding."

"No." Cindy's face flushed bright red as sobs burst from her lips. "He told me I'd be dead within the week and I'd better do it while I had the chance."

My brow furrowed, pinching together. "Raphael sounds like an ass."

"I don't want to die," she said. "I'm single."

Lord, I wasn't about to go into romance with her. Like my life was any less of a mess in that department. "Have you talked to the cops yet?"

"Why, are they cute?"

"I didn't mean for a date," I said, shaking my head.

"If we mention this, you know they'll lock us up quicker than honey sticks to a bee's ass."

I had no idea what that meant. "That...sounds disgusting, but true, yes."

Brinkley told me that Rachel lost it because she died too much. Too many deaths scar the brain irreparably until one day it pops. But Cindy and I had far fewer deaths than Rachel, and the fact that we had seen similar hallucinations didn't make sense. Each mind is individual. Each of us would "lose our shit" as Cindy put it, in our own ways. One thing was for sure, we couldn't tell anyone this was going on. I had no intention of being locked up and fed mashed bananas for the rest of my life.

"Can you drive?" I asked. We needed to get out of this house so we could really talk.

"Sure," she said.

I had my shoes and jacket on when Lane caught us at the door. "Wait. Where are you going?"

"We have to run to the hospital," I told him. "I don't have much time before I'm loopy from the meds so I need to go now."

Gloria appeared with a packed dinner. I had no idea what it was but it was warm and smelled fantastic, like sweet tomato and basil—the last taste of summer.

"I'll be here when you get back," she said.

"Thanks." I accepted the food.

Lane wasn't letting me go so easy. The scowl said so. I don't know what came over me, the drugs maybe, but I was up on my tiptoes kissing him before I even realized that's what I'd meant to do. His mouth was hot on mine. He tensed, probably as surprised as I was because I'd never kissed him in front of anyone before.

I broke the kiss.

"I'll be right here," he whispered. But I pretended not to hear.

CHAPTER TWELVE

Dr. York entered the small examination room and barely glanced away from the file in his hands. He did reach down and help me up from the floor where I'd collapsed in part boredom, part pain pill high. He hit the lights, throwing us all into darkness. A heartbeat later a small light box fixed to the wall flickered and hummed to life. He tacked several see-through pictures up side-by-side on the box, the light beneath illuminating its shadows.

"This is yours, and this is yours," he said. He pointed to Cindy and me, respectively.

I looked at my fuzzy brain picture on the right. I blinked several times, trying to clear my head enough to comprehend what was being said.

"You see all this scarring," he said to Cindy. "Jesse's scarring has reduced somehow. By almost twenty percent."

He pulled another photograph from the file. "This was her picture from a year ago."

"I have no idea what this means," I said. Apparently, I'd been leaning backwards because the good doctor pulled me upright by the shoulder.

"It's not entirely healed, showing some small areas of damage here as we typically see in death-replacement agents, but it's certainly improved since the last scan. The damage is reversing itself, particularly in relation to the temporal lobe and cerebral cortex. You see here," he said. He pointed from my scan to Cindy's. "Every time an agent dies, they get a little tick mark like this on the brain."

"I thought we healed almost anything," I said.

"Your brain fixes your body, but the oxygen loss the brain experiences during each death can only be partially repaired. Small scarring occurs from the oxygen deprivation.

"And this scarring affects memory?" I asked, to be clear.

"Yes," the doctor said.

"They sure didn't mention that in the Become-an-Agent brochure," I told him. These so-called repairs might explain my sudden memory of my mom. It might also mean that more memories would come back to me sooner or later—for better or worse.

Cindy bit her lip. "It's also why we go crazy, right?"

"I do not see anything on the scans that indicate you girls are mentally unstable," he said. Then the doctor's eyes narrowed. "What exactly are you looking for?"

"We told you," I said. I rocked back on my heels and it was Cindy's turn to push me upright. "I've been having these terrible headaches."

"And you?" he asked Cindy.

"Just thought we'd use my brain, my completely normal, average and not-insane brain as a comparison for Jesse's test," she said, her tone an octave too high.

"How accommodating." He clicked his pen several times as if trying to decide who was full of more crap. "Well, to answer your question, no. There is scarring but it is typical given your occupation. I see no abnormalities. Physically, you're both fine."

He didn't smile. He studied us as if expecting us to confess the real reason for our visit. Finally he asked, "Anything else?"

"Nope, nothing else," Cindy said.

"Nothing at all," I added.

The doctor removed the X-rays and turned off the light box, leaving little spots to dance in front of my eyes. "If you don't have anything else for me, I need to go save Cooper."

Cindy placed a hand over her heart. Her accent thickened. "What happened to Cooper?"

The doctor pushed his reading glasses up and rubbed the bridge of his nose. "Bullet to the throat just under the mandible. The first five vertebrae of his spine disintegrated."

"Jesus, Mary, and Joseph," Cindy said. "How did this happen?"

"We aren't sure," he said. "We don't know if it was part of his replacement or if he was attacked like Jesse."

That explained why I hadn't heard from the charming Agent Garrison. Apparently, he had his hands full, as if chasing Brinkley or threatening me wasn't enough.

"I was shot like that once," I said. "You need a bone donor."

"Are you volunteering?" he asked. "Because we need a donor for that procedure."

"Uh, I can't regrow that much bone."

"We won't take up any more of your time," Cindy said, motioning to the door. "Go save Cooper."

After depositing a fresh piece of butterscotch in each of our palms, he disappeared. My eyes had drooped closed again. Cindy swore and plopped me into a chair.

"When you suggested coming to the hospital I thought you'd stay lucid enough to get through the visit."

"Don't judge me," I said. "I was in pain. I needed those pills. I'm not a junkie or anything."

"I'm not judging you. Half of America is on pills," she said. "But it's difficult to talk to someone seriously when they're falling all over the place."

"I'm sorry," I said. "I was trying to help you."

Cindy sighed. "You did. At least we know there isn't anything physically wrong."

"We know that?" I asked. I'd heard the words "brain damage."

"He said my scan is normal," she said.

"We could be physically fine *and* crazy," I said. "But at least we ruled out tumors, yes."

She folded her arms over her chest. "You don't believe in angels?"

"No." I knew something was up with my brain. Stuff in there was changing, but I couldn't help but be excited. Maybe I'd remember my dad next. Or maybe I'd spontaneously combust.

"Raphael isn't a hallucination," Cindy said, challenging me.

I didn't want to debate. "They might not be hallucinations, but that doesn't mean they're real."

She tilted her head. "Let's get you to bed. You're not making any sense."

"I am too," I said. I was high, but I knew what I was saying. Kind of.

"I'm listening," she said. Her lips puckered as if she had a mouthful of sour candy.

"Sometimes Gloria sees stuff, and it's not real," I said. "She calls them cues."

Mentioning Gloria's name seemed to give legitimacy to my ramblings. Her face lost its sourness and softened.

"She'll see an image that, of course, looks really real, but really it's more like a hint." I searched for the right phrase.

"Like information we're sensing in the universe, but don't necessarily understand."

"How can we sense things in the universe?"

"Like spiders," I said. "They take down their webs before there's ever a cloud in the sky. You know. They sense the pressure change or whatever and know it's going to rain. Animals know storms are coming, right?"

She was having difficulties deciphering my slurred words so I had to repeat myself twice until she got what I meant.

"So we're spiders," she repeated. "But what are we 'sensing'?"

"I don't know," I said. "But it's probably got to do with the replacement agents dying."

Cindy shifted her weight. "Cooper has been going on for months about how we're special. Replacement agents being natural evolutions of—"

"Cooper is an asshole and an X-men freak." I went on to explain what Brinkley had said to me about the agent attacks. By the time I finished, I wasn't sure if Cindy was in shock or if she was pissed at me for not making any sense in my drug-induced state.

"Come on," she said. "We're leaving."

The transition of scenery was instant. One minute Cindy was pulling me out of the chair in the examination room, and the next minute Gloria was laying me down on my bed at home. My bed was super soft and cool against my face. I squished a pillow against me and listened to them talk, while Gloria removed my shoes and tucked me under the covers. My eyes fluttered closed and their soft voices became disembodied sound waves, vibrating overhead.

"Where's Lane?" I asked into the pillow.

"I sent him home," Gloria said.

I pouted my lips out to show my disapproval.

Cindy didn't give a shit about my boy troubles. "She said there've been killings."

"You think it's connected to Raphael and Gabriel?" Gloria asked. There, she'd said it. Just put it all out there. No turning back now.

"Jesse thinks we're picking up, uh, a disturbance in the force or whatever."

"It's possible," Gloria said. "I've long since believed that my visions weren't supernatural. I'm sensitive to the world around me. I sense the natural order and can predict how it will play out based on the present course. Humans are habitual. Every single one of us is traveling on a trajectory created by our own habits whether we realize it or not."

Cindy kept talking, probably happy to speak to someone with comprehensible speech. "Why are Gabriel and Raphael so different if they're illusions? Wouldn't they reflect the same information if they're both signals?"

"These metaphorical angels could be different aspects of the same situation or they're somehow different based on your personalities—"

"Or?" Poor Cindy turned downright frantic.

"Or they're really spirits with goals and intentions, manipulating you for a particular aim."

"That's real comforting," I said into the pillow. "I've always wanted to be a puppet."

"Do you think they're spirits?" Cindy asked her.

"No," I said. Gloria didn't answer.

I peeked my eyes open in time to see Cindy sink into the chair in the corner. "If they are angels, let me add that I'd buy it if they were. I'm Christian, so it comes with the package. But if they are angels, why are they different? Wouldn't they want the same thing? Wouldn't they both follow God's will?"

"Did Raphael have a tie that changed colors like a mood ring?" I asked.

"No."

"Jesse, honey, what's your point?" Gloria asked, pulling the cover down to see my face.

"If they have tie preferences they have taste. And if they have taste they are different from each other, right?"

Gloria turned to Cindy. "What makes you think they're different?"

"Gabriel is helping Jesse whereas Raphael is—he's really pessimistic and mean." Fresh tears crowded the edge of her words. God, I didn't want to see that. I buried my face deeper in the pillow.

"Maybe that's the way you perceive the situation," Gloria said. "You've no reason to suspect he wants something bad to happen to you."

Cindy must've made a face because Gloria gasped as if repulsed. "What happened?"

"When I came to see you I was upset," Cindy said.

"Yes, I thought Jesse might comfort you."

"No, that's not what I mean," Cindy said. I heard her earrings jingle as she shook her head.

"I came to you because I was afraid."

"Did Raphael touch you inappropriately?" I asked.

"Jesse," Gloria said.

"I hear that's what they do," I said. "Isn't that why they got kicked out of heaven because they got frisky with the ladies and didn't stop when God said no?"

Cindy wasn't in the mood for jokes. "Raphael told me to go the church on Broadway. He wanted me to confess to the priest there. If the Church is responsible for these attacks, that'd be the worst place to send me, right?"

"You don't know that's what he meant," Gloria said. "I misinterpret signs all the time."

"Can you be both Christian and—like us?"

"Don't be silly," Gloria said.

Cindy got really quiet, whispering. "Maybe I'm damned."

"You are not," Gloria said, shaking her. "Don't be ridiculous."

"I thought it was beautiful," she finally said in a whisper. "I was six when they televised The Amalgamation. The Truce my momma called it. Do you remember it?"

"No," I mumbled and it is true that I didn't remember the Church uniting.

"For hours, they showed clips of all the faiths, pledging allegiance to one another. Every single one of them in countries all over the world. Hour after hour. Priests, ministers, pastors placing their hands on the Bible and pledging fellowship, then their followers. Each church would keep doing things in their own way, but now they acknowledged each other as equal. Can you even imagine it? The Church, they even referred to themselves collectively. It was everything Christ talked about. No more fighting."

"I bet the Muslims loved that."

"But that's the point." Cindy shrieked. "In accepting each other they accepted everyone else too. The point of The Amalgamation was to end all religious warring. It was Christianity's attempt to end the rivalry once and for all, and it worked."

"Because they had their new devil," I said.

"What I remember is martial law," Gloria said. It was her turn to sound nostalgic. "Necronites shuffling the streets, turned out by their families. We were mobilized immediately to settle the civil unrest but it wasn't enough. Tanks—rolling down our own streets."

"Get back to your story," I insisted. I didn't like where this was going. "About Raphael."

"I went to the church," Cindy said. She stared at the floor as if she were envisioning a scene. "I sat down in a pew and started to pray. Then one of the clergymen approached and demanded I come with him."

"He probably wanted to offer you counsel if you looked distraught," Gloria offered.

Cindy shook her head. "The way he grabbed my arm, he wasn't trying to comfort me. He was practically dragging me away."

"Where would he take you?" Gloria asked.

"I don't know," she said. "Someone came in and called his name. I pulled away from him and ran."

"You need to tell Garrison," Gloria said. "It may help the investigation."

"He didn't really do anything wrong," Cindy said, biting her lip. "It was just a feeling."

"Priests are creepy," I muttered into my pillows.

"Why would Raphael send me there if he knew I'd get hurt?" Cindy asked. "The church is only two blocks from where Cooper got shot. Raphael knew exactly what he was doing."

"Are you sure Gabriel doesn't mean you harm?" Gloria asked me.

I snorted. "If he were really trying to save me, you'd think he'd have said something before I almost got my head chopped off."

"But if they're angels—" Cindy said.

Gloria interrupted her. "Just because they've got wings doesn't make them angels."

"You know," I said. The shady blob of an idea in the back of my mind solidified. "If we want to know what's going on with the angels, I know who we can ask."

Cindy squeezed my leg. "Who?"

"Rachel."

CHAPTER THIRTEEN

"Do I look slutty?" I tugged at the short skirt that came way too high up my thighs. After a nice, long sleep in which I lost the night and most of the next day, I woke in a much better mood. Better yet, I woke up with a plan.

We were at Gloria's place, a squat one-story pile of bricks. Unlike my subdivision, all of these houses were exactly the same. I imagined they all had three bedrooms, two baths with detached garages and decent-sized yards. Ally, Gloria, and I congregated here because we knew we could talk without being overheard.

Safe in Gloria's bedroom, they dressed me in Ally's heels, a black skirt and tight shirt. The shirt did something magical to my breasts. My hair tumbled down in wild, tousled waves. Ally had glopped on a lot of eyeliner, so it looked weird to me. That was probably because the most makeup I wore was lip balm on any given day. Mascara if I felt fat.

"You need to look the part," Ally said. "Just a girl going out with friends."

"I know, I know. I have to look like I'm there to party, not skip town. I want them to think I'm using my suspension to let loose."

Ally handed me a shoulder bag that could be mistaken for a huge purse. "This is all you get."

I unzipped the top part of the dark bag to see inside. I had a wad of cash, a toothbrush, deodorant, and clean underwear. I also had a different, more respectable-looking, shirt.

"If I give you a bigger bag it'll be too obvious," she said. "Just make do with what you've got."

"There must be $200 here. I'll only be gone for a night," I said. *Unless of course I'm arrested for murder—then it's the rest of my life.*

"I emptied your piggy bank into the Coin-Star machine. It'd look too suspicious if any of us withdrew a chunk of cash right now," she said.

"I suggest you avoid public places with video cameras," Gloria added.

"You basically want me to drive straight there and back on cash only?" I asked. "And to stay out of sight."

"I'd go with you, but they'll expect that," Ally said. "Just go to the funeral and come right back."

Okay, so maybe I hadn't told Ally the whole truth. Yes, I was sneaking out of town to attend my mother's funeral. I was also planning a detour to St. Louis so that I could question Rachel. St. Louis was only an hour away from my mom's place. I could do both.

Gloria kept her mouth shut.

"You guys watch too much television," I said and tried to keep my tone casual. "I don't think they're monitoring my every move. I'm not on FBI's most wanted or anything."

"Be careful," Ally said. I didn't like the sad expression she gave me. Ever since I'd resolved to go, she'd been giving me this same pitiful look.

"Cheer up, would you? I'll be back," I said.

"You have the night to get there and the day to spend with Danny, but try to get back by five so you'll be home before dark. If we're lucky they'll think they just lost track of you for the day. No harm, no foul."

I adjusted my boobs the way I'd seen Eve do it. I had to admit, it was a pretty fantastic trick. "Quit worrying. I promise I'll be quick about it."

"Directions are in your bag," Ally said with the renewed, devastated tone. She bit her lip.

"Are you sure you want to go? That woman didn't do a damn thing for you."

"I have to check on Danny," I said, my heart aching. "I want to know who'll be taking care of him. It's the least I can do."

But what the hell would I say to him was the real question. I felt like I had to apologize for missing most of his childhood. I'd always thought my mother had told him I was dead, but it turned out he'd known all along. What excuse had she given him for my absence? What lies had she told the kid?

I did one more turn in the mirror. "I can't walk in these heels." What I meant was, I can't run fast in heels if something went wrong. It was bound to go wrong, right? I can't skip town, evade the authorities and visit a mental patient and expect no drama.

After exchanging the heels for a gray sneaker and a blue sneaker, I organized my getaway bag to make sure I had everything. Gloria walked us to the car and gave me another squeeze. She didn't say anything, her face golden in the streetlight.

Shivering against the chilly fall night in my scant skirt, I climbed into the car the second Ally unlocked the door. Our headlights illuminated the cop car as we pulled out. Two pairs of beady little eyes glared back at us, like raccoons in a dumpster.

I gave Gloria a little wave as she waited in her driveway for us to leave.

The cops did a U-turn and followed us. "Surprise, surprise."

Ally's dark eyes flicked to the rearview mirror. She drove straight to the warehouse, cops on our tail. It wasn't until she parked the car in the back lot that she spoke to me again.

"Got your license?" she asked.

"Of course." I got carded for everything. I felt like I was perpetually under the you-must-be-this-tall-to-ride line. Going somewhere without ID wasn't really an option for me.

"Okay." She gripped the wheel and tried to twist it in her hands as the cop car came to a stop adjacent from us in the dark lot. They stayed to the right, probably for a good, uninterrupted view of the entrance. Not the least bit discreet. Ally didn't take her eyes off of them. She spoke again. "You don't have to do this. Seriously, we can send your mother a huge bouquet."

"I want to go," I said. And I needed to know more. "You can't make up a funeral."

Waiting around to be killed or going completely insane wasn't an option. Everything with Eve's accomplice, Brad Cestrum, Atlanta, and the replacement agents dying was beyond my control, but I did have control over what was wrong with me. I was exploding things. I was hallucinating. And if I didn't get proactive about these angel sightings, it was going to get worse. So I couldn't do anything about the investigation or the murders, but I sure as hell could deal with the angels and put my energy into figuring out if I was crazy or not.

And then there was Daniel.

Ally pushed the hair behind my ears and leaned dangerously close. "Please don't go. I have the worst feeling about this."

"I'll be careful," I promised, and the intimacy of the dark car pressed in on me, drawing my attention to little things that I usually didn't notice. The soft sound of her breath. The heat of it on my cheek. The smell of her shampoo.

Ally looked so beautiful in the shadows with only the stray orange light from street lamps—her cute, tiny ears and eyes turning from black to gold. I found myself leaning toward her, catching the scent of peppermint gum. I was warm and dizzy from it. I wanted to kiss her, but I stopped. Ally had told me not to confuse her and this was exactly what she meant.

I opened my eyes, completely unaware that I'd even closed them as I leaned in, she was right there. Her long lashes collected the orange light and she waited for me to make my move. And despite the invitation, I knew better. I knew better than to hurt one of the most important people in my life by dangling a commitment I could never give her in front of her face like a cat toy.

"I love you," she said. It wasn't the first time she'd said it.

"I love you too," I said. And I meant it. I pressed myself against the door, pushing myself out of the car with what little restraint I had left.

At the entrance to The Loft a tall girl with dreadlocks extended her hand. "ID, please."

I fished it from the top of my bag, doing my best to hide the other contents.

She angled it in the neon light of The Loft sign above the doorway. Satisfied, she passed it back to me between two fingers. "Five bucks." Maybe I looked older with all this makeup.

I gave her the cash. She pushed open the heavy metal door as if it were light as cotton candy.

The inside of the club was all smoke, shadows, and flashing colored lights. A full spectrum of prismatic colors cut through the air in rotation, guided by the colorful balls in the ceiling that seemed to dictate the rays' trajectories. If Ally, or anyone for that matter, said a word to me, I couldn't hear it. Not over the chest-thumping bass and techno treble flooding the room in repetitious waves.

Ally pulled my hand, urging me away from the door. We headed for the girl's bathroom, the only place quiet enough to talk. Umbri and Kyra, Ally's friends from her old job, were in the bathroom already when we walked in.

Umbri and Ally used to work together at the same coffee shop. Once they became after-work buddies, Ally met Kyra, Umbri's best friend. They'd been hanging out for almost a year before I came into the picture.

I pointed at them. "How did they—?"

Ally held up her phone. "I texted them." She checked under the stalls for feet and, satisfied it was only us, slid the deadbolt into place.

"Very cryptic like," Kyra said.

Umbri read her screen. "Meet us in the bathroom. Come alone."

Both Kyra and Umbri moved forward with wide eyes. They tenderly pulled my gauze down with *Ooos* and *Aahhs*.

"Girl, you are so badass," Umbri said. She was Japanese-American with short spiky hair falling forward into her eyes. Her eyes almost seemed closed when she smiled this big.

"I saw you on television and I couldn't believe it. Ho must've been off her meds," Kyra said. She flipped her brunette ponytail off her shoulders as she leaned closer to inspect my wound. "You know, it's not as fun calling her a whore when she's actually a whore."

Ally tugged me away from them. "Worst part is we don't know why she did it."

That wasn't my "worst part" of that experience.

"Ally says you need a car to leave town for a while," Umbri said. She turned to the mirror and applied more glittery lipstick. As she moved in the light, I realized she was covered in glitter.

"Yeah, the cops are watching me. They can't know I've left town."

"Wow, I think this is the most trouble you've ever been in, right?" Umbri, having fixed her eyeliner, abandoned the mirror to give me her full attention.

I nodded. "Hands down."

"Even more than that time the dog ate your finger and we had to wait until it—"

Ally held up her hands to intercept. "They disinfected it before it was sewn back on."

I wiggled my right middle finger to emphasize that it was as good as new.

Kyra looked like she might puke, though I couldn't imagine her doing anything as unladylike as hurling her guts up. Kyra was the tallest of us, with the long, lean body of a dancer. Her complexion actually had some color to it; whereas I was as pasty white as can be. I blamed my poor circulation.

"You can borrow my car," Kyra said. "I don't even care if they arrest you and impound it."

Kyra was a trust fund baby, so this was probably true.

"I'd rather not get arrested, thanks," I said.

"Check it. Here's what we'll do," Umbri said. "Kyra will go out and get her car in an hour or so, whenever the crowd gets pretty thick. Jesse can slip through the back exit. They'll go back to Kyra's place, drop her off, and Jesse will be on her way."

"But what if someone sees Jesse get into Kyra's car?"

Kyra snapped her fingers. "The east door is dark and out

of the way. You can't see it from the road and if I roll down the back window I can pull right up against the exit and you can leap through the window into the backseat."

I wasn't sure about this leaping idea. Hell, I wasn't even sure I was capable of leaping. What was I, a lemur?

"What if someone suspects and follows you?" Ally asked. She tugged the end of her hair.

"If I think we're being followed, Jesse can hide in the car until it is safe," Kyra said. "Or if it looks like it won't work, she'll have to stay the night at my place. She'll come inside with me and act like it was the plan the whole time."

"Sounds good to me," Umbri said. She moved to unlock the bathroom door, but paused to wait for us.

Ally's brow was furrowed, signaling an intense internal processing. Finally, she agreed.

At Ally's approval we left the bathroom, reintegrating ourselves into the throbbing masses.

There were glowsticks in addition to the glitter now. I figured out the sticks were like fire, if moved real fast I could write my name in the smoky darkness.

Umbri was a great DJ. Honestly, I didn't know much about DJs, but everyone else seemed impressed, which made me impressed. She looked totally at home up there on the speaker throne.

When Ally wasn't hovering awkwardly beside me on the dance floor, she was at the bar throwing down shots, which was a sight unto itself. Ally rarely drank anything more than an occasional glass of wine with dinner.

At one point, she returned to the dance floor crying, and threw her arms around me. It made us look like we were slow dancing, even though the music didn't quite suit.

I didn't know why she was so sad.

Had Garrison said something to her? Was she in trouble too and decided not to tell me? Brinkley? I didn't know, but did my best to comfort her, threading my fingers through her hair.

Kyra appeared to our left and squeezed my shoulder. Remembering what I was about to do made my guts churn. With one last desperate hug from Ally, I was off following Kyra out of the crowd to the dark and empty part of The Loft.

The leaping wasn't easy, even when the car was stationary. I banged my elbows, knees, and scraped my shins on Kyra's window sill as I climbed through. I hoped no one inside the club saw my little shimmy because I think they got a pretty good view of what was up my skirt if they had been watching. I didn't hurt my neck though.

"Thank you so much for doing this," I said to Kyra as I squished myself through the narrow space between the two front seats with about as much grace as a three-legged dog.

"What are friends for if not to help you evade the law?" She batted her big brown eyes mischievously.

"Break laws, hide your dead body, and find missing pets. Those sorts of things I think."

"Those too," she agreed. "But Winston hadn't gone far."

I lapsed into silence and Kyra nudged me. "Nervous?"

"A little," I admitted. "And I hope I'm not doing this for the wrong reasons."

Kyra shrugged, turning on her blinker with a flick of her wrist. "Your mom died and you haven't seen your brother in years. What other reasons do you need?"

I meant Rachel. Why was I going back to see Rachel? It wasn't just to ask her questions, was it?

"Chances are this won't go well," I said. "Hello, I'm Jesse, Danica's zombie daughter. Remember me? Then someone has a heart attack, I replace them and I'm a corpse on the living room floor." I'd already envisioned a fabricated version of some distant relative, who looked like a standardized '50s housewife, breaking a teacup and fainting just before I pop up and brush myself off, post-mortem.

It'd be cool if I could do that.

Kyra laughed. "Yeah, but I get why you want to go back. People have these weird ties to their families, even when their family is crazy like mine."

Kyra's parents were art dealers, running a large firm with offices in New York, Philadelphia, and San Francisco. Her family's income made my cushy-suburban life look pitiful by comparison. After all, they could afford to pay for her apartment on West End Avenue, a lovely sky rise with a great view of downtown. They were also paying for her Ph.D. in Art History.

"Okay, I've got to ask," she said, breaking the silence. "It's killing me and Umbri."

I was surprised by her playful switch in tone. "Just ask me."

"Who do you love—Lane or Ally?"

My jaw hinges broke leaving a gaping hole where my mouth should've been.

"Oh come on," Kyra said smacking the steering wheel. "Who are you in love with? I voted for Lane; is it Lane?"

I angled all the heating vents away from my blazing face. "I'm not in love with anyone."

Her grin got crazy huge. "Oh my god, are you sleeping with both of them?"

"No."

She frowned as if she didn't like this answer either. "It's obvious they're both madly in love with you."

"And it's obvious that dating either of them is the worst idea ever."

"But you've slept with Ally," she said.

How did she know this? Did Ally talk to Umbri?

"So if you sleep with her again nothing will change."

Ally must've told Umbri. I was going to kill her. "Sleeping with Ally almost ruined our friendship," I said. "And I don't sleep with more than one person at a time anyway."

"So you are sleeping with Lane," she declared. "Is he amazing? I bet he is amazing. He has the hottest ass. It's so cute I want to squeeze it every time—"

"Oh, god, Kyra, just stop." I pretended to count the streetlights.

"And Ally sleeps in your bed. You've got a hot single lesbian sleeping in your bed and you don't do anything?"

"We cuddle but that's it. Sometimes she reads to me or gives me a massage if I'm sore."

Kyra smirked.

"What?" I asked.

"That sounds so—" she pretended to search for a word. "*Gay*."

I remained defiant. "I'm not in a relationship with anyone. And Lane and I have decided to stop having sex."

"You've got *two* someones, but you're not getting laid." She frowned. "That's so sad."

"When was the last time you got laid?"

"Saturday and don't change the subject. Umbri thinks you should be with Ally and I want you with Lane," she said. "So you're going to have to choose one of them because we've got money on this."

I scoffed. "You make it sound so easy."

We pulled into her driveway. She hesitated in her seat, not getting out. "You know what?"

I had my hand on the door handle, ready to get out and switch places with her. "What?"

"I want to come with you. Let's road trip it."

My eyes searched the area. It didn't look like we'd been followed, but I wasn't any good at this sort of thing. "You could get in trouble if they catch you with me. And don't you have work?"

"It's not like I can't afford the bail," she said. "And I'm all caught up with work. I can spare a day."

I must have looked doubtful.

"I'm serious," she said.

Ally hadn't come because Garrison would certainly have an eye her. Kyra was different. Our lives were separate enough that her absence might not raise any suspicions. "Are you sure?"

"Absolutely, this is a big deal. I don't think you should go alone and I'm in the mood for a road trip."

"You want to hound me about Ally and Lane."

"There's that too," she said, with a cutesy head tilt.

"And Ally probably begged you to go," I added.

Her grin widened, but she neither confirmed nor denied my accusation. I relaxed, unaware that I'd even been tense. Had I really been afraid of going alone? Even if I did want the company, how was I going to get Kyra over to St. Louis to see Rachel?

"OK," I said finally. I was already formulating a new plan in my mind. "I'll drive."

CHAPTER FOURTEEN

As we pulled away from the tiny two-pump gas station in a nameless town, a large green Interstate I-64 junction sign caught my eye. I had to make my move. Now or never.

"Have you ever been to St. Louis?" I asked.

"When I was a kid," Kyra said. "I remember going up in the Arch and being terrified because of how much it sways in the wind."

"You want to go again?" I asked. I think my smile was too big, too urgent. "It's only 80 miles away."

"Your mom's funeral starts in four hours," she said. "We hardly have time for sightseeing."

"We can bum around the city for a whole hour or so and be back in plenty of time," I said, smiling. I hoped I wasn't overdoing it.

Kyra didn't look interested. "I don't think we should change the plan."

"Here's the truth." I had to confess at least part of my plan. I don't want to sight-see. "I used to live in St. Louis and I had this best friend, Rachel. She was more of a mentor really. Anyway, she got sick and now she lives in a hospital. I really want to see her."

Kyra hesitated, so I resorted to sticking my bottom lip out a little further.

"For an hour?" she asked.

"Less," I said. "We can probably even squeeze in the Arch if you want."

"I'd rather go to the Saint Louis Art Museum. They have the world's largest Max Beckmann collection, but there's no way I could be in and out of that place in an hour."

"But you'll take me?" I asked. I was careful to keep my bottom lip thing going.

"Only if you swear not to tell Ally," she said, taking the exit onto I-64W St. Louis. "If she knows we deviated from the plan, she'll kill me."

"I'd replace you, no problem," I said, happily bouncing in my seat. "Oh, and one more thing."

Kyra's shoulders tensed.

"When I say hospital, I mean mental hospital."

"Oh my god, Jesse."

"You don't have to go in," I added, quickly. "And I swear I won't be very long."

Kyra swore under her breath, but she didn't turn back. I took that as a good sign.

It wasn't that difficult to find St. Louis Psychiatric Rehabilitation Center. Mostly because Kyra had GPS, but also because the GPS failed to tell us everything, like in telling us which entrance to use. My memory made up for the rest. I'd only been here once, on our last day in St. Louis, but it was memorable.

I was out of the car, and Kyra hadn't moved out of the driver's seat. "Aren't you coming?"

"You said I didn't have to!"

My heart sped up at the idea of entering alone, but I

couldn't blame Kyra if this wasn't her idea of a good time. Asylums are super creepy. Still, I kind of expected her to go in anyway. Ally would have.

"I'll be right back," I said and reluctantly closed the door.

A large sweeping entryway with columns stretched up several stories. The urge to run back to the car was unsettling and definitely ominous.

The building itself was a square box of bricks and looked like it should be an old school or orphanage. A green and gold dome sat on top, pointing suggestively at the sky. Inside the look of last century prevailed with white cinder block walls and bland tile that squeaked beneath my sneakers.

I couldn't remember where she was in the building but I found a plaque on the wall, one with a black background and movable white letters. I refrained from moving them around to make dirty words and instead searched for the ward I needed.

On the fourth floor I was confronted by a large reception desk, manned by a squat nurse with a beehive hairdo. I imagined her wearing her hair like this for the last five decades.

"We don't have visiting hours except on Wednesdays," she explained.

"I'm from out of state. I drove from really far away," I pleaded. I bat my eyes. "Please."

"Who are you here to visit?" she asked.

"Rachel Wright."

She looked at her chart again and asked for my name. I gave it to her before it even occurred to me to give a fake name.

"You're on the authorized list, and you do have an out of state address, so I'll let it slide this once, hon," she said with a tight smile. "Just sign this check-in sheet, please."

I wasn't sure why my name was on the list unless Brinkley put it there. I stared at the columns and hesitated. I didn't want it to be known that I was here, but if I wanted to see her, what choice did I have? I scribbled my name as illegibly as possible. That way if anyone wanted to use this sheet in the court of law, there was no way in hell they could prove it was my signature. "Where is she?"

"Wait here and I'll ask her where she wants to see you," the nurse said.

Where she wants? Since when did they let the mental patients decide things? I was puzzling over this when Queen Bee reappeared, holding a door open for me.

"Down this hall, fifth door to the right, hon," she said. "She's in her room."

"You're going to let me visit her in her room?" I asked. My shock must've been apparent. "Alone?"

"We put a chair in there for you." She shooed me down the hallway toward an open door at the end and returned to her paperwork.

I had no idea what I expected to see in Rachel's bedroom or what state I expected Rachel to be in, but this wasn't it.

As the nurse promised, they'd brought in a chair and sat it by one of the beds. Two twin beds rested side by side, one empty, one with Rachel in it. Rachel had her back against the wall and her knees pulled close enough to her chest to balance a pad of paper on her knees. Between the beds sat two end tables, one for each bed.

"Don't be scared," Rachel said, dark eyes peering over the edge of her knees. "I've had my medication today."

I must have made a face because she burst out laughing.

"Oh, Jessup, come on. Lighten up," she laughed so hard tears stung her eyes. "I'm kidding." She put her pad of paper on the bed. It was a sketchbook similar to the one I'd given Gloria. With her hands free, she motioned me into the room. The fact that she was catatonic and drooling the last time I saw her made this lively Rachel more than a tad shocking.

I stepped into the room.

"A little closer," she motioned. The side of her hand was black with charcoal from her drawings, but seeing charcoal all over her hands was better than blood any day. "Let me get a good look at you. You haven't aged a bit, not that we do, of course."

I got a good look at her too. Her hair was the same chin-length bob, sleek and black as crow feathers. Her eyes were black marbles in her olive face and I'd almost forgotten about the Monroe mole on her left cheek. Scrub-like pajamas and no makeup didn't compare to the vibrant clothes and bright lipsticks that Rachel used to wear: lots of red and fuchsia, which always made her dark features that much more exotic. She wasn't as glamorous as I remembered, but I guess living in a mental hospital will do that to a person.

"This is the part where you pay me a compliment," she said, pretending to be affronted. "Have I taught you nothing?"

"You look well," I stammered and tried to blink my way out of shock. "Way better than I expected."

"Yeahhh," she said, drawing the word out. "I've come a long way in the past two years, thanks to Brinkley."

"Sorry." I thought she was being sarcastic because he'd put her here.

"For what?" she cocked her head playfully to one side. It was so old-Rachel that I smiled. "I'm grateful for all he does for me."

I wasn't following her. "What has he done for you?"

"He visits. He brings me goodies and makes sure I have the best food and doctors. Patients like me have no families to speak of, yet I have three separate volunteers who come and spend time with me. One of them, Andrew, is so cute."

She batted her eyes as if she truly believed she was

spoiled. God, I'd never realized that I'd learned my mock modesty from her.

"You look so surprised," she said, laughing again.

"Because the last time I saw you, you were practically unconscious. And the time before that—" I blurted. Immediately, I took a step back. I'd read somewhere that if patients are confronted with their afflictions, they flip out. Or at least that's what I thought I'd read in one of those articles Brinkley made me read, hoping I'd understand my clients' aversion to dying. That's what I expected Rachel to do, flip out in denial and attack me.

"I'm really sorry about that," she said. "I didn't have good control back then. The power was overwhelming, but I've learned to control it. I can only hope you'll forgive me for the past."

"What do you mean 'the power was overwhelming'?" I grabbed the back of the metal chair, but kept it between us. She was beginning to sound crazy again.

"You know what power I'm talking about," she said. "I know you came here for answers. Even if you aren't awake yet, you know you're different."

I spent most of my time as a corpse. Of course I knew I was different. "What do you mean I'm not awake? I'm talking to you, aren't I?"

She leaned in close and studied me. I didn't feel particularly safe, hiding behind a chair.

"I see," she began. "Someone just flipped your switch. You're still warming up." She returned to her drawing. "I, for one, am very excited, given who you are and all."

"Why are you whispering?" I asked. *Because she's crazy.* "And what do you mean who I am?"

She stopped drawing and frowned. "His daughter."

"Whose daughter? Brinkley's?" I asked. I wasn't sure why Brinkley popped into my head.

Maybe because he was the only man old enough that both Rachel and I knew.

Rachel burst out laughing. "No."

Then more and more laughter until tears blurred her eyes.

"This was a bad idea," I said. "I don't know why I thought coming here was the answer."

Rachel's hair fell forward into her eyes and curled under her chin. "Because you want to know about the angels."

That stopped me. And the sing-song tone of her voice put me on edge. She was so normal five seconds ago, that I'd almost forgotten she was crazy. Worse, I felt strange in Rachel's presence, which I could only describe as electric. My skin seemed to shiver against my bones and my mouth went dry. Even though I was convinced she was obviously completely insane, her words stirred something inside me.

"Can't you just tell me?" I asked.

She pointed at the drawings on her walls, the ones I'd casually overlooked when first entering. I knew the people in the pictures, including Ally and Gabriel—two people Rachel had never met.

Anger rose fresh up my throat and threatened to consume me. I tried to focus. Seeing Gabriel's face on the walls was enough to remind me why I was here. "Some hurt and some help. That's what you said. Tell me about the angels."

She glanced at me over her sketchpad but remained silent. It took every ounce of self-restraint not to knock the notepad out of her hand and demand she speak to me. Scared that I might actually lose my temper on someone who was as mentally fragile as a child, I turned to leave.

"Wait," Rachel called out, sounding terrified. "Don't go."

"You don't want to talk," I said. I kept my voice tight, restrained. I couldn't be mean to her.

She put the book down. "Can I at least have a hug?"

No way. I wasn't even comfortable sitting beside the bed. How could I let a crazy person wrap her arms around me?

Go ahead.

The command was clear in my mind, seemingly more urgent with her outstretched hands groping the air for me.

Do it.

I crossed the room, one step after another. I was within her reach but she didn't grab for me. She only opened her arms wider and invited me in. Was she compelling me with her mind or something crazy—no.

You can trust her, Jesse.

I recognized the voice but I didn't acknowledge it out loud. A mental asylum was the last place you'd catch me talking to my hallucination.

Then I saw him, sitting in the empty twin bed. One ankle crossed over the other as he slouched against the wall behind it.

"Come on, Jessup," Rachel pressed, wiggling her fingers. "Didn't you miss me even a little bit?"

"More than you know," I whispered. I meant it. This was my chance to apologize for real. "I'm so sorry for what happened to you. I blame myself. If you hadn't worked so hard to train me, replacing so many people—"

Rachel pulled me off my feet into her bed. My heart tightened in panic as her arms closed around me.

"You were worth it," she whispered and pinched my ear lobes and then my cheeks, an old comforting gesture.

Tears welled up in my eyes. I was torn between guilt over her condition and fear that it was only a matter of time before I ended up right here beside her.

"You will be the one to save us, Jessup. I've seen it." Rachel's arms, soft at first, coiled tighter. It was like feeling a boa constrictor slowly tighten around my neck. So slow that I didn't realize I was in trouble until I couldn't move. I tried to jerk away from her, but she only tightened her hold.

Her voice was so soft that I had to quit squirming or risk losing her words in the shuffle of our clothes and the bedding. "You must listen to your angel and only your angel. He knows what you need better than you do."

"Wh—"

She squeezed me hard enough to force the air out of my lungs and cut off my words. "They're watching you, Jessup. And listening. Be careful of what you let them see. Keep your power secret. Trust only your angel."

My heart was a thunderous roar in my temples. Combined with her death grip, the room was reduced to spots around me. It reminded me of Eve's attack in the worst way. Claustrophobic. Suffocating.

I gagged on my own spit, choking. She let go of me and air rushed in like a high wave pounding the sand. How in the hell was she so strong? What were they feeding her? I stumbled to my feet, trying to breathe. Granted, I probably made it worse by struggling.

A loud ripping sound echoed off the white walls as Rachel tore the picture she'd been working on out of her notebook and folded it up.

She thrust it into my hand. "Choose carefully. You'll need her the most—in the end."

I wanted to open the picture, hoping it would make her words clear but she placed a hand on mine, stopping me. "Time's up."

Gabriel didn't look relaxed. He stood, ready for anything. *You must go.*

I don't know how he did it, but I saw the men perfectly in my mind. Three goons who looked like big trouble, harassing the Queen Bee at the desk. Even though the desk was down the hall and out of sight, I saw the image perfectly as if we were standing right beside it.

"Thanks," I whispered to Rachel. I wasn't sure what I was grateful for, her not choking me to death probably. Whatever the reason, I felt like she'd done me a big favor. I slipped the paper into the back pocket of my jeans.

"It's always good to see you," she said and a sudden wide grin broke across her face. "And I'll see you again, Jess. Good luck."

The desk lady with the beehive squealed. "You can't go in there."

I ducked across the hall into another room and found myself staring at a middle-aged man in a flower-print dress. He was sitting on the bed and a woman was squatting in front of him, putting makeup on his face. They were both patients.

Scared they'd leap up and go crazy on me, I blurted a compliment. "You're beautiful."

"You can't look yet," the woman demanded in a gravelly voice. "He's not ready."

"I won't peek," I promised, focusing half my attention out the small glass window set into the door to see two men duck into Rachel's room. The other half of my attention remained on the two mental patients crouching behind me.

As soon as the goons entered, the door snapped shut as if slammed from the inside and I heard the strangest sounds. I yanked my door open and darted across the hall to save her and Rachel's face appeared.

She smiled through the tiny window and flashed me a thumbs up. I dumbly stared past her grinning face at the two unconscious guys that she'd piled up on the adjacent bed. I had a feeling Rachel's gifts were not limited to mediocre drawing or speaking in riddles.

I reentered the main room and found Queen Bee arguing with the last man. I pulled the hood of my hoodie up and yanked the drawstring to cover most of my face creeping past him on my toes. I prayed the whole time that my shoes wouldn't squeak or that Queenie wouldn't yell at me to sign out.

Just before I exited through the large double doors, the sole of my shoe dragged against the tile.

I froze.

The man arguing at the desk turned and caught sight of me. He yelled to his unconscious buddies. I ran as fast as I could, hoping he'd wait for his back-up that wouldn't come. I cut into the corridor and ran past the elevators to the stairs.

I'd never moved so fast in my life. I reached the bottom of the stairwell and I felt great about this. I was brilliant, I was quick, and I was made to survive, as if NRD gave me no other choice.

I threw open the door, cut through the last stretch of the first-floor corridor, and popped out the side exit. Kyra's car sat in the distance, my beacon of salvation.

Someone grabbed me from behind, two arms engulfing me.

"I'll cut you," I screamed. I thrashed like a landed fish as large hands lifted me off my feet, kicking. "I'll cut you with my mind powers."

"Since when do you have mind powers?" Brinkley said.

I stopped thrashing and he dropped me. I spun around. He'd grown some scruffy jaw hair. His blue eyes were puffy from lack of sleep and I'd never noticed so much gray on his head before. Whatever he'd been doing to keep me safe, he'd been doing it instead of sleeping.

"What the hell are you doing here?" he asked.

A heavy door slammed somewhere and Brinkley took that as his cue to drag me by the elbow toward Kyra's car.

"What the hell are *you* doing here?" I screamed as we

raced across the lawn to the parking lot. "You've been keeping secrets."

"I followed you. Now get in the car," Brinkley said. He tried to tear Kyra's door open but the car was locked. The click of it being released sounded and Brinkley tried to stuff me inside. I clung to the door, refusing to be stuffed into the car, and Kyra gasped.

"People are trying to kill me because they know things about me that I don't. Unless you're trying to get me killed talk to me."

He yanked on the door again, but I pushed against it. "Get in."

"No."

"Stop fighting me and get in the damn car," he demanded.

"No, I'm not leaving until you tell me what you know. You owe me that much. If I'm going to die, I better know why."

"There will be no share time." Brinkley jabbed a finger over the car at the three big men running our way. Big men, like body builders big. "They're going to kill you if you don't get into this fucking car."

With one violent push, he shoved me into the car and screamed at Kyra. "Drive!"

Kyra was terrified. Having probably never been screamed at by a stranger, here she was with an angry one in her face and three others running toward her looking equally as violent. No wonder she froze up.

"Drive or I'll yank you out of the car and drive her myself."

Kyra snapped to life and started the car. I grabbed Brinkley and begged. "You have to tell me. I have to know what's going on."

"Go to the funeral."

"You don't understand, okay. Something is wrong with me. I see—"

"Go to the funeral and I'll meet you there." I must have looked doubtful. "I promise, just go," he added.

It was hard but I let him go. Kyra punched the gas and backed up in a single squealing movement. She hit something which I hoped was a bad guy. I couldn't see and Kyra didn't care enough to check. She was already out of the parking lot and halfway to the entrance by the time I managed to turn around in the passenger seat and search the parking lot through the back window.

I didn't see anyone in the parking lot but Gabriel, his wings spread wide, menacingly, as he watched us go.

CHAPTER FIFTEEN

"No more pit stops!" Kyra screamed. Her eyes were wide, knuckles white, and hands shaking.

"But I really have to pee," I said.

"Should we even go to the funeral?" she asked, her voice cracking. "I know it's your mom and all, but there's no point in getting yourself killed. There are other ways to say goodbye."

I'd given her the short version: I was visiting. Some guys busted in. Brinkley demanded I get the hell out of there because these guys weren't necessarily nice.

Clearly, I left a lot out.

"Brinkley told us to meet him there," I said. "I don't think he'd tell me to go there if it'd put me in danger." Not to mention that wherever the hell Brinkley was, that's where I wanted to be. He had some questions to answer. "And if I'm not there he'll think something happened to us."

Kyra maneuvered us back the way we came without any more questions. Ally blabs when she's scared. Apparently, Kyra gets quieter than a mime.

The closer we got to my mother's house, the more corn I

saw. We must have passed a million rows of corn lining the two-way road between the last town and her house. The faded blacktop didn't even have a line dividing it into two lanes. Only the corn and a small, one-story house could be seen every mile or so.

My heart pounded the second Kyra turned onto the gravel driveway. The house itself was modest, but nice. White siding with black shutters and a red door hauntingly similar to the incomplete sketch Gloria had shown me in her book. Mom hadn't changed the house much in the years since I'd left. She'd planted more flowers, which were enjoying their last days of warmth before winter.

A red station wagon and a beat-up truck with a toolbox and tire in the bed sat parked near the door. No dogs barked and no one came out. Kyra looked from the address on the directions, to the address by the door.

"This is it," she said, turning to me. "Are you sure about this?"

No, I thought. "We'll be fine."

Then we sat—neither of us eager to move. Kyra gripped the steering wheel. I stared at the house, waiting for someone to appear. Technically, the funeral wasn't for another two hours. There weren't many cars so maybe people hadn't shown up for the wake yet.

"We could stay in the car," she said, and turned toward me. Color was returning to her cheeks, but her eyes were still a little too wide. I had a feeling she'd never road trip with me again.

"We can't," I said and got out. I couldn't go straight into the house because I was practically sick from adrenaline. I was so torn up from Rachel's visit that I couldn't imagine seeing my little brother yet. I leaned against the hood and surveyed the area.

No sign of Brinkley.

The property was really beautiful in the morning light. Water and hills framed one side of the house and what appeared to be miles of corn on the other. Lots of trees and open sky, no neighbors that I saw, though I was sure they were around. My eyes were drawn to the swarm of crows circling high above a scarecrow perched alone in a distant field.

Kyra's car door shut behind me and I jumped. "It's really quiet out here," she said.

"We could use a bit of quiet," I mumbled.

"We were at a mental hospital," Kyra said. "I guess we should've expected it to get crazy." Bad joke, but we both snickered. Then we laughed so hard tears spilled from our eyes. I was pretty sure we were losing our shit.

"I don't even know what happened back there," I admitted. Not just with Rachel, but who the hell were those guys? "I'm going to take a walk and try to shake some of this off. You want to come?"

"I'll stay here in case someone comes out," she said. "Are you sure you should be anywhere alone right now?"

"Look around," I told her. "I don't think anyone can sneak up on me way out here."

I walked away from the house into the woods, watching my feet kick at the fallen pine needles. The air smelled of dry cornhusks, and it was much cooler than in Nashville, though we hadn't traveled that far north. I breathed it in deeply and my lungs chilled. Then the packed dirt trail narrowed into the dense tree-line.

A crow cawed, loud and sudden above my head. I swore.

"I've had enough excitement today. Thanks."

He cawed again as if in response, which only spooked me more. I moved deeper into the woods away from it. I followed the black feathers littering the path until ahead the trees thinned, opening up to a clearing. It was like the pines formed a border around this one circle between them. I recognized it immediately from Gloria's charcoal rendering of it.

The circle was large with a thick layer of pine needles and forest ferns hiding the ground. Black feathers were everywhere—in the straw-colored grass, in the shedding trees. In the middle a large black Labrador sat on its haunches, big brown eyes watching me, velvety ears begging to be petted. I took a step forward, hand outstretched, hoping it was friendly. And it flickered. The air shimmered as its shape changed, stretching into the shape of a person. With wings. Gabriel. His arms were folded over his chest. His mouth moved, but I couldn't hear his voice.

"So that creepy bird by my mailbox, that was you?" I asked, stepping closer. "Are these the 'other forms' you meant? Do you always choose black? Should I keep an eye out for black cats, bats, and bears...?" His tie went from black to red and my voice trailed off.

I followed his finger, gazing up in the direction he was pointing. For a second, I stared at the sky. I didn't see anything. No clouds or birds or planes.

This was where I died.

Someone had come in and cleared the collapsed barn away. The grass had healed up for the most part, but the tops of the trees had a faint outline of black charring from where the high flames licked the branches seven years ago.

I lay down on the pine needle bed and looked up through the branches at the sky beyond them. I'd seen this same sky as I lay dying. It was lighter now, of course, being closer to dawn, yet there was no mistaking it. I measured out the lengths between the trees and thought hard about the way the scene had looked—Eddie at one end by the open door, me reclining on a pile of hay, staring at the stars through an open hatch in the roof.

This was the exact spot. This is where it happened.

My chest tightened and I held my breath. Tears formed in the corner of my eyes. Gabriel's face appeared above mine.

"Do you remember?" he asked.

"I died here."

"Do you remember?" he asked again and his mouth moved, but I couldn't hear him. "You must remember him."

Gabriel plunged his hand through my chest. I couldn't breathe. I don't think he was actually touching my lungs or anything since he wasn't entirely here, but he might as well have. It hurt that badly. I wasn't sure if that was because of him touching me or if I was in pain from the outpouring flood of memories.

"Don't fight me, Jesse." He lowered his mouth to mine, his soft lips real and hot. "You must remember, if only a little."

His kiss had the desired effect, or at least, it made me let go of the pain enough to be confused.

It all came back with the force of a broken dam. We're talking a sensory overload, tons of repressed memories flooding back all at once.

I remembered my mother, hair and eyes like mine, the same freckles. I remembered her cotton dresses and white lace gloves, in a tiny church that smelled of old books. I remembered my mother's locket, the tilt of her wide-brimmed Sunday hat. All of her, down to the perfume she wore.

I remembered how she fixed her hair for my father and how I'd sat underneath her vanity, watching her through the glass top holding her brushes, her combs. The way her face was lit in the vanity's light as she would look down and smile.

I remembered my father's funeral, a closed cedar box. In life, my father had smelled of cedar and motor oil. The night after his funeral, my mother removed the cedar satchels from all our closets, the ones that kept the moths away from the clothes. For another week the house smelled of cedar, but not oil.

I remembered my mother crying every night. She thought I was asleep, but I'd creep down the hall and watch her through the small crack in the bedroom door. Sometimes she wore his clothes. Other times she crushed them to her face, smelling them with urgent, ragged breaths, and crying into the sleeves.

I remembered my mother remarrying in the same church, in a tiny ceremony, to a tall man named Eddie much older than her. His graying hair and narrow eyes, and the way I felt colder when he entered a room.

I remembered my little brother being born. I remembered how my mother put him in my arms for the first time and called him Daniel.

I remembered Danny, three-years-old, climbing into my bed because he didn't want to sleep alone anymore. He said he didn't like the tree outside his window and the way it would scratch at his glass to be let in.

I remembered how Eddie made Daniel sleep in his own bed, whipping him if he didn't.

How Daniel had cried, never having been whipped. It was the first time I'd felt useless, without anything to offer. I might as well have been whipped too. In fact, I would have preferred it.

How Eddie looked at me as I did my homework or tanned in the backyard, getting coconut-scented lotion all over my scattered books with sticky hands.

I remembered the first time he came into my bedroom at night.

I remember trying to tell my mother, but she called me a whore and a liar, words I'd never even heard her say.

I remembered her threatening to throw me out of the house.

I remembered a younger Ally, promising to run away with me. I waited all night with a bag packed under my bed, straining to hear beyond my window for her voice or a tapping against the glass.

But Ally hadn't shown. I woke that morning to the sound of his voice in the kitchen, my bag packed at my feet. I remembered the panic and the sinking desolation in realizing I was still trapped.

I remembered slipping out at midnight with my mother's sleeping pills, his cigarette lighter and a whole bottle of Jack Daniels. I'd already drank down all the pills with the Jack when he found me. He demanded his usual price for his house, his food, his generosity. That night I hit him in the skull with that bottle and the lighter from my pocket did the rest. It's amazing how flammable a barn can be, full of dry hay and splashed with alcohol.

The smell of burning flesh. The guttural animalistic howl of a man burning to death, or the way flames furled up in sharp spikes as they eat a man—or the rush of power I felt knowing he'd die—even if it took me with him.

But I'd forgotten that I'd wanted to die. I'd forgotten how much my mother had hurt me.

I'd forgotten how close Ally and I were. I'd forgotten that my decision to abandon Danny was made long before I woke up to Brinkley's offer and the knowledge that I could never go back to that life. It was made when I took those pills, never intending to come back.

There was one other memory.

And the way Gabriel slowed it down made me think it was important, as if this was what he was looking for.

I was little and lying under a car with my father who was telling me what different parts of the car were. The harder I tried to see his face, the more it disappeared in the shadows of the car above us. But his laughter, like a good-natured rogue in one of those swash-buckling movies, his laughter I remembered. And the way I blamed him for dying too soon. If he hadn't gotten his stupid ass crushed, Eddie would have never married my mother, never entered her house, and never tortured me.

More memories existed, surely, because I felt the pressure of them trying to spill in, but Gabriel must have decided this was enough. It was like he reached in and shut off the valve, ending the flood drowning me.

I jerked straight up to my feet. My face was so wet with tears I couldn't see. I paced the circle screaming like a caged animal. The crows flew up from the trees at the sound of it, their feathers raining down slow like black ash around me.

A twig snapped and I whirled to find Brinkley at the opposite edge of the clearing, about where Eddie died.

"Are you okay?" he asked. He slowed down as he approached, the way you would approach an animal you suddenly saw in the woods.

I screamed out everything I remembered.

"Is that why you chose me?" I demanded to know. I wiped my runny nose and tears on my sleeve. "You knew I was a cold-blooded killer. That I'm a heartless, coward who'll do any kind of depraved work for enough money. Fucked up beyond all repair, right? Why not die for a living? I wanted to die anyway. That's why you won't let me out of my contract early because you know I deserve this. I deserve to die over and over and—"

"Stop," Brinkley said. He was much closer to me.

"That's all I am," I yelled.

"That's what happened but that's not who you are," he said. "I chose you for who you are."

"A masochist? Someone willing to kill herself even when

she didn't know she'd survive." I was wild and burning on the inside.

Brinkley grabbed me by the arm and yanked me into a hug. It was beyond awkward and stiff and he swore under his breath the whole time but he didn't let go of me.

"If Eddie was a rapist, was my father some terrible criminal too?" I pulled away, nearing the full height of my hysteria. "A homicidal maniac? Serial murderer, terrorist or what? God only knows what he did before the car crushed him. Did you watch me since childhood waiting for me to prove I was evil?"

"Jesse, stop," Brinkley said. He held me out at arm's length and shook me a little bit. "None of that is true. Your father was a good man before he died. He had a wonderful daughter who is a good person too. I didn't know you existed until I got the call from one terrified mortician claiming that he thought he had one of those people on his table."

I wiped tears out of my eyes and swallowed some snot. "Rachel said you chose me because of who my father is. Then why did Rachel say that? What did she mean?"

"Your father died when you were eight years old," Brinkley said again, letting go of me. "But that doesn't mean he stayed dead."

CHAPTER SIXTEEN

The house was filling up fast and it wasn't that large to begin with. Mrs. Danica Phelps was stretched long in a dark box with velvet lining in the corner of the living room. Having seen plenty of coffins on display at Kirk's funeral home, I could tell this particular coffin wasn't top of the line, but it was well-made and chosen with love, which is to say, it wasn't cheap either. Danica must've had good insurance, had saved some money or come into money since I'd left home.

I felt claustrophobic in the squat one-story house, rubbing shoulders with people I didn't recognize as I squeezed through the front door, kitchen and hallway leading into the living room—dizzy with what Brinkley had told me.

My father was a necronite.

It wasn't out of the question, given that NRD had genetic markers. Because of when my father died, he would have been one of those swept up by the military in the tail end of the "protective custody" campaign. Brinkley claimed Eric Sullivan broke out of his military internment camp years before rights activists demanded their release and had been under the radar ever since. His current whereabouts and identity were unknown, and though I accepted this as truth, I also believed Brinkley had theories he wasn't sharing.

He'd made sure the house was secure before leaving me alone in it, but I didn't like Brinkley leaving at all. He couldn't tell me much about my father or even about the guys that had chased me at Rachel's asylum. At this rate, I was going to die an idiot.

"Go straight home after this," Brinkley said and disappeared out the back door. I stood by the coffin and looked down into the face of the woman lying in it. The smell was overwhelming, artificially-fragrant with hints of musk and beneath that, chemicals. I searched her face, her waxy skin, closed eyes and thin lips.

Her hair was chestnut brown like mine and her skin relatively smooth. I found myself wondering what Kirk would think of her body: had the mortician done a good job? Were her hair and clothes done right? What would he think of this coffin? An at-home viewing?

I also wondered why my mother never considered death-replacing. Was she worried about the price? There were financing programs. Or she could have called me. But maybe that's the reason she never considered it.

She didn't look real. At least, I didn't look at her and think *this was my mother*. I saw a wax statue stretched out in a box. I touched the top of her hand, the one folded over the other on her stomach, and shuddered at how cold it was. I searched my new index of memories for anything labeled *Mom*. The thing I noticed was my memory of two separate mothers—no, not anything creepy like a body snatcher mom or anything. But there was definitely a stark difference between how my mother was before my father died and after. The *before mom* was happy, beautiful and young. After, she seemed to age too quickly, worry too much, and become annoyed at every little thing.

I was bothered by other reasons too. I'd seen a lot of death. Hell, I'd been a lot of *dead*. Yet this was really weird for me. The idea that life did actually end for some people, specifically, for someone I knew. That she wouldn't just wake up.

"Strange, is it not?" a man asked as if reading my thoughts.

The sudden deep voice in my ear made me jump. "W-what?" I stammered. I was suddenly very self-conscious of how long I'd been standing at the coffin, staring into it.

"It's strange seeing death after you spend so much time overcoming it," he said.

He slid into the conversation with the ease of a man who held appearances. He was handsome. Maybe ten years older than me, he couldn't be more than thirty-five. His clothes were clean and pressed, his hair pushed back out of his eyes. This man was so clean that I was embarrassed that my unkempt appearance was such a sharp contrast to his togetherness. I felt like the sloppiest of slobs, even if it was because I'd been wearing the same clothes for two days and only just escaped a mental hospital.

"Forgive me, but you are Jesse Sullivan, correct? Danica's daughter?"

"Yes," I managed to say.

"And are you not a death replacement agent?" he asked.

I nodded and glanced around the room self-consciously, wondering if anyone else here knew who I was. There were no pictures of me in the house—I'd checked—and I didn't recognize any of these people. I had kept an eye out for Danny but hadn't seen him yet, or any children for that matter. Maybe funerals weren't an event you brought children to. Maybe Danny was locked in another room being fed cookies.

"Oh don't worry. I don't think anyone knows about you. I'm the oldest friend here." The stranger offered his hand. "I'm Mr. Reeves. I knew your parents."

I shook his hand. "Eddie wasn't my father."

"I didn't mean Mr. Phelps," Mr. Reeves said with a smile. "I know your father, Eric Sullivan. And that you're beautiful like your mother," he said.

I found this compliment hard to digest. "Thank you."

"Except in some of your facial features, which are more like Eric's."

"How did you know my parents?" I asked.

"You couldn't know Danica and not know Eric. They were inseparable, once upon a time." His voice trailed away wistfully. "Pity that I can't remember a thing about him. I do love to reminisce. But it's been over fifteen years."

I really didn't want to talk to him if he had nothing useful to say, but I was sort of pinned between the wall and my mother's coffin.

"I can see I've made you uncomfortable." He smiled slowly. "I'm sorry to stare, but the last time I saw you, you were a little girl. You're all grown up now and it's a bit overwhelming for me. Time flies, as they say."

"Sorry, but I don't remember you."

"I don't suspect so," he said. His eyes seemed to burn, making me writhe uncomfortably. "Like I said, you were very young."

He leaned forward again, exuding charm. I caught a whiff of his cologne as he whispered into my ear as if sharing a dirty secret. "May I ask you a personal question?"

"Depends."

"Were you a Jack-in-the-box?"

Jack-in-the-box was what we called NRD-positives who were buried and woke up in their coffins. Cemeteries had reinstated the practice of bell-ringing, where strings ran from the coffins to a bell on the surface. If they were alive to ring the bell the caretaker would dig them out.

"No, you can't ask me a personal question." I searched the room again, praying for Danny to pop up. Kyra had lingered near the car in order to give me some privacy, but now I wished I'd made her come in. She'd know how to get me out of this conversation. Would anyone in this room come to my aid if I screamed?

Mr. Reeves intentionally overlooked my discomfort and continued to run his mouth.

"I've heard necronites can move things with their minds, alter reality around them, and even teleport. Anything you can think of—a necronite can do it," he said.

I thought I might have heard that one thing in a movie. "Like jump from one place to another?"

"Yes," he answered. "Some can even resurrect corpses from their graves and control them like an army. They can freeze time with their willpower alone."

I blinked at him in utter disbelief. I burst out laughing, more out of nervousness than anything else. More than a few heads turned my way. Good to know I could draw attention if needed.

"You shouldn't believe everything you hear," I warned Reeves.

"Just some of it?" he asked with an arched eyebrow.

"Jesse!" a small voice cried out and as I turned, two thin arms wrapped themselves around me. The top of a head bumped my chin and the smell of boy and home cooked food overwhelmed me. Once I peeled my captor off of me, the very first thing I noticed were big hazel eyes, exactly like my own.

"Daniel," I said and squeezed him hard against me so that his toes came up off the floor. My God, he was so small when I saw him last and now he was as tall as me.

Daniel. Daniel.

I turned to shoo Mr. Reeves but he was gone. Thank God. Still, I gave the room a once over. In his absence, I felt better. The room cooled and it was easier to breathe. I also felt steadier. The nauseous, dizzy, and sick feelings slowly left my cramped body. I squeezed Danny in relief.

"You came," he said in the same desperate tone. He refused to let me go. "I didn't think you'd come."

"Of course, I came." My breath scattered a few chestnut curls on the top of his head. He'd grown up to have the same unruly waves and freckles as me. "How are you? Are you okay?"

He pulled away from me finally but held my hand. I felt strange about it, but I didn't pull away from him. I was willing to give this kid anything he needed right now.

"I miss her," he said. "But I understand that God needs her now."

It sounded like something my mom would have taught him to believe. "Are you okay though? Where are you going to live now? Who's going to take care of you?"

"Uncle Paul and Aunt Jody," he said. Aunt Jody was Eddie's sister—one of the few names I recalled, but no real memory of her existed.

"Are they nice?" I asked him, fearing the worst. I knew I was in no shape to take custody of a child right now, but I'd be damned if I was going to let this kid end up with anyone depraved.

"Uncle Paul and I fish a lot and he lets me drive his truck through the fields. Aunt Jody can be a little OCD about keeping the house clean, but she's a really good cook and she's helping me catch up on my homework. They don't live too far away so I won't have to change schools or nothing."

"Anything," I corrected. His description didn't scream molesters or child abusers, so my shoulders relaxed. "It sounds like you'll be happy with them, Danny. I'm really glad."

I spoke too soon. He teared up and his little lip quivered. "I wish she didn't die though."

"Me, too, buddy," I told him, even though I wasn't feeling too sad about her death. There was nothing of the woman I knew in this box and nothing of this house that I felt any emotion for except the barn and that was burned to the ground. Maybe it was the room full of people. Maybe it was not talking to her for seven years, I'm not sure. I knew that whatever I expected to feel about this—I didn't. My pain was completely unrelated to the corpse. My regrets came from somewhere else.

"I want her to wake up," he whispered. "Like you did."

I saw this orphaned kid staring at his mother with tears in his eyes and it broke my heart. "Oh, honey. It doesn't work that way. I wish it did, but it doesn't." *Because I inherited my NRD from my father.*

"Why didn't you come home?" he asked. "You could have saved her."

I should've seen this coming. I looked him straight in the eye so he'd know I meant what I was about to say. "It wasn't because of you, Danny. Okay? I promise it wasn't because of you. Mom and I didn't get along."

"But we missed you."

No way in hell mom missed me.

"Did you think I wouldn't love you anymore because you're a zombie?" he asked.

I bit my lip and swallowed a laugh. Anytime anyone uses the word "zombie," a hot rush of angers fills me head to toe. However, hearing it come out of my little brother's mouth, with his voice still sweet and pre-pubescent, made me smile.

And he was old enough to handle at least some of the

truth. "Mom told me not to come back. I guess she was worried I'd hurt you."

"That's not what Mom told me," he said. "She said you got a job and moved away. She says that's what grownups do."

"She talked about me?"

"All the time," he said.

"No way," I blurted. And she couldn't tell me this shit? "What did she say?"

"She was proud of you," he said.

I kissed the top of his head and squeezed him again. I used the little guy to hold my shaking body in place. I didn't know what else to do.

I saw Kyra coming through the back kitchen door and she gave a little wave. I was out of time.

Danny must've sensed the change. "Please don't go. I promise it's okay. Aunt Jody doesn't like zombies, but Uncle Paul doesn't care. He says God has a plan for everything."

"I can't stay," I told him. "Let me get some things in order and I promise to visit."

He squeezed me tighter.

"I promise I'll call more, write more, email, whatever you kids do these days. Do you text?" I asked him.

He shook his head. "I don't have a cell phone."

Christmas present, check.

"Tell your uncle that I have money and if you need anything, he should call me," I said, handing him one of my crumpled business cards. Then I shoved the wad of cash Ally had given me into his hands. "Take this too and put it away for just in case."

His eyes were huge. I'm guessing he'd never seen so much money at one time. "In case of what?"

"Anything," I said. "If you need me, you call me okay? Hey, how did you get my number the first time?"

"It was in Mom's address book."

Jesus, Mom. Really? You kept tabs on me for seven years, told people how proud you were, but you couldn't even manage a phone call?

I gave him one last hug, amazed at how easy it was to coddle him. What had I expected, him to be aloof? Distant, maybe, now that he was an orphan.

But the fact remained, it really was time to go. I'd seen the corpse. I'd checked on the boy. If I stayed any longer, I ran the risk of getting caught or having one of those dramatic family member blowouts that I'd been worried about to begin with.

So I turned my back on my mother's house, knowing I'd never see it again.

CHAPTER SEVENTEEN

I sobbed like a baby all the way back to Nashville. I'm sure Herwin would call it years of repressed anger and depression working its way to the surface. Worse, I was drowning in all that Rachel and Brinkley had said, seeing my little brother all grown up, that I was the one who half-orphaned him, and that my Mom might have loved me after all.

It was too much.

I told Kyra what I'd remembered in the woods, leaving out the part about Gabriel. "When I hired Ally, she said we were friends in high school. I recognized her, but not as my best friend for like years. I hadn't forgotten about what a douchebag Eddie was, yet I'd forgotten her. That doesn't make any sense."

"You know you have brain damage," Kyra said. "How many years had you been dying before you saw Ally again?"

"Five."

Kyra made a there you go gesture. "Five years of dying. Of course, you'd forget."

"But why didn't Ally tell me we were best friends?"

Kyra shrugged. "She probably knew it'd be weird to bring it up if you didn't remember."

Somehow Ally had found me in Nashville, applied for my assistant position and then pretended like nothing had ever happened.

I fell against the seat. "God, I feel like such an asshole. Why didn't she tell me?"

"I'm sure she has a good explanation," Kyra said. "Just talk to her when you get back. Apologize if you feel you have to. Tell her you were brain dead from all that death-replacing but you're good now."

"I want to sleep and when I wake up, poof. All better."

Kyra pulled a pillow from her backseat and offered it to me, without swerving once. We lapsed into silence as I delved deeper into my own thoughts. Rachel, Brinkley, Gabriel, Ally, Danny, Eddie, my mother, my father—they each played on a loop in my head until I dozed off, exhausted from sleep deprivation.

Kyra thrashed me. "Jesse, wake up. Wake up."

My eyes focused first on the dashboard clock. Hours had passed and, ahead, the outline of Nashville's Centennial Park came into view. The cop car behind us, flashing its swirling lights.

"What do you want me to do?" she asked.

I gestured toward my ragged complexion in the visor mirror. "Have I *ever* had a good plan?"

"Good point," she muttered.

Kyra pulled over and turned on her emergency flashers. "Damn. We were so close."

"I think we should go with it. I'm too tired to make up a story."

"You can't lie for shit anyway," she said. "If they take you,

I'll call Ally and tell her where you are. She can ask her brother what to do."

Kyra fell silent. A tap-tap-tap sounded against her window. She rolled it down with a push of a button, and a waft of chilly air rushed in. Agent Garrison leaned down into the window, wearing his usual half-neutral, half-pained expression.

"Dare I ask where you ladies are heading?" he inquired.

"Breakfast," Kyra said. I guess that could've worked since it was noon and we still wore the clothes we'd worn the night before. Certainly we looked like we'd rolled off someone's couch, starved.

"Yes, can I please have breakfast before you interrogate me?" I asked. It was a sincere request. I'd only had gas station food—an orange juice and a sugar-laden snack cake since we left.

His eyes narrowed as if inspecting me more closely—my disheveled hair, smeared makeup and puffy eyes. "We won't keep you long."

"I guess that means no." I gathered up my bag.

After a little wave to Kyra, I slid into the back of the cop car with minimal grace, but managed to keep my skirt down so that Agent Garrison's partner didn't get a free peep show. Also, I tried not to let the overwhelming smell of leather and the fact that my doors didn't open from the inside freak me out. God, Eve had scarred me for life.

"So, am I finally being arrested?"

"That depends," Garrison said. He ran a hand through his hair. "On how well our discussion at the station goes."

"For the record, I maintain that I'm the victim here."

They clearly didn't agree nor did they indulge me chitchat until we arrived at the station—which was noisy. I didn't know how anyone got any work done with all that racket. A couple of officers glanced my way as we passed. I hoped they didn't think I was a hooker—excuse me, sex worker—with day-old eyeliner and the slutty schoolgirl-gone-bad look. Given that I looked young, they probably would peg me as some juvenile delinquent. Aside from these few glances, most of the officers were too busy to even spare a look.

Garrison looked through my bag and held my toothbrush up in the overhead lights as if it was evidence.

"Haven't you ever been clubbing?" I asked. "Girls always pack a toothbrush and their underwear in case we go home with someone else. No crime there."

His partner snorted as Garrison returned my bag. He couldn't prove I left town, especially since the directions were in Kyra's car and I'd given Danny my suspicious chunk of cash.

Agent Garrison sat in the seat opposite mine. His large metal desk stretched between us.

He opened a file and clicked his pen once so the ballpoint extended. The folder was terribly thick. I leaned over to see whose it was, and he slid it away.

"Is that whole file on me?" I asked.

He didn't answer. But unless I needed new eyes, I was pretty sure that was my name on the top tab and that some of the papers were written in Brinkley's handwriting. I had a record. That was something I needed to know. And Brinkley said he'd kept me under the radar.

"Where did you go last night, Ms. Sullivan?" Garrison asked.

"At what time?" I asked.

"The whole time," his partner said. He was downright mean and I wasn't in the mood for mean after the trip I'd had.

"Hi, I'm Jesse Sullivan," I said, extending my hand toward him. He jumped back as if I'd burned him. "I'm a real person with feelings, so maybe you can treat me like one."

Agent Garrison cracked a smile. Whoa. Too bad I didn't have a camera to capture that brief miracle. His face was a mask of calm again before his partner even had time to react.

"Can you get me a coffee, please?" Garrison asked. His partner wandered away without as much as a glance my way. I guess we disagreed on me being a real person.

"Wow, and I thought the good cop, bad cop thing was a cliché," I said. "Good to know some television gives it to you straight."

Garrison laced his fingers in front of him. "I think humor is your defense mechanism, Ms. Sullivan."

"*I* think I already have one government-issued therapist, thanks."

"This conversation is going to end in one of two ways. Either you'll cooperate and I'll let you walk out of this building, or you won't cooperate and I'll serve this warrant."

He tapped a piece of paper beside the file. That certainly got my attention. Did he really have a warrant? Don't they serve those when they arrest you, so why wait? Or was he bluffing to get me to talk?

Garrison spoke in a low, guarded tone. "Let me be clear. My sole objective is to discover who is responsible for the recent events and hold them accountable. However, interagency diplomacy is on its last leg. Detectives like Bobkins have little or no patience for our involvement, so I do not have much time—do you understand?"

I nodded. "Then why are you even working with them? Don't you have your own office?"

"The FBRD doesn't have a Nashville Branch," he said. "So I work with what I have. And if you refuse to help, let's go with the understatement that you won't like what comes next."

I tried to remember what Brinkley had told me about the

FBRD corruption. If Garrison knew what was going on, why would he feel any kind of 'pressure'?

"What do you want? To kill me and get me out of the way? Get promoted? A fat check? Why should I believe that you want to protect me at all? How do I know you aren't looking for my weaknesses?"

Garrison's face had a strange unreadable expression. "Did Brinkley tell you the FBRD meant you harm?"

If I couldn't lie for shit, there was no point trying.

"What else did he tell you?" he pressed as if I'd spoken. But Bobkins reentered the main office from the adjacent corridor, Styrofoam cup in hand.

"Nothing you want him to hear," I said and nodded in Bobkins' direction.

Garrison's intense gaze made my skin itch. I diverted my attention to Bobkins approaching.

Garrison's tone changed when he accepted his coffee. His veiled warnings from a moment ago hung mid-air between us, but he spoke as if nothing had been said. "When you left the club with Ms. Kyra Fenton, where did you go?"

"Back to her place."

"How long were you there?"

I'd stick with the truth as long as I could. "Not long."

"Do you know what time you left?"

"No," I said. "I'm not even sure what time we left The Loft."

"Where did you go next?"

"We stopped at Arby's for milkshakes." Technically true even if those two stops were hours apart. "But they were cleaning the machine so I didn't get one."

"When is the last time you saw your assistant, Alice Gallagher?" he asked.

The mention of her name was enough to make my heart jump. "Last night at the club."

"Have you spoken to her since?"

"No," I said. I definitely noticed this shift in the conversation. "Why?"

"Are you currently aware of Ms. Gallagher's whereabouts?"

"Aren't you aware of her whereabouts?" My heart pounded harder. "You've been following us for days."

"Ms. Gallagher left the night club alone. We quit tailing her in an attempt to find you," he said.

My heart felt like it was completing a series of 180-degree flops in my chest.

"Do you have any reason to suspect that she may have conspired with Eve Hildebrand to kill you?" he pressed.

"No," I asked.

"Are you aware that Alice and Eve Hildebrand are members of the same fitness club?"

I couldn't breathe.

"I'll take that as a no," he said, scrawling on the paper in front of him.

"Stop!" Several heads turned my way as Garrison asked me to calm down. "Just stop, okay. Why are you asking me these questions about Ally?"

Bobkins answered me. "We have tried to contact her but can't reach her."

"What do you mean can't reach her?" I dug in my bag furiously for my phone and called Ally twice. She didn't answer.

"No, no, no." I dialed a third time.

Garrison watched in silence.

I slammed my fist against the desk. If the police quit watching her in an attempt to find me, and something happened to her, I'd never forgive myself. When Bobkins came toward me I knocked him away, much farther than a tiny person like myself should have been able to move a man that size. For some reason, I thought of Rachel taking out those two men.

"Why didn't you protect her?" I screamed at Garrison. "You're an idiot if you think the people who want to kill me wouldn't go after her. Nothing would make me come running faster."

"Assuming you didn't orchestrate the attack yourself," Bobkins said.

My body turned electric. Something inside me moved and shifted and all I could think was *God, please let her be okay. I have to tell her I'm sorry. I have to tell her that after all that she did for me, all those times she consoled me after what Eddie did, when she told me everything was going to be okay, after all of that—*

You must calm down. Gabriel appeared behind Garrison, wings stretching out before tucking. *It is not safe to lose control here.*

I swallowed, inhaling quickly. I didn't think I was losing control. I wasn't hurling desks or choking people.

Garrison's eyes were wider than before which meant I was at least a little frightening. He motioned to Bobkins, but the officer objected. Whatever I was doing, Garrison saw it and Bobkins didn't. What was I doing? What was happening to me?

Ally is not yet harmed. Focus, Jesse.

Ally wasn't hurt. Yet. He'd said *yet*. Focus. Focus.

"Where did you see her last?" I asked. I couldn't remember the last question he'd asked so this was the best I could do as I slowly drew deep breaths in and out of my nose.

"I think you know where she is," Bobkins said. He wasn't happy about being pushed. At least, they weren't trying to arrest me for assault yet. "And I think you know what's going on."

"Yes, because we replacement agents love to kill ourselves off." As soon as the words left my lips, my stomach twitched. I guess I did have a history of killing myself. Garrison's eyes narrowed. I thought it best to add the very true statement, "Believe me, if I wanted to die, I wouldn't need Eve's help."

But Bobkins wouldn't shut up. "There's a guy in Auckland who's killed himself fifty-five times. He does it for kicks, just for fun."

I made a strangled sound in my throat as I fought to focus, but really I wanted to explode. "Uh, Bobkins, did you have a point?"

His fists blanched white, as if he'd like nothing better than to pulverize my face.

Garrison spoke up. "This morning at 8:47 a.m. Ms. Gallagher received a call of unknown origin. At 9:23 a.m., she disappeared somewhere near 4th Avenue."

"That means you don't know who called, right? Because that's not suspicious as hell." I put my head in my hands, laughed high in my throat. What was I going to do? How the hell was I going to find Ally?

Keep breathing, Jesse. Gabriel warned. My skin itched.

"Are you aware that over four hundred replacement agents have died in the last six months? Over a thousand in the last year?" Garrison asked.

"It's what we do, Agent Garrison." I squeezed my hair in my hands, pulling it away from my temples, hoping from some release of pressure.

"Dead, dead, Jesse," he said. "And not just death-replacement agents. Several of the necronites had not yet made their condition public. That means someone with power and authority is able to discover who is NRD-positive, even if they haven't reported their condition."

If Brinkley hadn't told me about these attacks, I might have wondered why we were dying. It could have been a virus depleting the necronite population, or a newly discovered medical "cure" that prevented us from resurrecting. Yet

Atlanta scrawled across my mind. Someone had decided necronites deserved to stay dead like the rest of humanity.

But who was doing it: FBRD, the Church, or the military?

I lifted my head from my hands. Gabriel was watching me carefully.

"We think these attacks are only the beginning," Garrison said.

Bobkins threw up his hands and turned away. I couldn't figure out if this was an elaborate dance between them, some kind of cop code, or if Bobkins was genuinely disgusted by Garrison's willingness to bring me into the loop.

Over one thousand of the unkillable, *killed*.

I wet my lips. "Maybe the military wants us back in protective custody to make super soldiers, or use us for biowarfare or whatever. If they scare us enough, maybe we'll run right back into their camouflaged arms."

"That's bullshit," Bobkins said, posturing himself like a gorilla. "No idiot's going to believe this shit."

Ignoring Bobkins, I met Garrison's eyes in a challenge. "Then there's the FBRD."

Garrison cocked his head to one side.

"You know why they're suspect," I told him. "Eve isn't the only one who gets around."

It was close to treason. The Bureau licensed me. They'd taken a high school dropout and given her a good paying job. I could be unemployed and under-skilled in a heartbeat. But I wanted Garrison to know about the rogue FBRD agent and his connection to Eve. I wanted him to start looking in the right place.

"Someone like Brinkley," Bobkins said, mocking my tone.

Garrison had the strangest look on his face—doubt, if I didn't know better. I was willing to bet that Garrison knew something was up in the FBRD.

"That's enough for now," Garrison said, pushing away from the desk.

"A few more questions," Bobkins said. "Then she can leave."

Garrison gave me a look. If I wanted to end this now, I'd have to speak up for myself.

"Look," I said, struggling to focus my eyes on his. I felt dizzy and lightheaded. That bizarre electrical surge had left me and I was cold. I shivered "I need sleep and probably a pain pill. So if you have to arrest me, then take me to a cell where I can lay down. If not, please let me go home. Either way, I can't talk about this anymore."

And Ally, I thought. I have to find Ally.

Garrison came around the desk and escorted me to the exit. Bobkins glared at me.

I was about to walk out of the exit and give Gloria or Lane a call to pick me up, when Garrison grabbed me roughly by the elbow.

"Hey," I said wrenching my arm away. I was so tired of being manhandled. "We already gave you the paperwork and I've done everything I can to prove I'm not a psycho. I don't know what else you want from me."

Garrison let go of my arm. "If you intend to look for your friend, I highly advise against it."

"I don't care what you advise. Your detective skills are crap."

"I highly advise against it," he repeated, stepping over my snarky attitude. "But if I were you, I'd ask Eve Hildebrand."

"How the hell can I ask Eve? She's in jail."

"She has visiting hours like every other inmate," he said. "Alice knew that."

Garrison disappeared back into the police station without waiting for a reply.

"How did she know?" I asked, watching him through the

clear doors until his dark shape melted into a torrential sea of others.

I realized what he'd so cryptically suggested.

She knew because she'd gone to see her.

Either before or after I ditched Nashville, Ally had begun her own investigation. I should have known that she wouldn't sit by and watch the world fall apart any more than I could.

CHAPTER EIGHTEEN

The Davidson County jail was in downtown Nashville, only a couple of blocks away from the James Robertson Parkway police station I just left. On my way over, I used my cell phone to call Gloria and ask her to pick me up from the jail in about an hour. She agreed, otherwise, I would have had to walk the mile to Lane's comic book store.

I popped into the McDonald's across the street. Good thing, considering I looked like the walking dead. I used the soap from the hand dispensers and those scratchy brown paper towels to clean myself, wiping at the smeared makeup and brushing my hair up into a respectable ponytail. I had a toothbrush and no toothpaste. But dry brushing was enough to remove the fuzzy slippers from my teeth.

At this point, I felt better except for the acidic feeling in my belly. I was worried about Ally, but there was nothing I could do for her yet.

The jail was a squat, brick building that couldn't be any more intimidating with its barred windows, strange noises, and bulletproof doors. The boxy shape and uninviting exterior made it look like it wanted to be a prison when it grew up. My heart raced and head pounded, and I got this terrible feeling as I entered the jail.

The desk attendant was nice enough as he asked me to sign in and take a seat. Once he gathered some papers, he told me to follow him to this room full of narrow glass cubicles. I took the plastic chair that he offered and stared through the empty glass. It was like a mirror, each side with a chair, small lip of a table for elbows and a plastic phone attached to a silver cord snaking from the wall. The only difference was no one sat in the chair across from mine. I was trying to figure out what that strange smell was, like old plastic and antiseptic. A guard walked through a door and plopped Eve into the chair opposite mine.

He tapped the glass to get my attention. "You've got fifteen minutes."

"That's it?" I asked.

The square block of a man exited without a word.

The last time I saw Eve she was straddling my chest trying to saw off my head. Her appearance hadn't improved. Her hair hadn't been washed in a few days and, without makeup and her miracle bra, she looked much older. Not to mention, orange was not a great color for her complexion.

"Your neck healed." She took a pack of cigarettes out of her jumper pocket and lit one with a match. I didn't quite know what to say. Eve gestured with her hands as smoke billowed about her face. "Did you come here for a good look or what?"

Asking me a direct question helped. I shook my head until the words came. "No, I want to talk about Ally—Alice —Gallagher, the girl that came with me to your replacement. Straight blond hair, nose ring."

She nodded in the direction the closed door. "You've got fifteen minutes."

"What did you tell her when she came to see you?"

Eve's eyes narrowed as she took a long drawl. "She didn't tell you?"

"She can't," I said. "On account that she's missing."

Her eyes widened. "Since when?"

"This morning."

Eve wouldn't look at me, lost in her own thoughts. "She asked about the man."

"Your last John?" I asked. Where the hell had I heard the word John? It sort of slipped out. Crappy TV probably. That's where I learned everything. "What's his name?"

"He was a first-timer. He didn't tell me his name," she said.

"Didn't you ask?"

"You saw us. We didn't do much talking, did we?"

She couldn't even look me in the face.

"You tried to cut off my head," I said and hit the glass hard enough to make her look up. "You could at least tell me what you know."

She blinked several times, pretending to care more about her cigarette than what I was saying.

"You're a completely worthless human being, aren't you?" I asked.

I shoved my chair back with an angry scrape across the hard floor.

"You're leaving?" she asked as if actually surprised.

"Uh, yeah. You won't tell me who the guy was, you won't tell me what you told my friend, and you won't even tell me why you tried to kill me. Not even a 'well, I had this knife and I wanted to see what you could do' or a pathetic 'Jesus told me to' or anything. God forbid a 'Sorry'."

I turned to leave but she banged her palms against the glass. When I turned back I saw her mouth moving in wide, exaggerated movements, but I couldn't hear her words until I picked up the plastic receiver again.

"Okay, I'll tell you."

I gestured to the phone I held as if to say I'm waiting, but I didn't sit back down.

"The guy told me his name was Brad Cestrum," she whispered. "I swear that's the only name he gave me. He found me. He made his appointment and gave me very specific instructions. I didn't see him again until that day in the hotel room. I don't know anything else about him."

"What did you tell Ally?"

"She asked why I did it. Did someone force me? What was in it for me?"

"And what did you tell her?" I eased back into my chair.

Eve's eyes welled up and her jaw tightened. "I can't tell you that."

"Come on," I said. "I can't figure out where she went if you don't give me clues."

"She's missing." She shook her head. "You'll be next."

"Why do you care?" I laughed. "You tried to kill me."

She wiped tears off her cheeks and cupped her hand over her mouth and the receiver.

"They have my daughter."

It took a moment for my brain to process the whispers. But as the words came together, my anger intensified.

"Are you fucking kidding me?" I asked.

She made a frantic waving motion with her hand. "Keep your voice down. Please."

I tried to let this set in but frankly it was too much. "I'm supposed to believe you're a victim? You tried to kill me, but you're the victim?"

Tears welled in her eyes again and I slammed the phone down. I took deep breaths while Eve just sat there and cried on the other side of the glass. Finally, once I was able to unclench my jaw, I lifted the receiver again.

"Look," I began, kicking myself the whole time. "It's clear that you've been forced into a bad position. I can't help you if you don't tell me what's going on. I know you're scared, but you have to be honest with me. Apparently, you can't or won't tell the authorities, but I'm not an authority. More importantly, it seems we are after the same people, so we can help each other out, right? But I can't help you, if you don't tell me what you know."

She nodded, wiping her face on her sleeve.

According to the clock on my phone, we had two minutes. "Talk fast."

She whispered so low that I could barely hear her. I was forced to press my ear to the grimy phone to make out her words. "Two months ago he found me and paid me to get information about you and your office schedule. I sent another girl into the office to ask questions. It was an easy $100. So when he asked me if I wanted to make more, I said sure. He said to get you to the hotel at the right day and time and he'd do the rest. Then the bastard took my daughter the day before the replacement to make sure I kept my appointment. And he told me if I wanted to get her back—I had to kill you myself."

"So he took her on the 19th?"

"Yeah," she agreed.

"They took your daughter and told you if you didn't kill me in the hotel room, they'd hurt her."

"I'm real sorry about your neck, but I'd do it again for my little girl."

"Yeah, yeah," I said, waving her on. I couldn't think about that or I'd get mad again. "So what happened?"

"They were supposed to return her to my momma after I was arrested but they didn't. Then he turned up here."

"Who?"

"Brad," she said. "He says my daughter is safe. He let me see her on his video phone. But he also said that if I confessed or told anyone anything, they'd kill her. I'm supposed to stick to my story."

"What's your story?" I asked. Tick, tock, tick tock.

"I know prostitution is wrong and I thought that by killing one of God's enemies, I would be forgiven and granted a place in Heaven."

"Did you tell Ally all of this?" I asked.

"She promised to find my daughter. But they probably killed her and my baby too."

"You don't know Ally," I argued. "She's head and shoulders above the rest of us mere mortals, so she's definitely smarter than the goons who threatened you. If she promised you she'd find your daughter, she will."

I hoped that Ally was hiding somewhere with the kid. And I didn't tell Eve that because for all I knew, she'd turn right around and tell Brad. I had a feeling she'd kill me herself right now if she had the chance—whatever improved her chances of seeing her kid.

"What's her name?" I asked. "Your kid?"

"Nessa," Eve said. It was the first time I saw her smile since I met her. A small but sweet smile.

The door behind her opened and the block-shaped guard yanked Eve out of the seat.

"Don't worry," I told her. I couldn't believe I was trying to comfort the person who'd nearly killed me. "We will find her."

Eve looked about as convinced as I was—not much.

Almost an hour later, I stumbled stiffly down the steps and fell into the passenger seat of Gloria's gold Buick, idling at the curb. I drew in a deep breath.

She waited until I closed the heavy door. "You need a favor."

"I need a favor," I confirmed.

"Just ask."

"I need you to view Nessa Hildebrand," I said. "Eve's daughter. I'm sure we can find a picture of her from St. Mary's yearbook, if you need."

"I already have a picture of Nessa," Gloria said.

"Why?" She was good at guessing the future, but I'd be real impressed if she was this far ahead of me.

"Ally asked for the same favor," she said.

Of course Ally was smart enough to enlist Gloria's help too. "Anything yet?"

"I'm working on it."

I was kind of hoping that Gloria had given Ally the information. At least it would've been likely that Ally was hiding with the little girl somewhere instead of kidnapped. Or dead.

I was scared to ask my next question. "What about Ally? Do you know she's missing?"

Her lips pressed together and she put the car into drive. "I'm working on that too."

CHAPTER NINETEEN

Once Gloria dropped me off, I took my last pain pill and went to bed. I stayed there, snuggled in a mound of pillowy fluff, and refused to get up. I was suspended from work, under investigation, everyone was MIA, and my mother had died.

But I woke around nine the next morning to someone climbing into bed with me.

Lane snuggled in, completely naked mind you, and pretended to be asleep. I poked his cheek until his eyes opened.

"I have two guest bedrooms," I said. "And I'm going to take your key away if you keep creeping up on me."

He stretched his arms high overhead. "Ally gets to sleep in your bed."

"You're not Ally."

"Quit reminding me," he growled. He grabbed my hips and pulled me against him. A wave of heat and clenching tension shot from my stomach to my groin. I shuddered and he took that as an invitation to roll me over and pin me, planting playful kisses on both of my cheeks. He even dared to sneak one under my ear.

Having not had sex for a few days, I felt ridiculously easy.

I pushed his chest forcing him up away from me. "I've got to look for Ally."

"God forbid you spend a day apart," he said.

"No you don't understand. She—" He covered my mouth with kisses, cutting me off. When I gave up, he kissed me under my ear again. Each brush of his lips erased the thoughts from my mind. The conflicting stress and desire escalated, until for no apparent reason, my vision changed.

"Whoa," I said.

"You want me to stop?" he asked.

"No—I—" I was dazzled by the layer of bouncy static between Lane's body and mine. It was like the colorful waves I saw during a replacement, but sharper with more contrast. The static was like an arm I could manipulate. And no sign of Gabriel or even an idea of how to change my vision back. Was someone dying?

"Oww. You shocked me," Lane said, laughing.

I thought about what I'd done—I had tried to "lift" the static like I would an arm. So if I—

"Owww, hey." He cleared the mattress as if in genuine pain.

"Oh my god," I said. "I'm dying."

"It's probably the sheets," he said, patting my thighs as if he could neutralize the static.

It was not the sheets. All the months of electrical mishaps became clear in my mind: smoking computers, blown lights and fuses. Oh God, it was apparent, on top of my emotional trauma, something was physically wrong with me.

"I'm going to combust," I said. And when I thought my terror might kill me outright, my weird vision returned to normal again.

"Oh thank God," I said. I crushed a pillow against my face, breathing deep breaths of relief. "I thought I was going to be stuck that way forever."

Lane arched an eyebrow and I tried my best to explain what had happened.

"You're stressed," he said. "Stress can really screw you up."

Stress—sounded like such a normal excuse that I accepted it immediately.

"You know what's great for stress? Presents." Lane handed me a box which I tore open. Throwing the tissue paper aside, I smelled them before I saw them. The smell of new shoes. Shiny black ones. I fingered the pristine white laces and marveled over how they matched.

"How was the funeral?" he asked.

"My mother dies and you buy me shoes?" I asked.

"I thought you'd love these more than flowers."

He was right. So I told him all about the funeral, even the weird guy who cornered me but I didn't mention Rachel or Brinkley. Secrets, secrets.

He walked out of my bedroom with the promise of breakfast, and he gave me a nice view of his bare ass as he went. I smiled into a pillow, thinking I'd have to tell Kyra later.

As soon as Lane was gone that moment of happiness dissipated. Stones filled up my stomach, sinking under thoughts of Ally—worry. Fear.

Coming off pain pills didn't help. I could detox fine. I'd been doing it for years. It didn't help that something terrible was happening. I had to remember not to let my emotions get the best of me.

Mechanically, I went through my morning. I found Winston asleep behind the entertainment center. I put him by his bowl filled with cheddar goldfish crackers on account that Ally was supposed to pick up dog food while I was gone but clearly hadn't. While I let him out to do his business, I tried to call Ally twice but I got her voicemail.

Winston presented his belly for a good scratch but gave up after enduring a few minutes of my pathetic attempt at a rub.

Was Ally really kidnapped? Should I be looking for her? Where would I look? And maybe she isn't kidnapped. Maybe she was hiding Eve's kid. What the hell was she doing? She would call to make sure I'd made it home okay—if she could call. So the real question was why couldn't she call?

Lane stuck his head out of the kitchen and called me to breakfast: oatmeal with brown sugar in it, cut fruit, and raisin toast. For himself, he made an egg sandwich with cheese. We split the pot of coffee.

"This is the first time I've seen you without the gauze," he said. He reached across my kitchen table and pulled down the collar of my shirt. "It looks good, a little bruised."

The sunlight filtered through the windows and back door gave his features a soft, touchable look. He was completely at home here, no shirt, only boxers, sitting in a pale wooden chair on the same corner of my kitchen table as me.

"Light bruising is to be expected," I said, quoting Dr. York. "I'm glad it won't scar."

"Scars are hot."

I bit my lip. "Have you heard from Ally?"

He sat his fork down gently but his jaw had tightened.

"She's missing." I told him everything Garrison said about her disappearance. He took my hand across the table.

"You hate her," I said, accepting his hand. "You're probably glad she's gone."

"That's unfair," he said. "Just because I dislike competition doesn't mean I want her to get hurt."

"There is no competition because there's no prize," I said.

Somehow what started as an I'm-not-worth-being-jealous-over argument became a full-blown confession. The words became water in my mouth. They flowed from mind to lips in one fluid movement and cutting the story off anywhere in between was as awkward as holding water in my mouth and trying not to swallow or spit it out.

I told him about Eddie, all that happened and how I made him pay the price for what he did to me, about my regrets over Danny and Rachel. I even told him about finding Rachel cut up on the floor, about all the craziness she'd preached about angels, and how it terrified me that I'm destined for a diet of mashed bananas. I didn't mention that I was actually seeing an angel, but I used the phrase 'half-crazy myself' more than once.

I also told him what Brinkley said about the FBRD, the Church and the military and how we have no idea who is pulling the strings. I even told him that my dad was a necronite but had never come back for me. I talked and talked and talked until my ass was sore in my seat and minute after minute ticked off the clock. Not once did he interrupt me.

"Wow," he said once my voice had fallen away and the kitchen had filled up with silence. "I didn't realize you had so much going on."

I snorted in response but we both remained silent for a long time.

"No wonder you can't commit."

After everything I told him, that was what he fixated on?

"And you love her," he added and there was something in his voice when he said it that made me look at him.

"She's my best friend."

"Did you ever sleep with her?" He looked up from his dirty plate and gave me the most pitiful puppy dog eyes.

My anger surged. "I told you that I killed a man, I'm

losing my mind, people want me dead and all you care about is who I like more? Unbelievable."

I wanted to put my plate away and get out of this chair but I couldn't bring myself to move. His silence held me trapped in this seat.

"Why did you break up with her?" he asked. His face was red but his voice was steady. He'd managed to get his guard back in place.

"We were never together," I said. "It was just sex."

"Like us?" he asked. But it didn't really feel like a question.

I grabbed my plate and threw it in the sink with a thunderous crash. "Yes because she gave me the same speech you did about not being able to fuck me without her feelings getting in the way."

He pushed back his chair and stood like he was going to leave. "I certainly have more respect for her now."

"And less for me?"

He walked away.

"I'm sorry," I yelled. "What do you want me to say?"

"For what?" he asked, his voice low. "What are you sorry for?"

"For being an emotional vacuum. I know you want more, but I can't give it to you. And I think it's really unfair that you force me to make a commitment now when my life is totally out of control."

Something in his shoulders relaxed. "Do you want to be with me?"

"Yes." I threw my hands up and gave a desperate shrug. "And no. It's hard to explain."

He turned to face me. "Then why do you sleep with me? Most girls won't sleep with a guy until they're sure."

I didn't know what to say. I didn't think "you're really good in bed" was what he wanted to hear right now. Apparently, I waited too long because he started up the stairs toward the bedroom. When he reappeared he was dressed with his keys and wallet in his hand.

A voice in my head screamed *say something say something say something*, as he moved back down the stairs and went straight for the door. It wasn't until he slipped on his shoes and his hand was on the handle that I finally blurted the only words I could think of.

"It doesn't hurt."

The near empty house echoed my desperation.

He let go of the door handle. "What doesn't hurt?"

"Sex doesn't hurt. What we have isn't complicated." I wasn't entirely sure where I was going with this. My head pounded, another symptom of the last pain pill fading away and I could barely think straight. "Worrying about people, caring about them, waiting for them to hurt me like they always do—I can't deal with that."

The color returned to his cheeks again, telling me I was going in the wrong direction with this. But I'd reached that point where I didn't care.

"You're punishing me for something I haven't done. I need this to be simple."

It was an eternity before he finally looked up and spoke. "It hurts me."

"I know," I said and I closed the distance between us slowly. I was afraid he might take off like a spooked animal if I moved too fast. But he didn't run away. "And I'm sorry."

"How sorry?"

"Sorry enough that I'm willing to try to do better," I said.

"I want you to date me."

My heart fluttered and the panic started to rise in my chest. I felt myself pulling away but I held steady.

"I can try dating you," I said. "If you can keep it simple."

"Just me?" he asked with a raised eyebrow.

"Just you," I said. *Probably.*

Promising Lane monogamy seemed like small potatoes and it wouldn't interfere with the promise I'd already made Ally about keeping my lips to myself. So why did I feel like I'd done something wrong?

"I'll think about it," he said and closed the door behind him.

CHAPTER TWENTY

I was crying when Cindy called. "Where are you?"

"Home. Why?" I said, and wiped my nose with my sleeve.

"I need your help. Can I pick you up?"

"Are you okay?" I assumed she didn't see Raphael all the time since Gabriel didn't stick around, but perhaps he'd shown up and told her to put extra money in the collection plate or adopt a Cambodian baby or something. Hopefully he hadn't told her to play with any sharp objects.

"I'm fine," she huffed. "I think I've got a lead and I don't want to check it out alone."

"Aren't the cops the ones who deal with leads?" I asked.

"I can't sit around and wait for someone to kill me," Cindy said. "Is that your plan?"

Healing my neck was my plan. Strangling Brinkley and Ally for worrying me to death was my plan. Lots and lots of therapy was my plan and, possibly, a new boy-toy. "Well, no, but—"

"Then help me," she said. "I don't trust anyone. I even

made my mailman open my mail for me this morning. That's how bad it's getting."

The idea of a frantic Cindy shaking her mailman and demanding that he open the mail cracked me up. "He must've enjoyed that."

"The Victoria's Secret Catalog maybe," she said. "He's got to think I'm nuts."

"How did you get him to do it?"

"I told him an ex-boyfriend threatened to send me anthrax," she said.

"And he still opened it?" I said.

"Look, are you going to help me or not?"

"Okay, okay." Bite my head off.

"We need to see Jacob," she said, stepping into my foyer thirty minutes later.

I recognized the name of Eve's cousin from the paperwork that Ally had gone over with me in detail by excruciating detail. "He isn't an A.M.P, but he gives psychic readings. How do you know him?"

"I don't *know* him," she said. "It's his name on my sign off sheet, which means it has to be a fake replacement too, right?"

"Probably." I knew Eve had faked Jacob's signature for our replacement, but I didn't know Jacob's name was on Cindy's replacement too. Was someone trying to bait replacement agents? Brad Cestrum was out there somewhere. It would also mean that the authorities were wrong about Brad only targeting me—and that I shouldn't be the only necronite under police protection. "Let me see it."

She thrust a piece of paper in my hands. There was Jacob's signature at the bottom of the page. He was the supposed A.M.P. for Cindy's client tomorrow, some woman by the name of Judy. It was the same signature on Eve's paperwork. Since I knew Eve forged Jacob's signature, who forged this one since Eve was in jail? Or maybe she did more than one before she was arrested? If so, why did she fail to mention this to me when I questioned her?

"Did you ask Frank about it?" I asked. Frank was Cindy's handler.

"The FBRD is conveniently holding him for questioning right now. Sound familiar?"

"Did they suspend you from replacements while they're investigating?" I asked. If someone was targeting agents, it would've been smart to protect all DR agents.

She shook her head no.

That made the FBRD look guilty as hell. "If Brinkley is right and the FBRD is responsible, maybe they hoped you would get yourself killed."

"Jacob doesn't even have a FBRD-certification."

"Somebody's lying," I said, certain. "If we can talk to him, maybe we'll get a better sense of what's going on. Maybe even who Brad Cestrum is and how he is involved."

"That's why we need to go over there and talk to Jacob. We need to drill a hole in his watermelon head and get some answers."

"Easy, girl," I said. I stepped into my new shoes and pulled on a black hoodie.

"Nice shoes," she said "So you're coming or not?"

I might not know where Ally or Brinkley was, but I was 90% sure Cindy was the next target. I couldn't let her wander off alone. "Sure," I said. "I'll go."

Cindy wanted to drive. Given she seemed a little less stable than usual, I thought that was a bad idea, but I let her anyway. She was a nervous wreck and that instability made me nervous. But hey, wielding a hunk of metal seemed to give her a false sense of control, so I let it go.

Whatever got her through the day.

"Let me ask you something," I said, trying to fill the

silence. She didn't even glance my way. "Anything weird going on with you?"

"Do you mean besides talking to an angel that no one else can see?"

I told her about my electrical problems and what Rachel and kooky Mr. Reeves had said about superpowers. She gave me a strange look. "Maybe I don't need a plumber after all."

"Please tell me why you think you need a plumber," I said.

"I don't want to talk about it."

"Why?" I said. I thought I was being awfully honest with my confession. It wasn't fair that she was holding back.

Finally she said, "Let's just say I have to be careful around toilets."

"Like they talk to you or—?" I pictured the lid flipping open and closed like a mouth.

"No. I just can't be in a bathroom if I'm emotional," she said. And that's all she would give me. Weird, because bathrooms, or sometimes my bed, were exactly where I hid if I was emotional.

Jacob's place was located off of Haywood Lane. It wasn't anywhere near as high class as Cindy's place or as legit looking as mine. I had a real sign and employees—Ally—but Jacob worked out of his mother's house, with only a little sign out front that said "Certified Psychic Jacob Willis" in black paint on a wooden board.

Who the hell certified psychics?

Cindy climbed the three-step cinder block porch and gave a few hard knocks. The screen door rattled and shook with each bang. But no one came.

"How do you know he's here?" I asked from the bottom of the steps.

"His momma told me," she said and knocked again.

A little kid opened the door. He had an orange stained

mouth and grubby fingers. The kid looked sticky. "Who are y'all?"

"We're looking for Jacob," Cindy said.

The kid looked her up and down. "Are you a patient?"

A large, rotund woman who dwarfed the doorway nudged the boy out of the way with a fearsome swing of her hips. "Client," she said. "He ain't no doctor."

"Mrs. Willis," Cindy said. "We spoke on the phone."

"He went down to the store. He'll be right back. Come on in and wait."

We filed into the small house one at a time. His mom pointed us around the corner to a small room that was set up for Jacob's "clients." The room was more like a dark nook, separated from the living room by a plastic beaded curtain. Inside the nook, two folding chairs sat beside a plastic covered card table.

His mom pointed at the empty chairs. "Just wait here."

Cindy leaned over and whispered once she'd gone. "The least he can do is talk to us."

Fifteen minutes later, Jacob, tall and thin, maybe in his late twenties turned up with a greasy sack in one hand and two cartons of cigarettes in the other. His sandy hair was slicked to his head. Big vacant eyes regarding us. His sunken cheeks and thin lips made him look more gaunt and angular than most. He froze. If he was psychic, he sure looked surprised to see us.

"Did I miss your appointment?" he asked.

"We didn't have an appointment," Cindy said. "We just need to talk."

The food sack hit the card table with a fat thump. He pulled out a huge burger wrapped in plastic. He flattened the sack with his hand, then scattered the fries all over it. With his food spread out in front of him, he took a seat.

"Do you know a woman named Judy Ludlow, or a man named Brad Cestrum?" she asked.

"I remember you," he said. "You asked me this on the phone."

"What kind of services do you offer?" I asked, hoping that if I showed interest—even flattery—he might be more willing to impress us with his knowledge.

He gave me a grease smudged price sheet. I could get a palm reading for $10 and a tarot reading for $25.

Cindy repeated the names. "Do you remember meeting them for a sign off?"

"No. I don't know anyone by those names." His eyes flicked to mine as he shoved a handful of ketchup covered fries into his mouth. He stared for a moment too long. "I have a feeling that you've got romance troubles."

"Really?" I asked. Was it written on my face or what?

Cindy tried to get his attention again, holding up her paperwork. "Can you verify this isn't your signature?"

Jacob ignored her, his eyes wide and dark. "All you've ever wanted was to be loved. So it scares you."

"Hey," Cindy snapped. "Answer my question."

"It's one thing to be adored," Jacob said. "It's another to love someone back. He adores you, but you love someone else, don't you?"

"Wait—" I said. "You saw all that on my face?"

Cindy slapped the paperwork down in front of him and put her whole body between us, stretching over the table and everything. "Have you ever seen this?"

Having broken the eye contact between us, Jacob was forced to give Cindy his attention. "That's not my signature."

"Can you verify that?" Cindy said. "Do you have anything you've signed that we can compare it to?"

Without those creepy black eyes burning through mine, it was easier to regain my self-control. Logic prevailed. He was a scam. So what if all I've ever wanted was to be loved? So did everyone. I probably smelled like Lane because we were just together and I didn't look happy, so there was probably trouble. A drunk hobo could guess as much.

Jacob pulled off a drape covering from a piece of neglected furniture in the corner. Dust billowed up into the air. He slid a fat folder from the cabinet.

"Here," he said. He lined up all three sheets side-by-side, two white sheets and a carbon copy, each signed by him. He even took a pen from his desk and signed again on the file folder itself so we could see all four signatures in a row. Cindy put her paperwork beside the sheets.

We leaned close, our eyes measuring every curve and shift of his signature. I broke the silence first. "They're different."

"So you don't serve as an A.M.P. on death replacements at all?" Cindy asked.

"Death-reading is not my area of expertise," he said with a wink.

Cindy straightened. "Do you realize someone has been going around signing your name? Do you even take proper steps to prevent identity theft? Do you know I could have been killed today under the false assumption that you, as an A.M.P., verified all these replacements?"

"How I run my business ain't none of your business."

"It does when people are trying to kill me," Cindy yelled.

Both Cindy and I turned toward the clicking beads of the moving curtain to find Jacob's mom in the doorway.

"Get out of my house."

She repeated herself when we didn't move fast enough.

"Do you have a hearing problem? I said get out of my house."

"Obviously we've misunderstood each other," Cindy said, her voice cooling.

"I didn't misunderstand nothing," she said. She reached

up and gave her blond ponytail a tug as if to say she were serious about hauling our butts out. I already figured that. I didn't need any displays of dominance to get the point. "I've been watching the news, knew I recognized you. You're trying to say my boy is responsible for that accident. You're saying he's going around trying to get people killed."

"Let's start over." Cindy assumed the voice of a lion tamer. "I'm Cindy. This is J—"

"Get the hell out of my house." She moved toward us. "Someone turns out to be special and you want to persecute them. Well, my boy ain't gonna be your sacrificial lamb."

"Wait a minute." I wasn't even going to point out the complete illogical mentality behind her reasoning. She knew she was talking to one of those persecuted victims, right?

Jacob slipped a card into my open hand. "In case you need help making your decision," he said in a whisper.

His mother edged closer. Cindy and I maneuvered around the other side of the table, away from the pair, moving back through the beaded curtain. Just as we crossed the threshold a picture on the wall beside the doorframe caught my eye.

Four people and a baby stood smiling: Jacob, his momma, and two women. One woman was a mystery. The other was Eve, holding a baby.

Here was my evidence. If I gave Garrison this picture, then he might believe our story about Eve's fake signatures even if she wouldn't confess.

"Yes, I got it," I squealed, snatching the picture off the wall and showed it to Cindy. "This is all we need."

Jacob's momma charged like a bull with a spear in its butt. "I told you to get the hell out of my house."

I pushed Cindy out of my way as I scrambled for the door. She got me back in the doorway, when she shoved me through the screen out onto the lawn. I hit the ground on both knees.

My knees connected with the dirt and gravel, as an explosion rocked the house. I bent down low and covered my head, inhaling the wet scent of earth.

"What in the Lord's name?" Jacob's mom said and stopped chasing us. Through the unhinged screen door and around the woman's thick calves, I saw a large spray of water pouring into the hallway. The toilet seat landed outside the bathroom, propped up at an angle against one wall.

"What the hell?" I asked.

"Don't ask," Cindy said and yanked me up out of the yard and pushed me toward her car.

We were in the car and pulled out of the driveway before Momma Mayhem made it down the stairs, cursing us for destroying her house.

Cindy didn't stop speeding until we were blocks away. "Holy shit!"

"Do you affect water pressure or something?"

Cindy bit her lip. "—or something."

"And you couldn't tell me that sooner?" I asked, my voice an octave too high. "Oh my god, I've been freaking out about spontaneous combustion and you explode toilets."

CHAPTER TWENTY-ONE

"We should talk about it," I pressed once we were safe at my house.

"No," Cindy insisted.

"You explode toilets. I explode electronics," I argued for the tenth time. "That's not fucking normal."

"Nothing is wrong with me," Cindy shouted. What little remained of her composure was lost. Her face was bright red and her hands shook in fists by her side. "If you say another word about it I'm leaving."

And that was that. I didn't want her to leave so I kept my mouth shut. But damn, it was hard. I felt better, knowing I wasn't the only one, but I needed to process.

We managed five whole minutes of silence, sprawled in defeat across my living room furniture, before she spoke again. Cindy pointed at the picture in my lap. "I can't believe you stole that."

"Eve might not tell the truth ever," I said, examining the picture more closely. "If I can show this to Garrison along with the falsified signatures, he might believe I'm the victim."

"Jacob might not have known she was forging his signature," Cindy said. "He looked surprised to see his name on our D.R.s."

"Or he could've been acting," I said. "You saw the way he totally tried to scam me."

I was shaking from my adrenaline crash. I searched the happy foursome for clues, staring at happy Eve holding a baby.

My eyes were fixed but my mind wandered. Eve's death wasn't a real death. I died for nothing. Worse, there was the possibility I'd have to pay the fine and go to jail. And Ally —*God*. I tried to breathe against the panic.

"Someone is baiting agents," I said. "I'm betting on Brad Cestrum. We could use your replacement to bait him, see how he likes it."

Cindy frowned. "It's too risky."

"You're right." That left us in the dark as to how to find the jerk from the hotel room. It was clear he was working to polish off the Nashville zombies, but why hadn't he come back for me? Was that Gabriel's doing? Or Brinkley's?

"Do you have any way of getting a hold of that agent who's supposed to be working your case?" Cindy asked.

"Garrison?" I asked.

"We should give him a call," she said. "Momma Mayhem can't chase him out of the house."

I turned the picture over so I wouldn't have to look at their grinning faces. "Mrs. Mayhem doesn't seem like the sort of woman to let a federal agent hold her back."

I called Garrison and he showed up with another fat folder in hand.

"What's that?" I asked, pointing at the bulging brown flaps. "Not my warrant I hope."

"We're in the process of acquiring that," he said, deadpan.

I couldn't tell if he was joking. I forced a laugh anyway, but was pretty sure it sounded nervous and awkward. I tried to offer the picture of Eve that I stole but he waved me away.

"I brought my own," he said. He unfolded the envelope flap and removed several large 8x10 photographs. He spread them side-by-side on my coffee table.

"Do you recognize him?" he asked, pointing to a middle-aged, bald man on the table.

"No," I said. I didn't like his blunt, irritated tone.

He turned to Cindy. "You?"

She leaned over the coffee table, peering closely. "No."

"This is Brad Cestrum," he said, turning back to me.

I pointed to a different photograph. "That's the man Eve introduced as Brad."

The photograph I pointed to was much less clear, an unfocused security cam photo rather than a staged portrait. The fuzzy photo was a black and white photograph of Eve and fake-Brad. In this picture, fake-Brad was checking out of some kind of store.

"This is the real Brad Cestrum," he said, again. He pointed at the middle-aged, bald man I'd never seen.

"But look at him," I said, trying to draw Garrison's eye back to fake-Brad's picture. "Doesn't he look familiar?"

He spoke as if he hadn't heard me. "We took it off a convenience store security camera."

Cindy handed me the picture I'd swiped from Jacob's place and nudged me. I offered it to Garrison again, hoping he wouldn't disregard me a second time. He took it and assessed with a thorough eye while I explained how we got it.

"You took this from Jacob Willis's house, 507 Kenney Street?"

"Eve fabricated her paperwork using her cousin Jacob's signature," I explained. "I have a couple of the signature sheets that prove his signatures don't match and that he knows Eve."

"We were chased out of the house," Cindy said. "She only took that by accident."

Cindy was sweet to offer me a cover story, but Garrison didn't look interested in arresting me for a minor theft.

I looked at Garrison's photographs. This whole situation was bizarre and surreal. A cop in my living room, showing me black and white photographs of someone who'd tried to kill me. Did this really happen to people?

"So the man in the hotel room isn't named Brad Cestrum?" I asked. "So who could he be?"

I couldn't make it any more obvious unless I told Garrison what Brinkley had told me, but that meant admitting that I'd seen Brinkley.

It was Cindy's turn to shuffle through the photographs. "My God, that's him."

Apparently Garrison and I didn't look nearly interested enough.

"Him," Cindy said. She poked the picture several times. "The priest I told you about."

Garrison snatched the second, slightly better photo of fake-Brad from my hands as if I weren't worthy of touching it anymore. He handed it to Cindy. "You've seen this man dressed as a priest?"

"A few days ago. He tried to get me to leave the church with him."

"He's a priest," I said, elated. "She identified him, so you can go pick him up, right?" I would've felt so much better if this fake-Brad wasn't lurking around. And at this rate, Garrison was going to have to look this guy in the face before making the FBRD connection.

"Are you certain?" he asked Cindy.

"Yes," we both said in unison.

"I interviewed all the listed priests and clergy members

last week. I didn't come across him." He gathered the photographs together.

"Maybe he's visiting from a different church," Cindy said, standing up because Garrison did. "They do that."

He tucked everything under his arms and hustled toward the door. "I'll see what I can find out."

"Wait." I touched his arm hoping to stop him. It worked but it was immediately apparent he did not like to be touched from the way he bristled and moved back. I released him. "Sorry. But look, so it turns out Eve's paperwork was fake. You can't really punish me for that, can you? How was I supposed to know?"

"Quit sneaking around," he said. "Or you'll run into worse than an irate mother."

"But I'm trying to get out of trouble here. I swear to you I didn't do anything."

Garrison leaned real close. At the last moment, he turned his head and whispered directly into my ear. "If you are so concerned with proving your innocence, I'd watch what you say over breakfast."

It took a moment for me to process this.

What had I said over breakfast? Everything.

I'd told Lane everything.

I either moved the phone away from my ear or risked losing an ear drum.

"Get the hell out of the house. Now," Gloria yelled, and Gloria never yelled.

"What? Why?"

I took another bite of my sandwich. I'd been standing in my kitchen trying to figure out what I could do—if anything—in the event that the police really did have my confession on tape. Call a lawyer, maybe? Make arrangements for

Winston?

"You have company coming," Gloria said. "You need to get out of the house."

"I want to finish my sandwich. Is that okay?"

"Move, move, move!" Gloria barked like a drill sergeant. "You've only got minutes."

"Is this a long trip? Do I need to pack?"

"Forget your clothes. You can't let them catch you. You have somewhere else to be."

My skin shivered. "You found her."

"But that won't mean anything if you don't get out of that house!" Gloria kept screaming.

I dropped the sandwich and grabbed my keys.

"Leave your car," Gloria said. "I'll meet you where you met Brinkley last. And leave the dog."

With this final warning she disconnected the line. The place I met Brinkley? She must've meant the trail behind my house. I heard sirens in the distance and I about shit myself. Those sirens might not have had anything to do with me, it could've been a fire for all I knew, but it was motivation enough to drop the keys and run for the back door.

I was almost out the kitchen door when I saw Winston lying in a heap of wrinkles by his food dish. Dinner wasn't for another two hours but he was very patient when it came to food. The sirens grew louder and I knew I should be running, but I couldn't leave him.

"Gloria's going to kill me," I said, scooping his chubby butt up. I ran out the back door, cut through the yard and hit the trail at full speed.

It wasn't easy running with forty pounds of pug pressed against my chest. Winston didn't appreciate it either, all his huffing and wheezing told me so. I apologized to him a million times explaining that I couldn't rely on the FBRD or the local police to feed him. They would've taken him for evidence for all I knew.

We had to stick together, for better or worse.

I traveled much farther down the trail than Ally and I had until I saw Gloria's car. My legs and lungs were on fire and my biceps threatened to give out on the pug, but we made it.

I had to balance Winston in one shaky arm while I opened the back door and put him in the car. I fell into the front seat panting. "God, I need to work out more. Lift weights, anything."

"I knew you were going to bring that damn thing," she said, throwing the car in reverse and speeding away before I even had the door shut.

"I couldn't leave him." I whined. "He's my baby."

"Well who's going to take care of him while you're off saving the world?" she asked with raised eyebrows.

I gave her a pouty lip.

"Honey, you don't want to leave your *baby* in my care," she said. "I disappear into my head for days at a time. I might come out to find that he's died of starvation or pissed on my floor."

I chewed my lip nervously. "Maybe Lane will watch him. We're dating now. I think."

Gloria didn't respond.

"So where are we going?"

"Somewhere they won't look," she said.

"They have to know I'm not home if they know what I said over breakfast. They're probably following you instead."

"Where is your cell phone?" Gloria asked.

I showed it to her. Her response was to snatch it from my hand and throw it out of her window. It hit the pavement with a sickening crack.

"Oh my god," I screamed, my head out the window. "I had a million pictures."

"Cell phones are traceable," she said.

"And my contacts."

"You had to ditch it."

"Then why did you let me take it to St. Louis?" I asked.

"I forgot," Gloria said.

I must have looked cynical. Gloria snorted.

"Contrary to popular belief, I am human."

"You're saving my ass now. That's what counts," I said, but I was pretty irritated. "So where's Ally?"

"I'll show you," she said.

During the drive, I made another attempt to use the shocky thing. After all, I might need that trick soon. When I failed to change my vision or go electric, I asked Gloria a few questions for ideas. She hypothesized that it was connected to emotions, a stress response. So I tried to think of things that made me sad, and when that didn't work, angry. Neither worked.

By the time we pulled up at Lane's comic bookstore, I'd accomplished nothing.

I hit the floorboard of her car. "Jesus Christ, Gloria. This place isn't exactly secret. It's attached to my office."

"No one is watching right now," she said. "And we'll only be here for a little while."

We entered the store and Lane knew immediately something was up. I kept spastically looking over my shoulder until I put a fat blob of pug in his arms.

"What happened?" He ushered his two regulars—the only current patrons—out the door and locked it. He flipped the sign to read CLOSED.

"You know all that stuff I told you over breakfast?" I asked. "My house is bugged and so now that's all on tape. Like police tape."

I let that settle in.

"I'm pretty much running from the law," I added, tugging my ponytail. "For, like, the rest of my life."

"You shouldn't be here."

"It wasn't my idea." I pointed at Gloria who wandered the store. My cheeks burned a little hotter. "You could get in trouble for aiding me, you know."

He smirked. "I've always had a problem with authority. We have that in common."

I was blushing so hard I thought my head might explode. "About earlier—"

He stopped me. "I get it. We'll take it slow."

"Oh God," I said. "Like no sex?"

"I need a minute to decide what I'm comfortable with and what I'm not," he said. "I'm not saying no."

I opened my mouth to argue that depriving me of sex would *not* be his best approach in securing fidelity—but he pointed at Gloria.

"Go talk to her and find out what's going on," he said, nudging me with a smile. "I'll watch the pug."

"But are we okay?" I asked him.

"We're okay."

I kissed his cheek. Then set off to corner Gloria at the anime display case. She looked particularly interested in the girl with a big sword and pink hair.

"Is that what you want Santa to bring you this year?" I read the box. "A Juko doll?"

Gloria jumped, jittery. I recognized her behavior.

"How much caffeine have you had?"

"Too much," she said. She must have been pushing herself hard to get the answers Ally and I asked her for. To Gloria, this meant no food or sleep, for however long it took. I'd seen her emerge from a pitch black room after days of silence and drink a gallon of soda straight from the bottle. The caffeine scattered her focus enough to cut off the visions. "About

Ally—"

She shifted the sketchbook under her arm as if it were a burden to hold. I didn't realize she'd carried it in from the car. I was too busy hefting around the pug.

She flipped open the book. "This is it."

The page was nothing but a black charcoal smudge across the entire page. It might as well have been blank.

"I don't get it," I said.

"Darkness," Gloria said, concerned. "Ally's future is darkness."

My heart pounded. "She's dead?"

"Not yet."

Yet, yet. Gabriel's words came back to me. She isn't harmed yet.

Gloria flipped through several sheets colored solid black. "She's here, somewhere right here."

The following five pages were various aspects of downtown. The river, the buildings, the church bells.

"Not here in the office," Gloria said, turning the page. Clearly she was irritated that I wasn't as perceptive as she was. "But she's close."

I was thinking hard and chewing my lips.

"She was coming back to talk to the police," she added.

"You saw that in your vision?" I asked.

"I got a call from her brother," she said. "He's driving down from Chicago to represent you and Ally. Ally told him she'd found the girl."

"If fake-Brad Cestrum was pretending to be a priest, they must be at the Church," I said.

"Could be," she said. "I hear those bells like they are right on top of me."

Please be alive, I thought. *Please, Ally. Please.*

Gloria leaned forward. "I have a confession."

She spat the words at me as if she'd been holding her breath.

"I hear people go to church to confess, but I don't think that'll get us in," I said, thinking about how I would get Ally back. If fake-Brad was there, he'd recognize me for sure.

"No, I need to tell to you the truth." She ran a palm over her head. "I screwed up."

I waved her on, hoping she'd get to the point.

"I'm so sorry, Jesse." Her chest heaved as if bucking some great weight.

"For what?" I asked.

"A month ago I saw Eve kill you. I didn't realize that was what I was viewing at the time. Sometimes visions have no time signifiers attached to them, especially in your case. I told Brinkley this and gave him the picture of the man behind it. I'm sorry I didn't tell you, but I didn't want you to change anything. If you change your mind, the vision changes and we end up in the dark again. It's like starting over."

I remembered the picture in her book of Eve beheading me and her turning the page quickly before I could get a good look. This time she showed me the same sketch but with the fake-Brad-priest in the room. Shit.

"It would have been fine if someone else wasn't manipulating the situation. I feel it. It's like watching someone weave a web around you, moving you into place. I had to do something, Jesse. I told Brinkley months ago. And I told Ally the night before you left for Illinois. I needed help to get you out of this."

"Who's manipulating the situation?"

"I put you in the trap," she said. "I've moved you, Brinkley, and Ally into the trap instead of out of it. I am the reason why Eve got to you."

"I didn't know there was another player. I swear I didn't," she said.

"I don't know what you mean by 'another player'," I said.

"Another remote-viewer," she said. "But he doesn't follow the rules."

"The bad guys have a viewer too?" I asked. Who could recruit a freelance viewer? I was back to wondering who was to blame—the military, the FBRD, or the Church.

Gloria gave me another picture, the most striking I'd ever seen. Ally, Brinkley, and I were somewhere dark. Shadowed stone surrounded a pocket of light cast by a lamp fixed to the wall. In the light, it was obvious I was dead, quite dead. Ally, collapsed on my chest, didn't look so well herself. Brinkley was unconscious or dead against a wall. A fourth person was also in the room.

Then it hit me. Gloria wasn't the only person who'd given me a drawing this week. I searched my pockets frantically and found Rachel's picture folded in the front of my jeans. Thank God, I'd been too busy to wash my clothes and had a habit of wearing my jeans several days in a row.

I unfolded the paper with shaking hands.

Gloria was a better artist than Rachel, but it was almost the exact same picture with one exception. In Rachel's picture, I clutched Nessa against my chest, trying to save her. And Ally was dead, her stomach dark with blood. In Gloria's version, there was no Nessa, only the unclear fourth person.

"Rachel gave me this picture when I was in St. Louis. She told me 'Choose carefully.'" I stared at the two pictures comparing them. "Shit, Gloria, I can't save them all."

I searched the pictures for clues. Ally. Brinkley. Poor little Nessa. Would I really have to choose? I could only replace one person.

"Why are these pictures different?" I asked.

Gloria pulled at her face as if exhausted. "If I drew mine before she did, the girl may not have been involved yet."

"When did you draw this?" I asked.

"Last night," she said. "It's like he knows me."

"Your drawing is the most recent," I said. "You're certain he's an A.M.P.?"

"He'd have to be," Lane said. He came up behind us and wrapped his arms around my waist. I didn't object. "That's the only way he'd see the threads."

"He's good," Gloria added, reluctant to leave her own thoughts. She met my eyes again. "He led me to believe I could prevent you from making this choice."

"What choice?" Lane asked.

"Do you have any idea who it might be?" I asked her. "Anyone come to mind?"

"What choice?" he asked again.

"Someone comes to mind," she admitted.

"I have to break into the church." I looked at the picture again. "And this is what I have to look forward to."

Lane snatched the two pictures from my hands. "You're not going."

"I have to go." I pointed at the horror scene. "If I don't everyone in this picture will die. Saving one person is better than saving no one."

Someone called out to me.

I froze. My first thought was cops, but the voice was too soft, feminine to be here to bust me. And it wasn't Gabriel because Lane tensed too.

"It's not the police," Gloria said, relaxing her shoulders. "But we don't have much time."

Kyra appeared in the hallway connecting our office to the comic bookstore.

"What are you doing here?" I asked. I pulled her into the store through the small hall connecting my office and the comic book store. I hoped she wasn't seen by any patrolling police. Worse, how did she get in? I sent Lane to check and he said the office had been unlocked. Ally wouldn't have left the office unlocked on purpose and she was the last one there.

"I was worried," Kyra said. "I called your cell and your house but you didn't answer. I couldn't get ahold of Ally either. I thought I'd drop by and see if you were okay."

The last time she saw me I had been carted away by Garrison. I should have called. "Sorry. They just asked some questions and let me go."

"I also came to invite you to my presentation," Kyra said. She looked at Gloria who came to stand beside me. "I know you might not want to come because it is in the church here, but you might really like it."

"You're giving a presentation at the church?" I asked. I pointed at the street beyond the large glass windows. "This church?"

She nodded, placing a beautifully gilded invitation in my hand. "I'll be talking about Baroque art and architecture. There are some really beautiful pieces inside the cathedral that I'm discussing in great length in my presentation. It's tomorrow night if you want to come."

Gloria squeezed my arm. "This is what we're waiting for."

I slowly grinned from ear to ear. "Hey, Kyra. I need your help."

CHAPTER TWENTY-TWO

Gloria stayed behind with the pug while Kyra, Lane, Cindy and I went to search the church quickly for Ally and Nessa.

I wasn't wearing any sexy tactical gear like ninja babes in the movies, though. Just jeans, my usual black zip-up hoodie and the new matching sneakers that Lane had just given me.

"So I am going to pretend to inspect the cathedral for tomorrow," Kyra said when we had a city block between us and the church. "The rest of you are my tech team, so if someone stops you, say you are looking for wiring or the fuse box or something. But how will you know where to look if you've never been inside?"

I pointed at Cindy. It was part of the reason why she'd been called in. I also hoped two necronites were better than one and meant more people would get out of this alive. I'd have to keep her away from the toilets.

Though Cindy didn't seem particularly focused. She hadn't said a word since we left the office. She was lost in her own thoughts. Or maybe she was having a visit from Raphael.

The way she looked worriedly over her shoulder and mumbled under her breath made me think so.

"I know most of it," Cindy answered. "But we shouldn't split up."

"We're adults. We can handle ourselves," I said.

"One: the place is huge, you'll get lost. Two: that's how people die in the movies," Cindy said.

"Can't we understand anything without a movie reference?" Kyra asked.

"The evolution of our culture will, of course, impact the evolution of our perceptional abilities and social understanding," Lane said.

"He means no," I answered.

"We're not splitting up," Lane said again.

"You're too old for tantrums," I said. "What's your problem?"

"Nothing is going to happen," Kyra added. "We've got a great cover story."

"Did you show them the drawings?" Lane asked.

"What drawings are you talking about?" Cindy asked. Everyone stopped.

"Gloria drew pictures of everyone in the church," Lane said. "*Dying*."

"First of all," I said, knowing if I didn't correct this immediately, I'd be going into that church alone.

"Kyra and Cindy weren't in the pictures. You weren't even in them. Secondly, I was the only person dying. And I can't not help Ally."

I was firm about this, hands on my hips and everything. I'd beat up Lane and throw myself through one of the church's windows if I had to. Well, I'd *try* to beat up Lane. At the very least, I would go alone.

"I wasn't in the pictures?" Cindy asked.

"No," I said and dared Lane to correct me.

"Then we're safe," Kyra chimed. "Let's go save the day."

"I go with Jesse," Lane said and yanked open the cemetery gate, the last thing standing between us and the small dark door tucked into the side of the church. "Kyra goes with Cindy. This way dying isn't an option for anyone."

"Fine with me," Kyra said and filed through the wrought-iron frame first. Cindy grudgingly followed.

We weaved ourselves in and out of the rough granite tombstones jutting skyward. I felt strange as we walked over the graves. Did I feel something stir underground? No way. It must have been the rumble from the main road or the leaves that crunched and hissed as we shuffled through. I wasn't stupid enough to let Mr. Reeves's dumb stories spook me. Probably.

Lane whirled around. "Go ahead and announce we're here."

"Sorry," I retorted. "I forgot to come by and rake the whole cemetery today on account that I was running from the law."

He whirled around and continued toward the door. I would like to add that he made more noise in his pouty shuffle and big boots than the three of us women made together. Yet, we arrived at the door without being seen. Lane reached it first and opened it slowly. He froze, surprised to find it unlocked. I was surprised too, looking to my friends for a possible explanation.

"What if they know we're here?" Cindy was glancing around us.

"Then we look stupid standing here deliberating," I said. I shrugged off thoughts of the spooky evil remote viewer watching my every move.

"Or it's because he's working," Lane offered, pointing in the direction of a gravedigger. He'd paused in his digging long enough to glare our way, or at least I thought so. It was hard to tell because his face was obscured by the dark shadows of the tree hanging over him. He was nothing more than a silhouette leaning against a glint of metal in the darkness. A shovel?

The faceless gravedigger creeped me out.

The church was huge from this angle, large and illuminated, towering over our heads like a colossal monument stretching into the heavens. The strategic lights highlighted the stained glass and stone in such a way that the building looked truly divine.

"It's beautiful," I said. "I hardly notice it when I drive by."

"The inside is prettier," Kyra said. "Come on."

Lane held back. "This is too easy."

"I *told* you this door would be unlocked," Cindy said. "It's the exit by the confessional. It stays unlocked until the church closes."

I pulled the door open hard, half-crossing the threshold. Lane grabbed my hand at the last moment.

"Stay close to me," he said. The tenderness returned to his face, and that was enough to soften me.

I leaned forward and gave his cheek a quick peck. "As if I have a choice."

CHAPTER TWENTY-THREE

Kyra was right. The inside of the church was more impressive. I was tiny walking beneath such a high ceiling and I couldn't stop looking up at it. Painted frescos and stained-glass windows hung overhead. Beams of dark polished wood ran from floor to ceiling, wall to wall. I saw a small, Asian woman polishing a pew and wondered if they were going to heft her up on a pulley to polish those rafters. I'd like to see that.

"You see these beams here?" Kyra pointed up. "Flying buttresses became popular in the—"

I nudged her, cutting her off. "This is not art appreciation class."

She looked crestfallen. "Right. Sorry."

A priest came straight toward us, his black robe swishing about his ankles.

Kyra was on it. Gracefully, she strode toward him, all smiles. In seconds she had him blushing as she made grand gestures toward the ceiling and smaller ones toward us. I held up my red-enveloped invitation just in case.

Cindy scoped out the area and then came close to whisper

in my ear. "I don't see the priest. You should duck out while he's not watching."

"Come on." Lane tugged my hand in agreement, trying to pull me from the allure of the ceiling and the little painted Christ-child in rich rosy hues.

"Remember we'll have to leave by nine," Cindy said. "They lock the doors."

With Kyra blocking the priest's view, and no one else in sight, Lane and I ducked under the velvet ropes barring a stone hallway. Immediately, we ducked left, out of sight. Lane took the lead, turning a corner into an identical hallway.

The walls and floor were the same stone as outside of the church. A long, red rug ran the length of the hallway, giving it a rather gothic look. There were several doors on each side before the hallway ended at a T, splitting into two directions.

Lane pressed his ear to the first door on the left and then opened it, moving inside. I did the same on the right. There wasn't much in the first room. No windows, so it reminded me of a cell. There was a desk with some papers on it, mostly receipts and thank you notes from various congregational members. Nothing that pointed me toward Ally or the black future we were trying to avoid.

I had similar results behind the next three doors. Each held odd pieces of furniture, a chair or chest. Others held vases, pictures of Jesus, and bookcases with Bibles and devotional hymns. But nothing I could use to determine Ally's whereabouts. The last door was locked. I pointed this out to Lane after he'd checked all the doors on his side of the hallway.

He wiggled the handle himself.

"Are we going to break it down?" I whispered. I made a kicking motion in the air.

He shook his head. At the end of our hallway, I leaned

around the corners in each direction of the T, but I didn't see any doors or people.

"I don't think anyone will hear if you knock softly," I whispered.

He shook his head again. Then put his lips right against my ear. "They wouldn't keep her this close to the front, in case she screamed."

Good point.

I followed him around the corner. I traced the entire length of the right hallway but found no doors except one at the very end. I pushed it open and found a staircase leading down into pitch black darkness.

I shivered. No way in hell I was going down there. Lane caught my attention by waving his arms and motioning me to follow him.

Turns out, at his end of the T-passage there was a door like the one on my end. But this one didn't open to a staircase. It opened to a bedroom.

A twin bed with rumpled white sheets and a down blanket sat tucked into the corner. It looked as though someone had just rolled out of it. The desk was neater than the one I'd seen in the other room. A small flower rested in the vase beside a lamp which was on, giving the room a soft glow, but Lane didn't bring me in here to see any of this. As I stared at this little living space, he was frantically jerking my sleeve and pointing at the bed. Ally's red coat.

I had a hard time dividing my attention between the coat and the painting on the wall.

In a large frame, there was a picture of Mr. Reeves, the creepy guy from my mother's funeral. He wore a nicely tailored suit much like the one I'd seen him in, except this suit was navy blue with a red tie. I soaked the painting up, not sure what it meant. What was the creepy guy from my mother's funeral doing here? Was he a church supporter? Was he a clergyman? Even so, why'd they hang a picture of him in a Nashville church?

I filed the portrait in the back of my mind under "Shit To Sort Out Later." I was a terribly simple girl when it came to problems and my plate was so full the vegetables were falling off.

Lane insisted we go back and investigate the dark staircase, since it was the only place left to look. We checked every inch of the basement, but no Ally. It was terrifying to be down here, because it looked the most like the room in the drawings. Pretty sure Ally was no longer in the church, we crept out. Kyra and Cindy were waiting in the parking lot, catty-corner to the cemetery.

"We only found her coat," I said. "You?"

"No," Kyra said.

"Wait. There it is again." Cindy's hands shot up.

"I—" Lane started but Cindy stopped him.

"Shhh." Cindy did a sort of twitch, side step. "There."

We strained to hear whatever it was Cindy was talking about. A phone suddenly vibrated and we all jumped. Lane pulled out his phone and saw Gloria's name on the display. He flipped it open. After listening for a moment, he handed it to me.

"Bobkins is here to serve your warrant," Gloria said. "Tell him where you are. You don't want more trouble."

She seemed to mean something by *more*. I tried to play along. "Put him on the phone."

"Bobkins," he said.

"So what are my charges?" I asked.

"Murder," he said.

Of course. "And who did I kill?"

"Eddie Phelps and Nessa Hildebrand. Eve Hildebrand gave a full confession today, saying that you killed her daughter and she was taking revenge."

My heart stopped. "Did you find Nessa's body?"

"It's only a matter of time."

I sighed, relieved. Maybe the little girl was still alive. Bobkins was an idiot and hopefully a misinformed one. Eve must've folded under the pressure.

"You can either turn yourself in or I can pick you up," he pressed.

"How thoughtful." My heart pounded like a jackhammer busting up concrete. *Prison.* "Why don't I leave the line open so you can trace my call?"

"Or you can tell me where you are?" he retorted.

What was a "resisting arrest" charge compared to murder? I couldn't cater to Bobkins anyway because I only had so much time to find Ally before they hauled me away. "Come and get me."

I put the phone in my pocket and left the call connected. If Gloria was right about this tracing business, they'd be able to find me. I wasn't sure why Gloria wanted the cops to come to the church, but if she thought it might help us, I was willing to go on a little faith. Faith was about all I had left to work with.

Lane, Kyra, and Cindy were making funny gestures and debating amongst themselves.

"What's going on now?" I asked. The reality of a confining cell in my immediate future seriously dampened my mood.

Lane held up his hand. "I heard it."

I listened until I heard it, a muffled banging noise. I had no idea where it was coming from.

"Is that what you're flipping out about? So what? Some squirrels are getting frisky in their nest."

"Big squirrels," Cindy muttered, her ears turned, straining.

Kyra's face lit up. "Oh my god, what if they put her in one of these trunks?"

Their eyes scanned the parking lot and the dozen cars filling random spaces.

"If Ally is in the trunk, we have to be quick," I said. "The cops are coming to arrest me."

"What?" Kyra and Cindy cried simultaneously. Oh, now they heard me. Lane pulled me closer, like holding me was going to keep me from going to prison.

I tried to make a joke. "I've always wanted to sit in a cell and sing, *Nobody knows the troubles I've seen*...Can one of you loan me a tin cup to rake the bars?"

"How much time do we have?" Cindy was already lowering her ear to the nearest trunk and knocking. No one appreciated my humor.

"Minutes," I said.

"We should run," Lane said. "I can hide you."

I pulled away from him. "I'm not leaving until we find her. Let's search the trunks."

Everyone took a car, doing a tap and listen sort of system. I'd knocked on three cars before Cindy yelled my name. We abandoned our cars and trotted over to the tan sedan furthest from the church's back door. It was parked conspicuously under a large tree, which rained dying leaves with each windy burst.

Cindy raised her hand from the trunk. "Well something's in here."

Kyra knocked on the trunk and a barrage of noise reverberated back. The noise was somewhere between muffled screams and shuffling noises.

"How do we get it open?" I asked, hesitating. What if it wasn't Ally? I'd heard stories about raccoons mauling people. Of course, I wasn't sure why someone would have a raccoon in their trunk, but I had theories. I always had theories.

Lane lifted a huge rock from beneath the tree and smashed the driver side window. The glass shattered, hitting the dark pavement in a shower of glitter. In the overhead street light, it looked gold.

"That works," Kyra said and opened the door. She pushed the trunk release button tucked up under the dash. The trunk popped open as the four of us crowded around to see what was inside.

Ally. She was bound and gagged with her hands behind her back. I pulled the gag out of her mouth as Lane lifted her from the trunk.

"I never thought I'd see you like this," I said. I held her coat open so she could slip her arms inside the sleeves once she was free.

"I never thought I'd see you again," she said as Lane put her on her feet.

Lane worked on loosening the ropes completely. Ally didn't look away from me once, tears rolling down her face as he worked. Her mouth was red, irritated from where the cloth had worked against her skin. As soon as the rope snapped she threw herself against me and kissed me full on the mouth.

And I mean kissed me, in spite of her wet cheeks and all. Was that her tongue? When she pulled back her arms went around my neck, crushing the coat between us.

"I have so much to tell you," she said.

"Obviously." Kyra tilted her head with a naughty smile.

Lane was not smiling. I did my best to ignore the attention and the warm tingles in my body. I looked down to hide my blush. If Lane was mad about this kiss and what doubts it must cast on my monogamy pledge, I was sure I'd hear about it later.

"Here's your coat," I said, offering the coat again. "You'll have to save whatever you want to tell me for visiting hours. The police are on their way to arrest me."

"That's perfect," Ally said. She grabbed me and pulled me toward the church. "Come on."

"No," I said. "We just came out of there. We can't go back in."

"We've got to get Nessa," she said. "I promised."

"Nessa is in there? But we searched everywhere." That'd be great. A living Nessa would exonerate me of at least one crime and throw doubt on Eve's confession. I hadn't worked out a plan for the whole killing Eddie thing though. But maybe I'd get less than a life sentence or the death penalty if I could prove it was self-defense.

"Jesse can't go back into the church," Lane said. "It isn't safe."

"If the agent is on his way, he'll be able to help," Ally said.

Ally dragged me to the back door, yanking it open. Lane grabbed a hold of my other hand. "No, you don't understand," he said. "There are these pictures that Gloria drew."

"Don't tug on me." I yanked my hands away from both of them and pulled my keys free from my pocket. "First of all, Kyra and Cindy need to get out of here. You'll be safer at the office with Gloria or at home."

"We can't leave you here," Kyra said.

"You'd better," I said. "It's two less people for me to worry about."

"I thought you wanted help?" Cindy asked.

"I want nothing more than to ask for your help." With Cindy's help I might be able to save at least two people if that horrible picture comes true. "But I can't ask you to risk your life. If they want me dead for being a necronite, then you aren't safe either."

Cindy hesitated but I could see the relief in her face. She would have stayed if she had to, but she couldn't be happier that I'd given her a way out. "But what about you?"

"I've got these guys to help me," I said, smiling at Ally and Lane. "I'll be okay."

There was also the problem of Cindy's strange behavior. If she was about to go all crazy like Rachel, I didn't want her to stay with us. One less thing for me to worry about.

Cindy led a reluctant Kyra toward the office, and I turned to find Ally all grins.

"What are you so happy about?" I asked her. "I'm going to prison."

"I'm so happy to see you," she said. She bit her lip. "I'm so happy. I knew they were going to shoot me and bury me in a ditch."

Lane huffed. "So did Jesse get a chance to tell you that we're—"

I cut him off. Ally was just rescued from a near death. She didn't need to hear that I was dating someone else right now.

"I'm glad you're okay too. I wanted to apologize for—*hey*."

I fell to the ground as Lane shoved me out of the way and took the full force of the shovel to his own skull. I didn't even have time to process his body collapsing to the ground beside me before I saw a steel plate whishing toward my face.

CHAPTER TWENTY-FOUR

When I woke up, my head was killing me. Not literally, but I wished I was dead so I didn't have to feel the massive lump throbbing on the side of my skull. My face was sticky with blood, but I reminded myself that face cuts always bleed profusely, so no need to panic yet. Again, I wasn't afraid of dying for someone, but I was worried about blacking out before I discovered what was going on.

Okay, maybe I was a little worried about my face.

As my vision blurred into focus, I saw the bed first. A twin-sized mattress like we saw in the room upstairs, sat to my right against the wall. Ally and Lane were tied up to chairs across from me with a dark door to the left. I jumped up and ran toward them only to be yanked back.

Something had me by the ankle—a little shackle equipped with a bell that jingled.

The door opened and a man entered as if I'd summoned him.

"Hello, again," he said. He was dressed as Cindy had described him, black robe and white collar. I tried not to think of him with his penis in his hand, standing behind Eve.

"Brad," I said. "I was wondering when the hell you'd turn up."

"My name is Martin," he said.

"Brad suits you better than Martin," I said. "Martin seems too goody-goody for you."

He smiled. "Did you enjoy watching us? I bet you did, you sick little bitch."

"Wow, such language for a priest," I said. "And actually, I was thinking if they offered sex-education in seminaries, maybe your performance would've been better. Five minutes? Come on."

His face burned crimson despite the poor lighting of this cramped room. Martin had an ego. Good to know. Maybe it would get the best of him like mine did me. I was sure going to try.

"I thought priests took a vow of celibacy," I said. "Do your church patrons know how you and Eve tricked me into dying?"

His face changed into something resembling pain.

"I'll take that as a no," I said. "So this is the part where I call you a kettle, because I think you're the one who enjoyed it. Oh, Martin, don't tell me. Was it your first time? Well, that explains some things."

"Shut up!" he barked.

Then it hit me. I realized where the hell I was.

The room spun and I grabbed my head to steady myself, failing to hold back the horror of where we were: stone walls, lamps casting playful shadows. Rachel and Gloria had seen this and if I didn't do something differently, I knew where this was going.

We would die down here.

All of us.

"Don't shout, Martin," I said, and tried to keep breathing. "That shovel gave me a headache, man."

"Shut up."

"Not much of a vocabulary. I thought seminary-types were well-educated." I wanted to keep him talking. To keep him talking meant time. Time meant possible rescue. Bobkins had to be on his way, right? But where was Lane's phone? It wasn't on me anymore.

Lane craned his neck to one side, and then the other. He was gagged like Ally. One of his eyes was swollen shut and purple. The other opened wide and the fire in it told me he was going to annihilate Martin first chance he got. I was quite happy to untie him and let him do it, except my little ankle bracelet only let me go so far.

When he saw where I was looking, Martin turned back. His eyes fixed on Ally who had woken up too. "Good."

The more of Martin's teeth I saw, the more nervous I got.

"Why didn't you cut off my head as soon as you knocked me out?" I asked, hoping he'd turn his attention on me. "That eager to tie me to a bed? Did you learn a few things from Eve?"

It worked and his eyes flicked to mine. "I know all about your kind. It's easier to kill you permanently if you're dead. Decapitation, of course.

"Right, I forgot you've got plenty of practice by now. You should know how to do it right." My eyes wouldn't stay open. I must've had a concussion from getting hit in the head with that damn shovel. I hoped my brain was okay. I couldn't save anyone without my brains.

"Just how much practice?" I asked, trying to stay awake. "Are you responsible for what happened in Atlanta—or anywhere else?" Though I doubted he killed over a thousand NRD-positives by himself. Genocide isn't a one-person job.

"I am a servant of God." He raised his chin. "I merely do his bidding. Now and always."

"Right now, it's not God helping you," I said. "It's my own stupidity."

He liked this answer. He pulled a third chair from the corner and placed it halfway between Ally and Lane, much closer to me than the other two seats.

"Is that for me," I asked. "Are you going to shoot us in the head like a firing squad or play more pop-goes-the-weasel?"

"This isn't for you," he said and rapped on the door twice. And the door opened I knew who it'd be. I'd seen the drawings after all—and I knew who was missing.

Boston and Swede carried Brinkley in, holding him under each arm, plopping him without ceremony into the chair.

Brinkley's face was in bad shape, bright blood running along the side of his jaw over, darker crusted wounds. Clearly, the torture had been going on for days. The sight of Boston and Swede and their smug faces made my insides boil.

"I can't believe it," I said, spitting hatred between my teeth. "Traitorous assholes. He trusted you."

Martin smiled.

My chest ached to see Brinkley slumped in the chair, and the swollen purple mass that used to be the left side of his face.

Bobkins, it's time to make your dumbass useful, I thought. *Garrison—anybody—hurry the fuck up. We're out of time.*

"He should have chosen our side when he had the chance," Martin said. "But he chose you and look where it got him. We tried to make him see that there are thousands like you, but he wouldn't listen. You aren't special at all."

The sad ache in my chest deepened, sparking into anger. "Brinkley is a good man. A loyal man. You wouldn't know anything about that."

Martin shrugged.

"Untie me so I can kick your teeth in," I said.

Martin came close, beyond my reach. His eyes boiled into mine. "I will untie you."

I covered one eye. "Ow, ow, ow. You poked out my eye with your nose, Pinocchio."

He bit his lip. "I want to see how funny you are when I let you go."

"You said you want to cut off my head. Of course, you won't let me go."

He grinned. A maniacal maddening grin that made him look carnivorous.

"See, I plan to stab your friends and let you choose which one lives."

My anger was completely replaced by a crashing wave of fear.

His smile doubled. "I'm going to stab them. And then I'm going to walk out of this room. From that safe distance, I'll enjoy the show. You'll run around frantic trying to decide who to replace. And once you do, once you're dead, I'm to come in here and cut off your head while the friend you saved, watches. I'll finish up by slitting their throat."

I didn't know what to say and I wasn't in the mindset to hide my complete horror. So he got the full satisfaction of my distress. He can't do that. He can't make me choose. He can't sit there and watch. Motherfucker. Motherfucker.

"*Motherfucker*," I said. "You can't do that."

The three of them laughed. Boston and Swede, the traitorous jerks, picked me up under the arms as Martin kneeled down and unlocked my shackle. As soon as my leg was loose I kicked Swede in the face, which he kindly repaid with a punch in the jaw. My hinges creaked on that one, ears ringing. I didn't think the jerk had broken it, but a bit more pressure and he'd have knocked my mandible out of socket for sure. The blow sure as hell didn't help my concussion.

"Don't do this," I said. It was as close to begging as I was going to get.

"Consider it done," he said with a smile. Boston and Swede threw me down on the bed and then stood close, waiting.

Martin pulled a knife from Swede's back pocket, where it'd been this whole time. If I'd known, I'd have done some carving of my own. The moment I saw him, I charged.

But Boston and Swede pushed me back down on to the bed.

"Don't ruin my fun," Martin said.

That's exactly what I wanted to do, ruin his fun. He might kill us, but I wasn't going to make it easy. But before I could plan my attack, Martin stabbed Lane under the ribs. Lane screamed, the white of his non-swollen eye expanding as he sucked in as much air as he could into his rapidly deflating lung.

I dashed forward and Boston picked me up, lifting me off the floor so even my feet couldn't touch. I had more than a few choice words for the traitorous SOB, but Martin, after dealing Lane a second stab wound, moved on to Brinkley. He stabbed Brinkley in the stomach twice. Brinkley grunted, but was so out of it from the previous beating I don't think he felt much. Then Martin went to Ally.

He came around the back of her chair, bending forward to press his cheek to hers.

"I know she's your favorite," he said. He took a deep breath, smelling her hair. He slid the blade down the front of her chest, popping off one shirt button, then two. With her right breast exposed he cut across her collarbone and chest, a long line of red bubbling to the surface. She kept her mouth shut, refusing to cry—her brown eyes shut tight. He slid his hand into her shirt and kissed her neck.

"He told us where to push if we wanted you." Martin

tapped her collarbone with the knife tip as he spoke. "We had to kill your mother, of course."

I wasn't sure I'd heard him right. I couldn't think past Ally as I moved from option to option, desperate for a way to save her.

"Didn't you think it strange that your mother had an accident in the middle of your investigation? We needed to separate you from your stronghold. With you gone, we could divide and conquer." He gestured to Ally. "When she came running through that door, it was like a gift from heaven."

"Who helped you?" He had to mean Gloria's nemesis, if she ever had one. Whoever the hell this other player was, he knew that if I left, Ally'd jump on the chance to find Nessa. And he knew that Gloria would tell her where to look. And of course, I'd come running after Ally.

Gloria was right. He'd manipulated us like pawns.

"I can give her a matching scar if you want," he said, ignoring my question. "A makeshift autopsy here and now?"

"Don't you fucking touch her!"

He moved his hand further down and cupped her breast. "Just think, if you save her, I can have a bit of fun with her before I slit her throat. You think I need practice fucking, do you?"

"Don't touch her!" I screamed again, more piercing reverberations ricocheted off the walls.

My vision changed.

At first I thought I was blacking out. It's happened, you know, high levels of stress and people faint. Yet I could see, in a weird disconnected way. It wasn't exactly the usual aurora borealis of color waves preceding a death, but more like what I'd seen in bed with Lane, only enhanced.

Everything was static, the embodiment of bombarding particles colliding with one another in torrential waves. It was like watching the hint of a television show on a blocked channel. The static of my body pulsed in time with my panic. It was ever so easy to shove that panic out, far, far out and penetrate both Boston and the Swede who held me.

It happened like it had with Lane. The men fell to either side yelping. Even though Martin was far away, he convulsed and dropped his knife. Back on my feet, I ran for Martin, but one of the men grabbed my pants' leg and I fell flat on my face, teeth probably cracking against the stone floor. I saw stars for a several seconds, giving Martin time to regain his footing and the knife.

When I saw him again, Martin's eyes were wide. "What the hell was that?"

"I don't know," Boston said. He held onto me, though more gingerly this time.

"She shocked me," added the Swede.

I tried to do it again, gather the static and shove it out, but all I could do was cradle my jaw and swallow the blood in my mouth.

Martin didn't move for a moment. He stared at me as if he'd never seen me before.

Then he stabbed Ally in the guts.

There was no pleasure in his face. His movements were mechanical. He couldn't get out of the room fast enough, leaving me alone with my three dying friends. I pulled myself to my knees, trying to stand. A wave of dizziness took me. I crawled to Lane's chair and pulled the gags out of his mouth.

"Save Brinkley," Lane said as I untied Ally and Brinkley's gags.

"No one's going to die, but me." I barely saw them through my tears, wiping them out of my eyes as fast I could. "The cops will be here any minute now. Just hang on. Someone will come."

"Of course you want me to die," Ally said. Her eyes were down, unfocused. Her breath grew uneven.

Lane whispered, losing air. "If you survive, Jess, they'll keep coming for you. You'll need Brinkley to keep you safe."

"Both of you shut up," I said. "You're fucking idiots."

Finally on my feet, I shuffled back and forth between their chairs, watching blood pour out over their thighs, pooling on the floor at their feet. Brinkley's blood was the first to touch the floor. I assumed this was because he was a big guy. Already half-pulverized, I couldn't believe he had any to spare. The sight of a growing puddle made me wail louder. I searched the room for anything I could use to stop the bleeding. Aside from their clothes, I had nothing. The bed was stripped and not another scrap of cotton existed. My feet squeaked as they slide over the wet stones.

"Nessa," Ally murmured. "They're going to kill her."

"Goddamn you!" I yelled through the slot in the door where Martin and the others watched. I heard their laughter seep through the cracks while I paced.

"I can't," I said. "I can't bury any of you."

I circled the room twice, laying a hand on each of their chests. They were cooling, sticky, but none of them had the pull of death yet. My mind raced. This couldn't possibly be happening to us. How did we end up here? We knew this would happen. Why couldn't we manage to stay away?

"I'm sorry I didn't tell you I was going to look for her," Ally whispered.

"Don't do that," I said. "None of that last confession crap. We're not dying here."

I removed my shirt and shoved it against her stomach, adding as much pressure as I could. I waited, but I didn't feel the pull. I paced again, touching each of them, feeling as though I was playing the most bizarre version of *eenie-meanie-minie-mo*. Something stank, putrid. Whatever it was, it was on my hands. My stomach turned and I dry heaved twice.

I untied Lane, feeling stupid I hadn't thought to do so

sooner. Then I untied Brinkley and Ally. "We're getting out of here. I promise. Someone's coming."

Without the ropes holding him in place Brinkley fell forward onto the floor. He wouldn't be walking anywhere. Ally couldn't stand, trying once before collapsing back into her chair. Lane could stand, but he hissed through his gritted teeth—clearly in a lot of pain.

"I'll save whoever goes first," I said, helping Lane to steady himself. "But the other two of you will have to fight. Kick, scream, whatever you've got until someone comes, okay? Do you hear me?"

I looked at Brinkley nearly unconscious and Ally clutching her belly. What the hell was I saying?

Lane kissed me full on the mouth, holding the back of my head with his free hand. He smiled. Before I said anything he shuffled to the door and leaned near its opening as if taking a guard's post. He'd volunteered himself for the first attack, for anything coming through that door. I couldn't look at him or I was going to fall apart. Adrenaline only took me so far.

"Listen," Brinkley said. His first word and he was fading fast. I felt it in my bones. I kneeled between Ally and Brinkley, not touching either of them yet.

"You didn't prepare me for this, asshole." I wasn't talking about death and I wasn't talking to Brinkley. Dying was what I did best.

It didn't scare me to die.

Whenever I died I'd wake and the people I loved would be there—but not this time.

I would lose someone tonight.

"Just hold on, okay?" I begged Brinkley. "I promise to quit being an ungrateful little ingrate if you pull through this."

"That's redundant, ungrateful ingrate." Ally murmured. Leave it to her to care about English on her death bed.

"You led me here to die," I said, speaking to Gabriel. As if

I conjured him, the room changed and grew warmer. Feathers rained into the room like fallen ash. I looked up to find Gabriel standing behind Brinkley and Ally. His tie was midnight blue and matched his eyes. The utter sorrow in his downturned eyes could never make me believe this was anything Gabriel wanted or planned.

"I hear someone," Lane said from the doorway. He was sliding down the wall to the floor.

"Help us," I said. I wanted Gabriel to be real, to have real divine powers. Ally's breath became labored. I reached for Ally and pulled her from the floor into my lap. I rocked her gently.

"Please don't do this to me."

Choose who you will take with you. Choose the one who will help you most in the desert ahead.

Gabriel echoed Rachel's warning to "choose well." But I couldn't choose, not between Ally and Lane, if it meant the other had to die. And I couldn't give up on Brinkley, now that I knew how much he'd sacrificed to keep me safe in a world that was against me.

How the hell could I give up on any of them?

The only clue I had was Rachel had used the word she—and I only had one *she*.

But Rachel could be wrong. She had drawn Nessa in the room after all and Nessa wasn't here.

Death came when I pressed my cheek against Ally's cheek. I felt the pull when it'd begun. I was replacing her, feeling that string tighten in my navel and the suction of the mini black hole. Ally's head fell back as she gasped for air. Then I heard Brinkley beside us, lapse into ragged breaths.

I couldn't replace them both. I reached out and tried to grab him anyway, willing to try. But I couldn't reach him with Ally in my lap. I was tethered to her now, and she'd be the one I followed into death.

Lane coughed and blood creased the corner of his mouth. I couldn't do anything for him or Brinkley. I'd only followed Ally and that tightened navel string, down, down, down—Gabriel never taking his eyes off me. Those watery eyes—that great abyss—seemed to widen, ready to swallow me whole.

At first I resisted. I thought, *but what happens next?* Anything was possible. Even if I saved her, they could kill us all. Or worse—they could keep her alive. And I knew sometimes alive was far worse than dead.

It was like closing my eyes at the worse possible moment, in the middle of chaos. It felt stupid—my eyes should be open. I should be ready.

But what else could I do? This was my only option—praying that somehow, despite the odds, we would survive this.

All I could do was save her. Save her but—*I choose them all*, I told Gabriel. *I need them all.*

And as if in response, he spread his wings wide, and enveloped my world in darkness.

CHAPTER TWENTY-FIVE

Gabriel held me in his warm arms, too warm for a person's—as if he were made of sunshine itself. His feathers smelled like rain, but were as soft as wisps of smoke. I breathed him in before I opened my eyes.

"Oh God, I'm dead, aren't I? *Dead*-dead. The final sha-*bang*. A ghost on toast, right? Kaput," I said, my eyes still closed. "Like the real deal."

"No," he said, smoothing my hair away from my face. "You're in the hospital. Again."

Too much time with me and he'd inherited my sarcasm. I finally dared to open my eyes and take in my surroundings. I saw the usual: bed, vitals monitor, too much fluorescent light —and that antiseptic hospital smell.

"Am I really in the hospital or is this some kind of out-of-body near-death experience?"

"You are not dead," he said, patiently. "I promised to keep you safe."

"You weren't much help when Martin carved us up like pumpkins."

I shot upright in bed. "Oh my god, where are they?"

"You're awake." A nurse rushed into the room and turned the volume on my wailing heart monitor down. "I'll notify the doctor."

I snatched her wrist. "Where are they?"

"Let go please, ma'am." She tried to pull away, but I sure as hell wasn't letting go.

"You're hurting her," Gabriel warned.

"Where are they?" I demanded again. "Did you bring anyone in with me? There were three of them with knife wounds."

She reached over and jammed the nurse-call button by my bed.

"There's a white guy, late twenties named Lane Handel," I continued. I wanted her to answer my question. "A young woman, blond hair named Alice Gallagher, and an older guy mid-fifties, James Brinkley."

"Let go of me," she said and yanked free. After a nervous glance at the fried monitor that I apparently zapped, she disappeared out the door cradling her wrist.

"What happened to them?" I asked. Gabriel blinked big eyes at me. "Tell me or I'll start plucking your feathers out one by one."

"You were saved," he said, completely unaffected by my threat.

"But what about Ally?"

"You successfully replaced her."

I released a breath I hadn't realized I'd been holding. "And Lane and Brinkley?"

A knock on the door stole my attention. The doctor walked in. "Who were you talking to?"

"Are they okay? Are they here in this hospital, can I see them?"

"Are you next of kin?" the nurse asked, the one with the red wrist.

"I'm going to next your kin if you don't answer my question," I said.

The doctor came to the edge of the bed. It wasn't Dr. York. It was some young guy who I'd seen around. "You need to remain calm, Ms. Sullivan."

I grabbed his arm and yanked him toward me so hard he flinched.

"If you don't tell me if my friends are dead or alive I'm going to shock the living daylights out of you."

"What's an assault charge on top of everything else?" a voice asked from the doorway.

Agent Garrison stood there. He had a bandage on his head and a look that told me that if I knew what was good for me I'd shut my pie hole. I admitted it was enough to make me pause.

"That is a terrible way to treat the man who patched you up," Garrison added. He came into the room, standing beside the doctor-nurse duo, and I still couldn't get over how short he was.

"I'm sorry," I muttered, releasing the doctor. I smoothed his ruffled lab coat with my hands and forced a smile. "Post-traumatic stress or whatever."

"Do you need to examine her before she leaves her bed?" Garrison asked.

"Yes." The doctor removed his stethoscope from his shoulders, but it was obvious he had little interest in touching me after my violent spiel. Regardless, he did his job dutifully, and so did the nurse who checked my blood pressure with a cuff and played with my fluid bags. Though I'm sure she'd found pleasure in stabbing me with a new needle.

"A little dehydrated," the doctor finally pronounced. "But she'll survive."

"Can she bring that with her?" Garrison pointed to my

fluid bag and to the IV connecting it to my arm. When he lifted his hand I realized his right arm was bandaged too.

"It has wheels," the nurse answered. She helped me from the bed, then offered me the slender metal bar supporting my IV. I turned toward the bed but Gabriel was gone. I didn't know at which moment he'd left. Perhaps he didn't like being threatened to have his feathers plucked.

Their jobs done, the nurse and doctor left, leaving me alone with Garrison who motioned for me to follow him. "We need to talk."

I shuffled after him, my legs stiff and cold.

"You haven't read me my rights yet," I said. "Is that a good sign?"

"You will go to jail," he said. He shuffled through the critical care unit as if he was stiff too. "I can't prevent that."

"I didn't kill Nessa, if she's even dead, and what I did to Eddie was self-defense," I told him. "Surely there's a way to prove that."

"I'd worry more about her if I were you," he said.

I looked up, and there was Ally in bed with her blond hair spread over a pillow like Sleeping Beauty. I hobbled over to her side. I searched the monitor for answers. Everything looked okay from what I could tell, but I had no medical training. At the very least, I knew she wasn't dead.

"Please tell me she'll wake up."

"It's only the anesthesia. She came out of surgery. They removed her spleen and stopped the bleeding."

"She won't need that, right? She'll live okay without it?" Spleen, what's a spleen? Why do we have spleens?

"She'll be fine," he said. Then after a moment, "I need to ask you some questions."

"Ask away." I wrapped my hand around Ally's. I would've given anyone anything right then. I was so happy she was okay.

Garrison pulled up two chairs, opposite each other beside Ally's bed. He gestured for me to sit and I did, but I didn't let go of her hand.

"You will have to tell me what happened," he said.

"Do I need an attorney present?"

"Do you want one?"

"I don't want to make this any worse for myself than it already is."

"We have your confession of murder on tape," he said. "You can't make this any worse."

"Because my house was bugged?" I asked. Garrison didn't answer, but instead gave me the blank cop face I'd gotten so often from Brinkley.

Gabriel appeared on the other side of Ally, watching her sleep with a curious expression. He didn't warn me to keep my mouth shut. And Ally was alive, wasn't she? Here's to hoping I really had an angel on my side.

I told Garrison what happened.

I started from Eve's attack and reaffirmed that I hadn't known that was a fake replacement, nor had I ever met Eve or Martin. I told him about Gloria's drawings, the mysterious A.M.P. and how he'd manipulated me and everyone I loved into the trap he'd set in the church's basement. I told him Martin confessed to killing my mother, or at least wanted me to believe he did. I tried not to dwell on the idea that maybe my mother had been right all along. It was too dangerous to let something like me back into the house and if she had done it sooner, maybe Danny would be dead by now.

I explained how Martin used my departure for Illinois to bait Ally into the trap, knowing damn well I'd follow right after her. I told him Brinkley's theories about whether it was the Church, the military, or the FBRD. I even told him about Eddie and why I burned the barn to the ground with both of us inside. The only things I didn't admit were electrocuting everyone in the basement and the fact that I had conversations with an angel.

There was only one place I could go if I confessed to insanity.

He listened to everything without interrupting "Where did you find Ally?"

"In the trunk of a car, in the parking lot out back," I said. I described the car. "We broke the window."

"That's where you were when Bobkins called you," he said.

I nodded. "Ally wanted to go back inside for Nessa."

"But you didn't find her?"

"No," I said. "We were smacked in the face by a shovel, probably by the creepy guy digging the grave. Then I woke up in the basement."

"We have the men you described in custody," he said. "All three of them."

"Martin stabbed each of them in the stomach or at least it looked like the stomach from where I stood. He wanted me to choose who I'd save and when I was dead, he was going to make that person watch me get my head chopped off."

"Martin worked for the FBRD," Garrison said, gauging my reaction. "But I think you already knew that."

"I practically tattooed it to your forehead," I said.

"Did Brinkley conspire to kill you, along with Martin and Eve?"

"No," I said. My chest burned. "No, he was protecting me this whole time. For the last seven years."

"I want to ask your opinion on another theory," he said and clicked his recorder off.

I sat up straighter in my seat, my back killing me.

"Let's start with a necronite who gets herself killed by a couple of church fanatics to make it look like an attack. When she wakes up, her accomplice is missing. Now the pressure gets high, so she returns to the church to reinforce her cover. She lets another accomplice, Martin, stab the only witnesses, and leave them for dead."

"What's my motive?" I asked. "What the hell would I gain by letting myself get killed?"

"All kinds of things," Garrison said. "Notoriety. Public attention. Maybe you want to discredit the Church."

"Do you really think I would have saved Ally instead of Brinkley, if he was my accomplice?"

"No, I believe Martin, with the help of the Church, manipulated local prostitutes into deceiving replacement agents. I am not yet sure if Martin acted alone, or under orders, or to what extent the Church is involved. But I do know they killed a little girl to prove their point."

I touched my chest. "Nessa is dead?"

He looked away, speaking to his shoes without lifting his head.

"Regardless of the truth, Bobkins has formed a strong case against you. Local authorities like him want to make an example of you. He hopes it will send the right message to the public, "Don't fear them, replacement agents are held accountable, too."

I arched an eyebrow. "Partial decapitation is an extreme cover story."

"You're the only necronite who has survived an attack, and you happen to be the only one with connections to the Church."

My voice caught in my throat like a doorstop wedge. "I haven't been to church in decades."

"Your father's position discredits you."

"My father?" I sat up straighter. "You know my father?"

He stared again, penetratingly, one of those I'll-figure-out-if-you're-lying-to-me stares.

"I don't remember him," I said. "If you know who he is, you've got to tell me."

Agent Garrison fell quiet again. "If you don't know then I shouldn't tell you."

"Why?" I asked him. "Does Bobkins know?"

"No," he said. "And that's a blessing."

"Why won't you tell me?" I said.

"Because all I have is a theory and because you will be much more convincing on the witness stand if that's where you hear it for the first time. Though I'm not sure they will bring it up. The last thing he'll want is a public paternity test, especially now that your condition is public as a result of Eve's attack."

He had to be an important man, I thought. Otherwise, public reputation wouldn't be such a big deal.

Garrison read my thoughts. "If the Church is somehow involved, I imagine he will pay dearly to keep his name out of this case."

"So he is involved in the Church somehow," I said. "Do you think that they are responsible for the necronite murders?" If my father was a necronite himself, why would he be okay with the murders?

"I'm sorry it took us so long to get to you," he said. "We tracked Mr. Handel's phone to the church. We rushed the place and heard you screaming, but those corridors are confusing." He held up his cut hand and pointed at his head. "We had to fight our way in to get you out."

"Do you believe me?" I asked. I felt vulnerable.

"I believe your story," he said and it was the first real sympathy I saw in him. "I think you were lucky enough to survive because you have people around you who care about you."

I lowered my head. Why did this make me feel so ashamed?

"So if you don't think I'm guilty, where does that leave me?" I asked.

"I will do my best to try and prove your story. I advise you to be honest in court and tell the judge everything. If what you say about Eddie is true, be ready to talk about that as well. In the meantime, you can expect to be held in the county jail for a few days without bail."

"When can I expect a pretty orange jumpsuit of my very own?"

"Once you heal," he said. He stood, dragging his chair back to the corner. "I'll do what I can."

"Can I see Lane and Brinkley now?" I stood to follow him. I clutched the metal bar for stability but Garrison didn't move or speak.

"Oh, are they still in surgery?" I asked when I saw his hesitation.

"No," he said, softly, his hand outstretched to stop me. "Brinkley and Lane are dead."

CHAPTER TWENTY-SIX

I went to jail like Garrison promised. When Bobkins picked me up, he had other cops with him. They read me my rights while I tried not to cry about it. I can't describe how absolutely terrible the Davidson County Jail was.

Handcuffs were horribly uncomfortable, and I had to wear them all the way to the station where the real fun began. They took my picture and my fingerprints, which I expected. I'd seen enough television to know that much. What I didn't know was that after that little welcome, they promptly stripped me naked, searched me, and hosed me down in a cold shower.

If that wasn't humiliating enough, I had to drag a crappy mattress and a toothbrush to a cell that I shared with a number of women until my name came up on the docket, meaning it was my turn to go to court—all this and an attractive orange jumper with county-provided underwear.

If sharing a cramped cell with eleven other people wasn't mortifying, let's not forget that all hygienic activities, the toilet included, must be done in plain sight of everyone else.

Yep. I had to use the bathroom in front of other people. If that didn't kill me, the food was going to.

Imagine my utter ecstasy when Ally showed up for visitation, six days in. They brought me from the cell to a separate little room and pushed me down onto a metal stool. Only a sheet of acrylic Plexiglas separated us. It was like with Eve but now I sat on the other side.

"You look pretty good, considering," she said, trying to be nice.

"You look like a dream come true," I said. "Please tell me I have a court date."

"It's only a couple of days until your hearing." Ally tucked a sympathetic smile into the corner of her lips. "You can make it."

I bumped my face against the glass but it was disgustingly sticky. I regretted my decision instantly.

"I brought you something that may help." She gave a small bag to the officer on her side of the glass, who came through a door and gave me the bag. I had to set the phone down in order to open it. Officer Nosey helped. He had to pull out every item and inspect it before letting me have it. There was a chocolate bar, two paperback books, and a small personal pan pizza with cheese and pineapple.

"Oh, this cheese will help." I wasted no time shoving half the pizza in my mouth. Jail food was worse than cardboard with salt on it. Dying was a great idea and admittedly not the first time I had it. Unfortunately, I couldn't find anything in the cell to off myself with—and the guards watched us too closely for me to hang myself with a sheet. "If I could kill myself, my jail time would fly by."

Ally started to laugh and then grimaced. Apparently, she wasn't fully healed yet.

"Okay, bad joke," I admitted.

"Is anyone being mean to you?" she asked. The tense lines in her face melted away after a few deep breaths.

"They were the first day," I said, starting in on the chocolate. "Then they found out I was a zombie. Now they won't come near me. Apparently, they have their own ideas of what that means. Sometimes I pretend to talk in my sleep, muttering brains, brains, that sort of thing. When I wake up they're all huddled on the other side of the room."

"How'd they find out?"

"This fat woman in my cell, Felicia, took my toothbrush and polished her toes with it. Then she told me to put it in my mouth."

"What did you say?"

"I told her no." I took another big bite of pizza. "She said she'd beat me up if I didn't."

"Oh, Jess."

"I told her she could kill me if she wanted, but when I woke up I'd turn her skull into a cereal bowl."

"And she believed you?"

"The guards told her I wasn't lying about being a zombie."

"At least they'll leave you alone now," she said.

I shrugged, finished the pizza in one last bite, and turned to the chocolate whole-heartedly. I knew I had to eat it all before returning to my cell.

"At least you got to see the service," she said.

Garrison had to pull strings and I had to wear shackles, but I did get to see the 21 gun salute. Brinkley's name was cleared because they assumed he'd been in Martin's capture from the moment he went missing. Frankly, I wasn't sure I'd ever forgive myself for being so snotty to the man who died for me.

The officer who brought me up to the visitation booth tapped his watch. I only had a few minutes left. I nodded and took another big bite of chocolate.

"Kirk's been saving Lane for you," she said. "Lane's mom let Kirk put him in a freezer or something. She won't give me Winston without your consent."

Not Lane. I couldn't think of him while I worked hard to keep it together in this place. The irony didn't escape me. Of course it figured that as soon as I commit, he died.

I changed the subject.

"Why didn't you show up that night?" I asked, wiping tears from the corners of my eyes.

"What do you remember?" she asked.

I remembered sitting in a dark room, all of my things removed, but the bed, desk and lamp for my homework. I remembered passing the nights alone, reading the books I had stashed under my bed.

"Just tell me your side of the story. From the beginning."

"I came by to see you, and she wouldn't let me come in," Ally said. "She'd never done that before. The next day at school we started making plans on how we were going to get you out of there. We were going to take my car to my brother's place in Louisville. We'd finish our senior year there. I left that night to come and get you and I blew a tire and hit a mailbox. Do you remember Ms. Beverly? Talk about crappy luck."

A vague picture of an elementary school teacher came to mind.

"She called the cops, my parents came, and I tried to explain everything to them, but they said I shouldn't be getting involved in your problems. You should've heard the lecture they gave my brother. He still refuses to go home for Thanksgiving."

"I remember trying to call you a million times the next day. You didn't answer. I thought you'd changed your mind," I said.

"No." She shook her head. "My parents wouldn't let me

near the phone. I managed to sneak a call once, but your mother wouldn't let me talk to you. Then I found out your mother spoke to mine at church. Then you were dead," Ally said. She was on the verge of sobbing. "Please tell me that you didn't kill yourself because you thought—because I—"

"No," I said. It was a lie. I *had* felt abandoned and *had* taken the only way out. But I couldn't put that on Ally.

"They said you died of smoke inhalation."

"Easy peasy compared to what I do now," I lied. I didn't want to hurt her.

I asked her the last question I had in my remaining time. "How did you find me?"

Ally pushed her hair behind her ears. "My senior year at SIUC, I had a class with Chelsea Whitehead. Do you remember her?"

I didn't. Ally shook her head like it didn't matter. "Anyway, she asked me if it was true, except I had no idea what she meant until she told me she'd heard a rumor that you weren't dead that you were"—and this is where Ally used air quotes and a valley-girl voice—"Like, one of those gross undead girls, or whatever."

I laughed.

"She remembered us hanging out in high school and I guess she thought I'd know. So, that's what started my quest. It took me some time to track you down. I finally found you in Nashville. My God, I was so nervous when I showed up at the office that day."

I sat up straighter. "How nervous?"

Ally licked her lips. "I walked into the office with this whole speech in my head, and there you were, trying to do fifteen things at once."

Yeah, I was a wreck in my pre-assistant days. Brinkley and I had just moved to Nashville.

He'd given me the office, but no real idea how to run it.

Worse, I'd lost my biggest source of support, Rachel. "I think I was vacuuming, making coffee, answering a phone call and trying to file at the same time."

Ally smiled. "Something ridiculous like that."

"You didn't have the somber, shell-shocked look of a client so I blurted out, 'Please tell me you're here to interview for the assistant's position.'"

I'd made up the position on the spot out of sheer desperation. I had to pay Ally out of pocket for a week until I convinced Brinkley to write it off.

Ally nodded, her eyes widening with recognition. "Yes, and that's what threw me. I was set to apologize and you didn't recognize me. And you were all witty and happy. It took me a minute to realize you'd forgotten everything and then I couldn't bring myself to tell you."

"I'm really sorry for forgetting," I told her.

"It was almost nice," she said. "Like everything was back to normal. We had a chance to start over."

The officer took my receiver and put it in its cradle before I could say anything else.

"Time's up," he said and pulled me away before I could even wave goodbye.

Someone banged against the glass. The guard stopped.

It was Garrison. He looked hot from running. He must have hustled over here to catch the tail end of my visitation. Garrison showed his badge and credentials to the guard and was granted extra time.

I used this opportunity to polish off the last of the chocolate, prying it from the guard's hand. I grinned hoping that little rebellion wouldn't cost me later.

He sank into the seat opposite mine and lifted the phone. "We don't have much time."

"What's going on?" I asked. Seeing him like this made my heart race.

"I was counting on a certain person's name coming up in court, but it seems that money has changed hands."

I was lost. "I don't understand."

"Just listen," he said, out of breath. He opened a large envelope and pulled out several pictures. Pressing them against the glass, he pointed to each one to make me look at it. "You told me you saw a picture hanging in one of the rooms you investigated the night you found Ally."

"Yeah, the guy from my mother's funeral, Mr. Reeves," I said. "I assumed he was a church donor. Don't they immortalize the bank roll that way?"

"Is he in any of these photographs?" He shuffled the pictures.

I tapped the glass. "That's him."

He removed the other photographs so only Mr. Reeves face remained pressed to the glass.

"You're sure?" he asked.

I shrugged. "That's Mr. Reeves."

"This is a picture of Caldwell, one of four leaders of The Church. He was elected to run the North American division and represent all of its regional needs. His three co-leaders run its worldwide affiliates and are responsible for the "upon-death" head severance practiced in their nations."

I looked at the picture again. "But he said his name was Reeves, not Caldwell."

"That's not important," he pushed. "What matters is that you say you saw this man at your mother's funeral."

I gestured at the picture again. "He said he knew my parents a long time ago."

He hesitated. "He didn't look familiar to you?"

It surprised me to hear him say that. "Yeah, but if he's the head guy, he's been on television, tabloids and all that. He'd look familiar when I met him, but he said he knew me when I was little."

He paused and I had no idea what he was waiting for. "What?"

Garrison hesitated as if he wanted to say more. "Are you aware that your grandmother's maiden name was Reeves?"

"Grandmother who?" I asked. I didn't remember any grandmother.

"Your father's mother," he said.

"So you want me to believe that this random guy at my mother's funeral was someone related to my father's mother?" I asked. "Then he's a million years old."

He gave me another moment to come up with a more logical explanation. Slowly, very slowly, pieces fell into place.

If Mr. Reeves was really Caldwell, Garrison said my father was a high-ranking Church official and Caldwell was at my mother's funeral.

Click, click, click.

"Holy shit." I sucked air. "You think Mr. Reeves—Caldwell is my—grandfather?"

Garrison looked as though he wanted to hit his head against the glass. "I'm having a hell of a time finding any old photographs of your father for comparison, but it seems that Caldwell might very well be Eric Sullivan."

When I didn't immediately blink or move he was forced to repeat himself.

"Ms. Sullivan, I believe your father is the head of the Unified Church."

CHAPTER TWENTY-SEVEN

I was in the closet, crying. Cliché, I know, but when I'd slipped into the black dress for Lane's funeral, I'd spotted a shoe on the floor. The hospital had lost yet another, no surprise there. Something about seeing the shoe by itself, all alone, and the fact that Lane had just given me this pair—I lost it. Gloria found me in the *closet*. Her face was a mask of sympathy as she knelt beside me. The clank of dishes beyond her meant Ally was in the kitchen, preparing for the guests.

"I made lasagna, garlic bread, and tiramisu for you," Gloria said, softly. "A lot of butter."

I didn't want to go to Lane's funeral. I didn't care if she had a whole meal prepared for all of us to eat beforehand. I didn't care about anything, but this shoe and how lonely it looked. I choked out a response. "I'm not hungry."

"Jesse, you have to eat," she whispered, cooing into my ear as she stroked my hair away from my face. My face was a sticky mess of snot and tears. "You can't skip meals. You'll make yourself sick."

She sat beside me on the closet floor. She moved a pair of

dangling pants away from her face and pulled me in close so that my head rested rather awkwardly against her large breasts.

I kept picturing Lane in his blue shirt, my favorite, the same ocean-blue of his eyes. Lane coming to my house at 2:00 a.m. with Chinese food. Lane asleep beside me when I woke up from zombie-dom. Lane who carried me when I was sore. Lane who baked me cakes with funny icing pictures. Lane, feet kicked up on the coffee table, asleep with the television still on. Winston, a fawn-colored roll of fluff on his chest as they both snored, who I could tell had entered a room by the sheer smell of him. Lane who let me be demanding and whiny every moment of everyday and still made me feel adorable. Beautiful. Wanted.

Lane.

"I can't replace him." I wrung the shoe between my hands like a wet washcloth.

"And that's the sad truth," she said. "You can't replace everyone."

My chest hurt. I doubled over trying to drag fresh air into my lungs. I couldn't catch my breath. I managed a strained "It's-all-my-fault" in between choking.

"No," she said. "It's my fault."

So here we were in my closet, both blaming ourselves. How useful.

With my chest pressed against the flat surface of my thighs, I drew my first long, steady breath. The doorbell rang. I lifted myself slowly from her arms and stood without looking at her because I knew it'd make me cry some more. I adjusted my dress with shaking hands and cleaned my face with a tissue from a box on my desk. I placed the shoe on my bed, unwilling to leave it alone in the closet and went downstairs to answer the door. I would have stayed in the closet forever, but with Gloria there it wasn't the same.

Kyra stood on the porch in her clean, pressed coat, soft brown curls wild, holding a bottle of wine. Umbri, who held a bottle of tequila, had exchanged her usual grungy, punk look for nice black slacks and a white buttoned up shirt.

"Oh honey," they said, encircling me in their arms before even getting out of the doorway. I fought the urge to fall apart again, leading them with a half-hearted wave into the kitchen.

"My God, something smells amazing," Kyra said.

"Look at that cake," Umbri said. She reached forward and finger-swiped the tiramisu before Ally could swat her hand.

"You went all out," Kyra said to Ally. She hung her coat on the back of her chair.

"Gloria did most of the cooking," Ally admitted, counting plates.

It was an impressive spread with cloth napkins and my good dishes. Sweet tea and water pitchers sat on the table with lemons in the glasses, big bowls of salad and bread beside them. The tiramisu sat elevated and looked impressive on a pedestal of its own, with globs of icing and chocolate shavings around the edges. Sunset basked the kitchen in a soft, orange glow.

"Who else is coming?" Ally asked.

"Just us. Cindy couldn't make it," Gloria said. "And Kirk has a funeral."

I went around the room, counting us. With Gloria, Ally, Kyra, and Umbri that made only five. Our party was depressingly thin. "Who's the sixth plate for?"

"Garrison said he may stop by," Ally said, taking the seat beside me.

"Why would the cop come?" Umbri asked with her mouth full. "He sent you to jail."

"Federal agent," Ally corrected her. "And no, he didn't."

"Garrison is the one that helped her get out of trouble,"

Kyra said, throwing her coat over the back of her chair. "He is the one that proved Jesse didn't kill Nessa and that what happened in the barn seven years ago was self-defense. Everything they tried to pin on her, Garrison squashed it."

"Just a year of probation," I said, knocking a crouton off my plate. Ally nudged me gently, trying to get me to at least eat the tiramisu. "The judge said it was to encourage me to stay out of trouble."

Everyone laughed. *Why was that funny?*

Everyone else was well into their salad and bread when the oven dinged, and Gloria removed a huge dish of lasagna. She sat the glass dish on a pot holder and cut through the melty cheese in one steaming slice. I continued to push salad around on my plate.

"I thought you were going to have to pay that huge fine," Umbri said. She had so much food in her mouth that her cheeks bulged on either side.

"The fine was waived," Ally said.

"Garrison did that," Kyra said, willing to take up the fight with Umbri again. "Garrison."

"If Bobkins had his way, I'd go to prison indefinitely." I took a sip of tea, something to distract me from the full dinner plate. Before I could set the glass down, the doorbell rang again.

"It's probably him," I said, standing. "I'll get it."

It wasn't Garrison—but it was enough to stop my heart.

Brinkley, my supposedly dead handler, stood on the porch, looking like his usual demanding self. Yet I barely noticed him holding Winston to his chest, cradled like a baby on account that my eyes fixated on only one thing.

Lane.

Lane stood beside him on my porch in a gorgeous suit tailored to his body, perfect down to sparkly cuff links and shiny shoes. His hair was cut, expertly styled, and in his arms he held a large bouquet of sunflowers, tulips, and pink-purple roses. I'd never seen him grin so big.

"Oh my god," I said. "First angels and now ghosts."

"If I come back from the dead, I've got to come back looking great, don't I?" he said.

It really was Lane.

"But you—" I swallowed the lump in my throat. "Are you—"

"Statistically, speaking," Brinkley broke in, keeping his voice low. "Everyone's met at least two necronites who are unaware of their NRD condition."

"Are you a necronite too?" I asked him. Winston, now on his feet and within smelling distance of the feast, waddled past my feet into the kitchen.

"No, just lucky," Brinkley answered. "And that agent Garrison is a good man who can keep a secret."

"So who the hell was in your coffin?" I demanded to know.

Brinkley smiled.

Lane crossed the threshold completely and lifted me up into his arms. My feet came off the floor as he squeezed me against his neck. The smell of him was enough to make me start crying again.

"Aren't you coming in?" I asked Brinkley over Lane's shoulder.

"I'll meet you in the back," Brinkley said. "I'm dead, remember?"

Lane gently placed me on my feet and shut the door. My reaction was nothing compared to the faces around the dinner table. Everyone's mouth hung open as we came into the kitchen. Ally, who'd been pouring a glass of tea at the time, was now pouring half the pitcher into Umbri's lap.

"Hey," Umbri yelped.

"I'm sorry," Ally said absentmindedly, and handed Kyra the towel.

"My funeral's been canceled for obvious reasons," Lane said. "But everyone looks great."

A general murmur of disbelief circled the table. Kyra flashed me a double thumbs-up and I knew she saw his newfound condition as another reason why I should be with Lane. My senses were coming back to me. The flowers Lane gave me wrapped in cellophane hung limply at my side. Then I pointed the bouquet accusingly at him.

"You've been gone almost two weeks. With stab wounds like that, you would've been dead two days tops and that's only if he'd managed to cut up some important organs," I said.

Lane slid in amongst the guests, not hesitating to make himself a plate. "Post-death evaluations and new status processing take forever. Surely you remember how lengthy death-replacement agent enlistment is. The interviews, the paperwork. Garrison's doing, by the way. He says Nashville is understaffed and could use me."

"So you let me think you were dead this whole time?" I said. "You couldn't pick up a phone and call me?"

"With rigor mortis, no, and you never told me how horribly painful that is. You complained, but Jesus, you were underplaying it," he said and leaned over the table for a piece of garlic bread. "And what is it with women and getting a phone call?"

I smacked him with the flowers, raining petals everywhere, and sending the garlic bread en route to his mouth sailing through the air. Someone gasped.

"How could you?" I said, tears streaming. "How could you just walk in here and pretend like it's fine?" More flower bashing. "Nessa is dead. She'll never wake up and you come in making jokes."

He came up cradling his jaw with a fire in his eyes that most men get when hit by a girl. Men don't, at least on a biological level, like a subverted patriarchy. Like that was going to stop me.

"If I had a gun, I'd shoot you in the heart and when you wake up from *that* I bet your ass, you'd call." To drive it home, I smacked him with the bouquet a few times more calling him every insult I could think of. Kyra turned as white as the table cloth.

Lane's face was red and he had a cut on his cheek when I finished. But his voice was soft. "I'm sorry. I would have called you if I could."

I threw my destroyed flowers on the floor.

"I need some air," I said and excused myself.

Gabriel appeared against the back door, watching us. I barely flinched. I was getting scary good at not reacting to his sudden appearances. He was scratching his wing, raining little feathers onto the floor. Did he have lice or what? I couldn't exit unless I walked through him, so I had to pretend he wasn't there. I was glad that he didn't choose that moment to turn solid.

The back deck was lit up with little TIKI-torches to give an island-at-night glow. Gabriel followed me in that creepy immaterial way of his. I offered Brinkley a lawn chair. He preferred to lean against the deck railing and I did the same. The air was cooling fast, curling itself around my bare legs. It would be winter soon enough.

"Let me guess. You really do have NRD but never told me," I said.

"No," he said. "I don't have NRD. Only a trusted few know I survived and we have to keep it that way. Which is why I've debugged your house and waited for the cops to stop watching you before showing up. Of course, that won't stop you from telling Alice."

"Probably not."

I moved further away from the door so that Brinkley

would be hidden from view. "What's to be gained by faking your death?"

Brinkley leaned over the rail. "This situation with Martin using prostitutes to kill replacement agents, it's only the beginning. I've known since St. Louis that something was wrong. I knew by the sloppy way the FBRD handled those murders in Atlanta."

An idea popped into my head. "Are you the anonymous caller who reported the murders?"

Brinkley smirked. "You're smarter than I give you credit for, kid."

I swept a curtsey. "So what do we know now that we didn't know before?"

"FBRD has been bought and paid for," Brinkley said. He spoke through his teeth like it pained him. I thought of Boston and Swede, the two jerks that Brinkley had called in to help him. God, it must've sucked when he realized they were on the other side. I don't know what I'd do if someone I trusted turned on me—someone like Ally or Lane.

"The FBRD is providing the information to the Church—your father—and the Church is doing the executing."

"How do you know?" I asked. "Caldwell could be unaware of—" My voice trailed off when I saw Brinkley's sad expression.

"Martin contacted Caldwell directly on a private line numerous times," he said. Gracefully, he shifted the conversation. "From what I can tell, only a limited number of FBRD agents are involved."

I couldn't believe that a legal organization established for the sole purpose of protecting us would turn us over to the bad guys. "Why would they do that?"

Brinkley searched my face. "I don't know. It is either Caldwell's agenda or the FBRD's. But Martin was reporting to Caldwell, not the other way around."

I couldn't look him in the eyes and for some stupid reason my throat was uncomfortably tight. "I'm sorry about your friends, the jerks that betrayed you. At least they're in custody."

Brinkley grinned. "Not anymore."

"They escaped?" I was so looking forward to a break from homicidal maniacs.

"Don't worry about running into them," he said with a malicious grin. "I took care of it."

I arched an eyebrow. "Is that what was in your coffin?"

His smile faltered. "The truth is, this is not the first time someone has come after you."

I was so tired of hearing about people trying to kill me. "Are you saying they've been trying to kill me for seven years?"

"I need you to understand," he said, seriously. "It is extremely important."

"O-*kay*, is that a yes?"

"I know Garrison told you about Caldwell being your father."

"Do you really think he is?"

"I haven't been able to prove it, but yes, I think so," he said.

"Why would he want to kill necronites if he is one?" I couldn't put these pieces together.

"I don't care about that as much as I want to know why he's targeting you," he said. "His own daughter."

Brinkley ran his hands through his hair. It was wonderfully reminiscent of times he found me exhausting, weeks ago, before my life got even more complicated than usual. "Why make you a priority?"

"How do you know I'm a priority? Maybe he doesn't even know about me."

Brinkley spared me another sad smile. "The pattern

suggests otherwise. It is like they choose their cities based on your location and they take greater risks trying to catch you. They make mistakes."

I wasn't sure what to think about it—the idea that my father was hunting me down and trying to kill me.

"So where does that leave us?" I asked. "What are we going to do now?"

"I'm dead," he repeated. "If I want to go any deeper with this, I can't be a law-abiding federal agent anymore. James Brinkley is officially off the books."

"Okay, you want to be dead so you can find out more, but what about me?" I demanded. "I'm not dead and they know I'm not dead."

He lowered his voice. "If you remain a death replacement agent," he began in a slow, cautious tone. "You can use your replacements and skills to get inside information."

"I'm not trained to be a spy."

"Don't underestimate what you can do. I'll train you." His tone softened. "I believe in you, Jesse. I always have."

"Very motivational, chief," I said and a sense of déjà vu washed over me. "When I saw Caldwell at the funeral, he didn't look older than thirty or thirty-five. You know what that means, right?"

Brinkley's eyes narrowed. "He's been dying."

"Yeah, but for who?" I asked. "And why hasn't anyone noticed."

"One of the many questions we'll have to answer," he said, turning to leave.

"That's it?" I asked. "That's how you're going to leave me?"

"Wait, no." He stopped and pulled a stack of comment cards out of his pocket, handing them to me. "I almost forgot."

Every single one of them was between 8-10 points. I

found it way easier to be furious now. "What the hell! You've been holding out on me?"

"In the military, we push our soldiers hard to make them strong. It's the only tactic I know."

I smacked his shoulder with the stack, secretly glowing from all the compliments I'd been denied.

"Haven't you heard of positive reinforcement, man?"

"You have to stay with me in this," Brinkley said and he looked worried that I might back out. "I'm giving you these cards now because I want you to know that what you do matters. Not just to me."

Damn. He got me.

"I'm sorry I always made it hard," his voice was as close to gentle as I'd ever heard it.

"You're killing me with kindness, man," I said.

An eruption of laughter from the kitchen caught my attention. Through the doors I saw Lane holding Umbri and Kyra over his shoulders like a barbarian conquest. He'd clearly picked them up and turned them away from the door so they wouldn't see Brinkley.

Brinkley grinned and slipped his hands into his pockets. "I'll be hard to reach for a few weeks, but they won't make a move until it all quiets down. Rest up until I get back. And Garrison is your contact if you need anything. He's been assigned as your temporary handler."

"You're dead and you still get to boss me around?" I asked.

"Of course." He descended the steps heading for the driveway.

"Wait," I yelled, leaning over the railings. "Are you the one that found Lane?"

"In Kirk's basement shaking a fist in the air screaming, "Yes."

My sad, tired lips crooked into a half-smile. "He's always wanted to be a zombie."

Watching Brinkley disappear, I had a feeling that from now on, he was going to be the sort of guy who only showed up when there's trouble. Like Gabriel.

Car lights spilled into the backyard as he pulled away. I turned toward Gabriel who was leaning on the rail beside me.

"Caldwell wants to kill everyone with NRD," I said. Gabriel's eyes filled with torchlight. "Why would he do that?"

His eyes narrowed. "You must remember him."

"So he is my father, huh?" I asked.

"He is much more than that," Gabriel warned. And a fire churned inside me.

"I don't have any mushy, fatherly memories of him if that's what you mean." I sighed. "Why couldn't he be my orthodontist or something? It'd be so much easier to take out an orthodontist. We will have to kill him, right? It's always kill or be killed with these things."

Gabriel was not a fan of my jokes.

"Tell me the truth," I said. I leaned my head against his arm. I felt safe. "In jail, I did a good deal of thinking. Raphael sent Cindy to the church knowing she'd be killed."

"Yes."

"Why would he do that?" I asked, but he didn't offer a reply. "You don't secretly want me dead, do you?"

"You must survive."

"Can't you tell me what I need to know?"

Gabriel's tie melted to the mysterious midnight color. "You are not ready."

"Come on. Knowing is almost as good as remembering," I begged, but it didn't work. I took in a deep breath of night air. "I can't be sure if you are real or not. I guess it doesn't matter. Either way, here you are, with that mood ring tie of yours."

He leaned into me and I felt the heat of him staving off the chilly air.

"What should I do, Gabriel?" I asked. I felt drowsy with his warmth.

"Be human while you still can." His voice held such sadness.

"Am I going to ever be not human?"

Lane burst through the glass door, clutching his side.

My heart hit my ribcage in a sudden thump. "Did you hurt yourself?"

"No." He offered me a large plate of tiramisu. "You forgot your cake."

I took it reluctantly. I wanted to finish this conversation with Gabriel and the jerk had interrupted. I must have looked gloomy at best when I shoved a forkful of sugar in my mouth.

"Straight hair, makeup, heels, and a dress—all for me. I'm flattered," Lane said. I turned a cold shoulder. "Are you going to be mad at me forever?"

I didn't answer.

He tried harder. "When I woke up my very first thought was of you."

"You're an ass," I said, with a mouthful of cake.

"I'm serious," he said.

"You probably thought of me in a perverted way," I said.

"I was pretty stiff," Lane said.

I jabbed him with my fork and he yelped.

"You deserve more pain than that," I said. I suppressed the urge to squeeze him to death, and I absolutely refused to let him know how happy I was that he wasn't dead.

"I should've known that flowers and a nice suit wouldn't be enough to win you over. But I brought Winston."

"I was about to sue your mother."

"She does love him," Lane grinned. He reached into his jacket pocket and pulled out an envelope. I shoved the last bite of cake into my mouth and traded him the scraped plate for the envelope.

I tore it open and my body tingled. "This is from Danny."

"Yeah, I guessed that by the return address," Lane said. Sarcastic jerk.

"Mail theft is a federal crime, you know." I read the letter hastily. "He wants to visit me. His uncle Paul even wrote a polite note too."

"Why not invite him down? I'll show him the store. Boys his age love comics."

I shoved the letter back into its envelope with shaking hands.

"Thank you," I whispered softly to Lane. Without a word he turned to reenter the house.

I called after him. "Did you agree to be an agent so you could keep an eye on me?"

Lane smirked. "Garrison is a very persuasive man."

"Are you sure you want to date me?" I asked. I braced myself for rejection again, knowing that Lane might think I'm even more trouble now that he'd seen me in action.

Lane took my hand and kissed it, sucking a stray bit of icing off the side of my thumb. It was weird to lean against Gabriel and have another man kissing me—weirder because one was invisible.

"I don't want you to change, Jess," he said. "If that's what you're worried about. I just want to take it slow. Get to know you in ways that aren't physical. Let me make you dinner. Hold your hand in public."

I exhaled a slow, steady breath. I hated PDA.

Ally came to the door wearing her coat and holding mine loosely in her grip. With a gentle squeeze of my hands in his, Lane slipped back inside.

"What are you still doing out here? It's getting cold," she said, shutting the door after Lane. They didn't even look at each other. Clearly, almost dying together hadn't brought them any closer.

I stared through the kitchen, watching Lane talk to Kyra.

"Are you okay?" she asked, brushing the hair out of my eyes. "You look upset."

I forced a smile. "I'm just tired."

Ally bit her lip. "We'll do what we can. We'll post notices online, give the replacement agents a heads-up. We'll get the word out. We might not get the whole world to accept necronites overnight, but we'll make it hard as hell for people like Martin to kill anyone."

"That won't buy you much time," Gabriel said, inspecting his nails. When my eyes met Gabriel's the image of Ally's kiss filled my mind, as if Gabriel himself were shoving it into my skull.

"That reminds me." I turned toward her again. "After we saved you from the trunk, why did you kiss me?"

"I kiss you all the time," she said.

"Not like that," I said. "In fact, you specifically told me not to kiss you like that anymore."

She smiled. "You realize Lane will be insufferable now. He'll want to set up appointments, have clients. He'll probably schedule your massages together."

She seemed even more stressed by this prospect of death-replacement agent Lane than I did. My problem was I did realize he'd be insufferable now. He had one more reason for his we-belong-together argument.

"Is it true you agreed to date him?" she asked.

"Is that okay?" I'm not even sure why I felt like I needed her approval.

There was an awkward pause as Ally's cheeks reddened. "What happened in the church?"

Sure, avoid the question. "You were there."

"I know what I thought I saw," she said. "Like you, electrocuting those guys who held you up. That's what happened, wasn't it?"

I'd prepared for this. "Static electricity."

She arched an eyebrow. "Static electricity?"

I nodded and shuffled my feet. "From shuffling around in that ankle bracelet. It's what I get for wearing mismatched shoes."

Her eyebrow went higher. "Uh, huh."

I huffed. "What do you think happened?"

"You get mad and stun people? A human stun gun?"

"Yes, because that's a better explanation than static electricity," I said.

"That was some hellacious static." Ally leaned against the rail, touching Gabriel and not even knowing it. He didn't seem bothered by her, just curious as always. Huh, a green tie might mean curious. So what the hell does midnight blue mean? And red—

Ally smoothed the hair away from her face, buttoning up my coat, then hers. "Maybe this is just the beginning. Maybe you'll be able to do all sorts of cool new things. Won't that make life interesting?"

"Yes, because my life was getting a little dull," I said. Then I remembered something Caldwell said while pretending to be Mr. Reeves. *Teleportation, electrocution, skeleton armies.*

Please, no.

"Caldwell is scared for a reason. Why else would he go through all this trouble with you?" Ally said. "I just wish I knew what he knows. And I want to know if he's got an A.M.P. up his sleeve like Gloria thinks. That'll be a real problem for us if he does and keeps coming after you. But you know, I think we learned our lesson there. I mean, we certainly won't make the same mistakes. Can you imagine—?"

Her voice sort of trailed away as I watched Gabriel walk down the porch steps with his hands in his pockets and disappear into the dark tree line. His green eyes burned in the darkness for a heartbeat as he looked back at me. Then nothing.

But this wasn't over.

"Caldwell's not scared of me," I whispered to Ally. I watched the darkness, waiting for a sign.

Ally brushed my bangs out of my eyes and then kissed me soft on the cheek. "Maybe he should be."

Did you enjoy this book? You can make a BIG difference.

I don't have the same power as big New York publishers who can buy full spread ads in magazines and you won't see my covers on the side of a bus anytime soon, but what I *do* have are wonderful readers like you.

And honest reviews from readers garner more attention for my books and help my career more than anything else I could possibly do—and I can't get a review without **you!**

So if you would be so kind, I'd be very grateful if you would post a review wherever you buy books. It only takes a minute or so of your time and yet you can't imagine how much it helps me.

It can be as short as you like and yes, I cherish every. single. one.

So please go to your preferred retailer and leave a review for this book today.

Eternally grateful,
Kory

Get Your Three Free Stories Today

Thank you so much for reading *Dying for a Living*. I hope you're enjoying Jesse's story. If you'd like more, I have a free, exclusive Jesse Sullivan story for you. See Ally survive her first death replacement gig, during her first week as Jesse's assistant. You'll also see how the lovable Winston came to be Jesse's loyal companion.

You can only read this story for free by signing up for my newsletter. If you would like this story, you can get your copy by visiting **www.korymshrum.com/jessenewsletteroffer**

I will also send you free stories from the other series that I write. If you've signed up for my newsletter already, no need to sign up again. You should have already received this story from me. Check your email! Can't find it? ➜ Email me at **kory@korymshrum.com** and I'll take care of it.

As to the newsletter itself, I send out 2-3 a month and host a monthly giveaway exclusive to my subscribers. The prizes are usually signed books or other freebies that I think you'll enjoy. I also share information about my current projects, and personal anecdotes.

If you want these free stories and access to the giveaways, you can sign up for the newsletter at ➜ **www.korymshrum.com/jessenewsletteroffer**

If this is not your cup of tea (I love tea), you can follow me on Facebook at **www.facebook.com/korymshrum** in order to be notified of my new releases.

PREVIEW OF DYING BY THE HOUR

You've just finished reading *Dying for a Living*, the first book in this series. Keep reading for a preview of the next Dying for a Living novel, *Dying by the Hour*

Jesse

When they describe female special agents in the movies, or in books, it's always like this: a sleek, cat-like body that slithers in tight clothing, gorgeous exotic face and a sultry voice that can lure any target into submission.

While I am a female agent, double agent even, I'm *not* sultry, exotic, cat-like, sleek or even remotely alluring. I'm an idiot wearing a clown suit. And I don't mean clown suit figuratively.

I am wearing a clown suit at a birthday party.

I have the red nose, the floppy shoes and this horn around my neck that honks obnoxiously every time a grubby kid with sticky fingers runs up and gives it a squeeze.

The *double* part is more complicated. Neither my official job nor my unofficial off-the-books job requires I wear a clown suit. Yet, here I am dressed as a clown because my current client Regina Lovett begged me to.

She apparently believes a clown is less terrifying to her daughter, the person she's hired me to protect, than just being a regular old death replacement agent. Death replacement agent is my "respectable" job—though that depends upon whom you ask. The double agent part of me is here to gather intel. This is the *only* reason I'm willing to jump through Regina's obnoxious hoops in order to keep her business. Usually I hold all the cards in a death replacement because without me, they *die*.

I'm not even sure Julia, turning four, will agree with her mother anyway. She's done a good job of keeping her distance from me, the red-nosed wonder, backing away slowly every time I offer her a balloon.

My floppy shoes squish against the ground saturated with six days of September rain. I rock on my heels and watch Julia twirl in her party dress, a good twenty feet away. It's a pretty lavender color, complete with lacey ankle socks and Mary-Janes. A tiny gray peacoat protects her from the elements. She looks like any other privileged upper-class kid, standing in a big, beautiful yard, her thick brown locks pulled up into curling pigtails that graze the top of each shoulder and the lacy white collar of her dress. A white fence establishes the boundaries around the property and along the edge of the fence stand a few large saggy trees that have seen better, dryer days.

The pool has recently been drained, a military-green tarp stretching from one end to the other. I can't help but look at it and wonder if Julia will fall through and crack her head open on that poured cement or something. Or maybe the birthday candles will ignite and catch her hair on fire.

Occupational hazard, I'm afraid. I spend lots of time pondering death.

A little boy, maybe a year older than the birthday girl, tugs one of her curly pigtails. She stops twirling, squeals, and takes off chasing him through the yard. It is a shame the kid will die today being as cute as she is and on her birthday even.

Unless I can change it, of course, and that's what Regina Lovett is paying me to do—without her husband Gerard Lovett's knowledge, I might add. Given my real reason for being here, I am perfectly fine with this arrangement. Gerard doesn't need to know about me. But what his wife said to him to keep him away from Julia's birthday, I have no idea. When I suggested she pick another day for the birthday party, since she knew this would be Julia's death day, she said: *but I've already sent the invitations. I can't just cancel now.*

The woman has strange priorities, but it's really her husband I have to watch out for.

Gerard Lovett, the religious freak that he is, would have never allowed me—*especially* me—to be his daughter's death replacement agent. The Unified Church has a particular view on people like me. It doesn't matter that I have the ability to sense death coming, the ability to see its sneaky blue fire and put the kibosh on all that. Taking help from a death replacement agent would be a sign that they didn't have faith in God. All high-ranking church officials like Gerard Lovett have to demonstrate the solidity of their faith at all times. I often wonder if they'd refuse blood transfusions too, having faith God would just add a few pints when he got a chance.

Or maybe it's because I don't go anywhere when I die that I can't be trusted.

I turn at the sound of a sliding glass door and see Regina appear cake in hand. My personal assistant Ally is with her. She holds open the door for Regina, and then slides it closed behind them both.

"Time for cake!" Regina exclaims. The smile she'd given me when entering my office with Julia's death report two months ago had been forced, practiced, the smile of a woman married to an important man.

Her smile is softer now and Julia abandons the boy she's been chasing for it. She runs toward her mother with renewed laughter.

I look away, focusing on something mundane—Regina's clothes. They're some kind of modern business casual, classy and feminine. Her mousey hair is side swept and elegant, curling at the ends naturally. She's attractive, not *gorgeous* like Ally, but she knows how to do herself up, glossing up her plainness enough without screaming *I AM TRYING, OKAY?*

I notice all of this instead of looking at her and Julia together. For me, it hurts to look at mothers loving their daughters. My mother is dead and we weren't speaking for years before that.

Ally leaves Regina's trail, escaping the children gathering like rats around the Pied Piper, and comes to stand beside me. She pulls her red A-line coat tighter against the chilly air icing our cheeks and gathers her straight blond hair, the color of honey butter. I'd have helped her free it from the collar, but before I could she'd already done it, and with a single toss her locks had spilled down her back. Her nose stud looks silver in the dull overcast sky, instead of sparkling like the tiny diamond that it is. Her brown eyes are equally muted from their usual vibrant amber to an unremarkable brown. Dull light aside, she seems radiant against all this lush, landscaped green, moist with rain. The light flush in her otherwise pale cheeks suits her.

"Are you cold?" she asks, nodding at my colorful polka-dot jumper.

The answer is yes. Cold air has collected in my thighs and stomach, where the fabric of my polka-dotted jumper feels thinnest.

"I'm wearing layers," I insist. Ally can be quite the mother hen, and I know myself well enough to admit I can't be alert and babied at the same time.

"Are we good?" she asks.

Do I sense Julia's death coming? Not yet. "For now."

We watch Regina arrange the cake table, and launch the birthday song. It isn't until I start singing that Ally nudges me.

"Quit that," she says.

"What?" I play coy.

"I hear what you're saying," she accuses. "You're replacing *birth*day with *death*day."

"It *is* her death day."

"You are so morbid," she murmurs, but she's smiling.

Happy Death Day, Little Julia.

"What does morbid mean?" a kid asks. This kid is pudgy, as tall as he is round and apparently uninterested in singing to the birthday girl. Also, his face is an unnatural green color from eating something made mostly of food coloring.

"Weird," Ally says. I am not sure if she is defining morbid or if she is as surprised by the ninja appearance of this kid as I am.

"Clowns are weird," the kid says, sucking on his sticky fingers.

"*You're* weird," I say. Ally nudges me with an elbow, but it's unneeded. This kid is too young to recognize an insult or he is just impervious beneath all that fat.

"I want a balloon," he demands.

I offer the big black trash bag to him, filled with animal balloons of every shape and color. When I took this job, I knew better than to improvise a skill I didn't have. So *voilà!*— a big bag of balloon animals.

"I want to see you make one," the kid groans.

"I want to see you leave," I say and stick the bag in his face.

Ally intervenes. "She can't make them because she has a bad wrist."

"Really?" the kid asks. He warms to her the way everyone warms to Ally.

I tell the kid, my cover story. "Yeah, carpel tunnel from all that juggling, camel riding, and whatever the hell clowns do."

"You said a bad word."

"I'm going to call you a bad word if you don't go away."

Ally is doing a decent job of keeping a straight face. She is also doing a great job of being pretty and convinces the little fatty to take a yellow "lion" and go get some cake. The words *before it's all gone* seem to work.

"You promised not to make the children cry," Ally says. She's not kidding.

"Sorry," I grumble. "I'm in a piss poor mood today."

"It's the first kid since Nessa."

And that's why Ally is my best friend. She knows what bothers me before I do. I let out a big exhale and the breathing hole in my red nose whistles, dramatizing my despair.

Nessa.

I've thought a lot about Nessa this past year, especially in the past month leading up to Julia's replacement. It was this time last year that I'd failed to save her. Granted, I hadn't been her death replacement agent, so technically my perfect record is still intact. But she'd also been just a little girl and I'd promised her mother I would save her from some bad people. When you have this ability to save people, and a perfect track record of doing so—when you screw up—

Yeah, I'm a sore loser.

"Nessa Hildebrand. Our first casualty of war," I whisper. An ache fills my chest and I look away from the kids.

"Are we calling it war now?" Ally asks. She let her own breath out slow, weary.

"Two sides. Good versus evil. Only one can win. That's war, isn't it?"

"Evil hasn't made a move in over a year," Ally whispers. "Openly anyway."

"Oh, they've made moves, I'm sure," I say. "Just not that we can see."

"That's a good sign though, right?"

Oh Ally, my ever optimistic companion. Just because someone hasn't stabbed her in a year, she thinks we're safe. I know better. I can feel them sliding through the dark around us, large and scaly, looking for the right moment to spit acid venom in our faces.

"Sure. That's a great sign," I say. I don't believe what I'm saying and she knows I don't believe it. But sometimes you say things to be kind to the people you love. It wouldn't comfort her to hear *We're all going to die, Ally. They came for us once and they'll come again. Harder and harder until they win, and God help us, I can't imagine anything worse than what we've already been through*—No.

Some things you don't say to people you love.

Besides the word *war* suggests a fighting chance. War means a prolonged battle where either side could come out on top. This isn't war. This is a death sentence.

Ally gives my hand a quick squeeze, bringing me back to the present moment, to a moment when I am just a clown at a little girl's birthday party.

"Go on," she says. "Get what you came for."

I cast a last look at Regina, Julia, and the others, then hand Ally the balloon bag.

"If they ask, I went to pee."

She gives a cute salute and I slip away. I take my huge floppy shoes off by the back door and creep inside, careful to slide the door closed behind me.

The kitchen welcomes me. A large island with a granite

countertop sits off to the left, and behind that, mahogany cabinets and a stainless steel fridge. The place looks like an ad in *Better Homes*, with only a few stray coats from guests and the occasional toy forgotten in a corner. Otherwise, it is pristine.

I turn on the bathroom light and shut the door, hoping to give the *occupado* impression should someone wonder where I am. Cover story secure, I creep up the stairs and down the hallway. My ears strain for any people noises—voices, footsteps, maniacal whistling, for anyone who might wonder why a girl wearing a rainbow wig is sneaking around up here.

But I hear nothing and see no one.

I place my hand on the door handle of Mr. Lovett's office and find it locked. Then I do what I've been taught to do. I pull two pins from my thick rainbow wig and slip them into the lock. I push against the bearing—turn, and *pop*.

It sounds easy, sure, but I've practiced a *million* times on a variety of locks purchased from hardware stores. A box of locks in the corner of a living room is a great conversation starter, by the way, and a lovely way to spend a Friday night alone.

Gerard Lovett's office is large. The desk stands in the middle of the room, directly opposite the door. The desk itself is immaculate, *nothing* like mine, which has piles of paperwork, junk mail, and bills needing attention. Behind his neat desk is a regal black chair, with a high back and wheels. The desk and chair itself are perched on top of a red and gold rug matching the red and gold drapes on either side of the fireplace behind the desk. One side of the room has a massive book case. The spines look unbroken, unread, and I'm not surprised to think of Mr. Lovett as a man who likes the appearance of being erudite rather than the actual reading. The remaining side of the room has a wooden chess set on a table between two more regal chairs, this time made of red leather.

Before entering the room I look around. I'm glad I do. Because up above me, sitting on a ledge above the chess set, is a camera. It isn't trained on the whole room, just the desk and the wall behind it, so if I'm lucky, I'm still invisible.

I admit I'm pretty freaked about the camera. I'm staring at its little black eye, trying to determine my next move when—*POP*.

I jump. My heart explodes in my chest, taking off like a rabbit fleeing a fox and I am about to run like hellfire back down the stairs and out the door. Then I hear a child crying. I swear, steady myself against the door frame, breath caught in my throat like a cotton ball and cross to the window to see what made the sound.

A balloon had popped and a child, devastated, is crying against Ally's leg while she searches the bag for one in a similar shape and color. She finds one and the girl brings her weeping to a raggedy, shuddering stop. Her face brightens. The smile still tight, turns into a half-hearted, lopsided grin and the sobs become a kind of gleeful hiccup.

"Je*sus*," I mutter. I swear I can feel my ovaries die.

When I turn back to the room I realize something is wrong. Not just that I'd run into the room without thinking and was surely caught on camera, but the room is suspiciously quiet. The hum and click of electronics I'd noted upon first entering the room is gone. The clocks have stopped ticking. Latent electricity in lamp wires, phone outlets, an answering machine and internet modem have all stopped. The camera too, of course. Everything still, everything quiet—the way a house is quiet after a power outage.

"Shit."

This time last year, when my life started to get out of control, and homicidal maniacs tried to kill me and whatnot,

I started to develop this new—I can't believe I'm going to say this—power. Unfortunately, there just isn't another word for it. It's not part of my weird death-replacement thing, but something that can't be explained scientifically by my NRD—my Necronitic Regenerative Disorder, a neurological disorder that allows me to die but not stay dead.

No, this is something else entirely.

It would seem I have some strange connection to electricity. It's not like I can control it. When it started last year, it was just a shocky thing—a static sort of electricity managing to blow light bulbs at the flip of a switch, or shock people quite a bit stronger than the usual I-shuffled-my-feet-and-now-*zap*.

It's evolved.

Lately, I can do this surge thing. When I'm startled, or scared, I send a shock out and *BAM*, electronics fail. So far I've only managed to blow up my own shit—bye, bye the possibility of morning toast or midnight margaritas, which is fine except now I'm blowing up other people's shit.

This is a serious problem.

I can't fall apart over fried electronics. I have to do what I came up here to do. I relax against the side of Mr. Lovett's desk and steady my breath. Once I feel somewhat together, I pull out a small Phillips-head screwdriver from my rainbow wig. I hold my hand above Mr. Lovett's computer listening for any kind of electric static crackling around my skin. When I feel none, I start to dismantle his computer.

Three of the six tiny screws are out of the computer, the ones that would release the hard drive from its little plastic nest, when all hell breaks loose.

A wave hits me. I rock back on my heels, topple, and hit the wall. My shoulder brushes something and I hear a crash. I quit moving, knowing because I can't see, I'll only knock more shit over if I continue flailing blindly.

"No, no, *no*," I whine as if that will make Julia's death turn on its heels and leave. Because that is what I feel—Death come calling.

I work faster.

First I reach out for the desk, find its edge and pull myself back to the computer. In my hurried panic, I start dropping the little screws on the office rug.

I have the last screw loose, but not completely out, when my vision changes.

The world dissolves from its usual solid self into a shifting world of color. The only equivalent I can think of is heat sensory, like the way they show it on TV or in the movies where someone puts on special goggles and then the world turns into an orange-yellow-red blob. This isn't exactly right, what I see in the moments before a death. I see more color and nuances, but it's close enough that you get the idea.

The problem with it happening *now* is two-fold. Problem one—I can't see the last freaking screw anymore. I can't clearly define *anything*, now that the world has reduced itself to something less substantial than an acid trip.

Problem two, Julia Lovett is about to die and I'm not close enough to save her. I can feel her out there, moving around in the yard, feel the pull surrounding her, centering and drawing close. If she dies and I am not near her, she can't be saved. Proximity is required for a death replacement.

The only thing I can do now is force myself to focus.

Even after my best effort, the colors are still there, making it hard to see. I have to rely on my fingers, the feel of grooves against the tips just to figure out what I'm doing, really hoping that it *is* the hard drive I'm removing.

I'm not a computer expert. I only know how to do this because Brinkley, my ex-handler, showed me on an old garage sale computer making me practice until I practically wept for a break.

Finally, it falls free of its case. Clutching the stolen hard drive in one hand, I rush back toward the stairs. I can't afford to be casual. I can't afford to take my time or even stop to turn off the bathroom light or open the door. In fact, I'm forced to crawl down the stairs the way a baby would, butt first so I don't fall. I make slow progress, but I can't save Julia's life if I break my own neck before even getting to her.

Somehow I manage to make it back to the sliding kitchen door and see Ally on the other side. Sure, she is a blur of color like everything else, but I *know* Ally. I know what she looks like even in this form. Maybe it's because I've saved her life once, or because she's been on a *bagillion* replacements with me, or even because she's my best friend. I don't know or care as I pry open the glass and croak her name.

Nothing.

Louder: "*Ally*."

She turns around and it must be the way I look because she comes running.

"Are you—"

"Here," I say. I shove what I hope is the hard drive at her and step fully into the backyard.

"Jesse, your shoes," she says.

"No time." I'm already walking to the edge of the brick patio stretching like a giant doormat away from the kitchen entrance. I'm searching the yard for Julia.

I find her colorful blur twirling again and I know it is her, because something isn't quite right with her "thermal" reading. A menacing black blur mars her color. She's out by the fence and I can't see anything around her that's of danger, but I know better than to let that assumption stop me. Something can fall from the sky at any second. Some insane driver could crash through that white fence. Hell, little Julia could be having a heart attack from all that twirling.

I run through the soggy grass, my socks soaking up the

cold rainwater. My toes curl. I run and Ally follows, but not too close, yelling, "Everyone back up, please!" She knows to do crowd control and create as much distance between me and the others as possible.

I have no idea if it works. I can't afford to focus on anything but Julia.

I run across the yard, arms out to grab her. Julia must see me coming and stops twirling for long enough to scream and run in the other direction. It isn't until I hear her screaming "Mommy the clown! Mommy!" that I realize *I* am the one terrifying her, a clown with a manically determined expression, rushing her at full speed.

"Come here!" I yell, unable to pretend like this was anything but urgent. "We don't have time for this."

And of course I'm right.

I hear Ally yelling. Something unclear, directed at Regina. People always want to rush in and save their loved ones from dying, but it only gets in the way and causes more casualties. After all, I can only replace one person at a time.

Death is different for everyone and I see it differently for everyone.

Sometimes I see death as a tiny black hole created inside a person, an empty swirling vortex sucking all the warm, living colors out of a person, leaving nothing behind that can survive.

Sometimes a hot-cold chill settles into the muscles in my back and coils around my navel before yanking me down into oblivion.

Then there are deaths like Julia Lovett's.

A death where I just have to throw myself out there and hope it works out. No vision guidance. No conscious effort on my part. Just faith that being who I am, *what* I am, the exchange will happen.

Julia has almost reached the fence when I grab ahold of

her. I hold her against my scratchy polka-dotted jumper while she screams and flails. I try to say soothing things: "I'm not going to hurt you. Gee-*zus*. Calm down!" My best efforts fall short as I look up and see my worst nightmare.

A tall, stupidly beautiful man, dressed in a three-piece suit, strides across Julia's yard toward us. With determined, dedicated steps, he unfurls his black wings on either side of him as he closes the distance between us. I haven't seen that shaggy dark hair or those animalistic green eyes in a year. Now here he is, walking straight toward me in all his angelic splendor.

"*Shit*," I say.

Julia quits squirming in my arms and turns her wide eyes up to mine. Her mouth is open in horror as if my profanity is the worst thing that's ever happened to her.

Before I can apologize something hard and heavy slams us from behind.

The entire world goes dark

Have you enjoyed this excerpt from *Dying by the Hour*? You can find and purchase the book at your favorite retailer.

PREVIEW OF GRAVEYARD SHIFT
by Angela Roquet

*"Suicide is man's way of telling god,
you can't fire me, I quit."*
-Bill Maher

No one cared about Lial Gordon, but you might have never guessed if you had seen his funeral. A herd of socialites gathered around his grave. A silk handkerchief dabbed an eye here and there. A eulogy fit for the President was poetically read, and dozens of white roses were tossed with a dramatic and well-practiced sympathy.

Lial smiled and rolled back on his heels. He looked a little too smug for a dead man, but he was a dead man just the same.

"Pigs!" he snorted. "I don't know half of them, but there's no doubt why they're here. Everyone wants a piece of my money. Ha! Wait until they find out they've wasted a perfectly good Saturday for nothing."

Lial was in a much better mood than he had been four days ago, when he came home early from his visit to New

York. He was the president of a reputable bank and often took trips to meet his most valuable customers. Unfortunately, he had just lost one of his best. He was looking forward to sulking over one of his wife's casseroles, but soon discovered he wasn't the only man enjoying her cooking.

He entered his master bedroom to find his best friend, and vice president of his bank, snoring between his wife's legs.

Lial didn't wake them. He quietly retreated to his library to find solace in a bottle of aged brandy. Then, in a drunken stupor, he gathered the cash from his private safe, all of his wife's jewelry, and anything else of value he could smuggle out of the house. He loaded it all into the trunk of his Rolls Royce and left.

After an hour's drive, he pulled off onto a gravel road and followed it back to a lake surrounded by woods. At one time, the place had been special. He had gone fishing there with his sons when they were younger. Now they only called if they needed money. Lial finished off another bottle of brandy while pitching bundles of crisp hundred dollar bills into the lake.

When he finished disposing of his riches, he got back in his car and drove home. Morning broke, and the sun glimmered into a rich dawn as he pulled into his driveway and found the traitors kissing goodbye on the front porch. They froze at the sight of him, and before they could compose themselves, Lial floored it.

He plowed the car right through the bay window and into the living room. The impact threw him into the windshield, where a piece of glass found his throat. He would have choked to death on his own blood, watching his wife and best friend run from the house, screaming like lunatics, if it hadn't been for the explosion.

That's how Lial Gordon died, and that's how he met me. Lial was pleased with himself. Not only had he taken care of his money and car, but now the house was worthless as well. Not many are as proud as he had been so soon after death.

'All right." Lial smiled and turned to walk away from the crowd of mourners. "Enough of this. I'm ready to burn in Hell."

The dead are strange. They always assume they can just walk into their afterlife. I reached for his shoulder and pulled him back.

"Hold still." If you had my job, you'd be grim too.

I pushed my hand into the pocket of my robe and found my coin. Rolling it three times, I said the word, and we left the graveyard behind.

There is no tunnel with a light at the end when you die, just a reaper with a coin, like me. Maybe to a human the passage over resembles a tunnel. To me, it's more like a womb, and we're being pushed into existence elsewhere. Humans are always in that infant-like state of shock when they see Limbo City.

Lial's smirking good mood melted as we arrived. My world is very different from his. But I have to admit, my shock to his world when I got my first coin was just as bad.

The coordinates I used pushed us out into the middle of the market area, shadowed by the towering architecture of downtown Limbo. Buildings crammed together down Morte Avenue, a collage of metal and stone. The old world charm of cathedrals and temples mixed with New York styled skyscrapers, imitating the human realm. Rusty streaks of light shot out from behind the city, strangling the illusion of a sunset. Limbo has no sun, but the fake light is welcomed by most citizens. Even the dead prefer to see what they're doing.

I sighed, wishing I had picked a different location. The

market was an unthinkable place to be on a Sunday. Crowds of souls picked through an assortment of goods shipped in from the afterlives. The innocent items like phoenix feathers and vases autographed by Greek gods were arranged out in the open, but if you looked close enough, you could find someone selling vials of holy water or hellfire under the table. Both substances required a license to carry in Limbo City, but most vendors didn't care, if you paid the right price.

Crones hobbled by, gaudy amulets swinging from their necks as they waved their salt-crusted fingers to lure customers closer. A patron bumped a table of herbs, and a horde of pixies scurried to gather them before they hit the ground. A trio of saints lectured outside a white tent, stressing the importance of keeping faith in the afterlife to a crowd of fresh souls.

The harbor would be busy too. It's always busy on the weekends. That's when the Sea of Eternity is the calmest. It used to be only Sundays, but less than a century ago, during the Colorado Labor Wars, two souls who had died in the Ludlow Massacre ended up working in the Three Fates Factory. They convinced the employees to go on strike until they were given Saturdays off as well.

The strike hadn't lasted long. The factory is responsible for pulling souls out of the sea and reinstalling them into the human realm. After a few days, the Sea of Eternity had swelled up around Limbo City and threatened to swallow it. The Fates quickly agreed to give Saturdays off, and the factory began running again.

The Sea of Eternity used to be a river, but that all changed when humans began dabbling in science. More atheists and agnostics die every day. It's their souls that fill the sea, making my job even grimmer. It used to be easy getting a lot of souls to their afterlives. It used to take minutes, but minutes stretched into hours, and soon I fear it will become days. I don't get paid enough to waste that kind of time. Like I said, you'd be grim too.

Taking Lial by the shoulder, I directed him through the crowd and down the main dock to my ship. He was my last soul for the day and I was ready to set sail. I had twelve souls to take to Heaven, eight to Nirvana, and four to Summerland. Not too bad for a Sunday. Unlike the Three Fates employees, reapers don't get weekends off. But if we save enough coin, we can buy ourselves a vacation.

"What are you doing, Lana?" Josie, my sailing partner, stood on the deck of my ship with her arms folded. Tuffs of black hair framed her oval face. The haircut was almost too short to be considered feminine, but she pulled it off with her delicate chin and ample pout. The fierce sweep of lashes around her eyes didn't hurt either.

She tapped her toe on the deck of my- well, our ship. We had gone in and traded our two smaller boats for something a little nicer and a little faster. A demon sold it to us, claiming Grace O'Malley had given it to him in exchange for some deed involving the possession of a queen. How fitting that two lady reapers should purchase it. It had been a little too expensive for me to buy on my own. Besides, it was nice to have some company other than a herd of disoriented souls.

"Sorry, I know I'm late. We stayed for the funeral."

I hated being lectured. Josie was a better reaper than me, and I didn't have a problem with that. What I did have a problem with, was her rubbing it in my face.

"No, what are you doing bringing that soul on our boat? I saw his file. He's a suicide and a non-believer. Where do you think we're taking him?" She tilted her head to one side and raised an eyebrow.

"By all rights, yes, he belongs in the sea. His soul is not

nearly dark enough for Hell to pay us anything worth our time."

"But?" she snapped.

We hadn't been working on the same boat for very long, but her criticism was getting old. She always had to do everything by the book, like something bad might happen if she bent the rules. I didn't bend them all the time, and I never outright broke them... much.

"I like Lial here, and I have a coin I've been saving for a rainy day. Nirvana should take it. He's had a difficult life, and I think he deserves a little enjoyment before being sucked up by the Fates and spit back into that pitiful reality again." I yanked back the hood of my robe so she could get the full effect of the face I made at her as I pushed Lial on deck.

"Nirvana? You mean that Asian religion was right?" Lial's fear mutated into curiosity.

"They're all right. We just sort you humans by how well you measure up to your individual beliefs." You can't imagine how many times I've had this conversation.

"Then why are you taking me to Nirvana? Not that I mind," he quickly added.

"Because I think you deserve a vacation, and Nirvana's laws are easier to get around than Heaven's." I patted his arm and opened the door to the sailor's quarters.

My first twenty-three souls chattered among twenty new faces, Josie's catch. My stomach knotted. She had twenty-four souls on her docket that morning, same as me, all preordered by their afterlives. This meant four were in the hold. We never put souls in the hold unless we're taking them to Hell. Most Hell-bounds try to escape. Can you blame them?

I scowled, wishing I had reviewed Josie's list as well as she had reviewed mine. I hated making deliveries to Hell. Lucifer never gave me any trouble, but he had been on vacation lately.

Gate duty had been turned over to Maalik, one of the Islamic angels.

Maalik had originally been appointed to watch over the Islamic hell, Jahannam, but with Eternity's growing demands, the rulers of Jahannam and Hell decided to adjoin their territories and utilize a single gateway.

Maalik made me nervous. He was too flirty and too pretty to be guarding the gates of Hell. I didn't trust him, and I didn't like that he was racking up so much coin with his ambitious work ethic. If he showed up in Limbo, I planned on hightailing it to Summerland until he left. I needed a vacation anyway.

Lial looked around the room. He was my most enjoyable catch of the day. I didn't regret staying for his funeral. Josie would get over it.

"I'll come find you when we get to Nirvana," I said. 'Meanwhile, talk to James over there. He's a Buddhist. He can fill you in on how to get through the gates."

"Hey, uh, thanks," Lial whispered. "I don't know why you're doing this, but I appreciate it."

"Sure." I laughed. Granting little favors almost made my job worth it. I closed the door behind me and found Josie waiting.

"Do you even know how many rules you're breaking doing this?" she grumbled.

I folded my arms. "It's not a big deal. Like the Fates will even miss him."

"You're jeopardizing both of our jobs, not to mention gambling with a ship that I paid for, too."

"Lighten up. I'm going to change before we take off. Where's Gabriel? Didn't he need a ride?" I wanted to change the subject before she listed off every rule I had broken since we started working together.

"He's late, as usual. Cocky jerk thinks the world revolves around him. He's probably still at Purgatory Lounge."

"I thought he quit drinking. He better sober up before we get to Heaven, or you know we'll get blamed for it."

"I know." Josie frowned. "You're redirecting souls without authorization, and now we're transporting a drunk of an archangel to make coin on the side. We might as well be demons."

"I'll go fetch him." I felt like a drink myself after Josie's little fit.

"If you're not back in twenty minutes, I'm tossing your refugee and taking the coin for your other souls," she warned.

"I'll be back in time. I just gotta change first. I'm not going inside Purgatory wearing my work robe." I looked down at the frumpy garment and sighed. While it looked good on Josie, it made me look like Marilyn Monroe's evil twin.

I headed for the captain's quarters before Josie could start another argument. She was a pain in the ass, but she was one of the few reapers I trusted.

Shuffling through my dresser, I found a pair of leather pants I had bought at Athena's Boutique. Athena had set up a nice little shop in Limbo after sulking for nearly a millennium over her decline of followers. It was doing her a world of good, and I was growing a rather charming wardrobe. A black tank top and my favorite pair of boots completed the outfit. I thought about doing something with my hair but decided I didn't have time. Josie was in a bad enough mood. If I was late, I knew she would make good on her threat to leave.

I cocked an eyebrow at myself in the dusty oval mirror next to our bunk and made a mental note to give Josie back the tube of cherry lipstick she had loaned me. Anemic hooker was not the look I was going for. I combed my fingers through my black ringlets and left.

Limbo City was just as crowded as the market and harbor. The Fates' employees were busy shopping. Fresh souls happily filled the streets and sidewalks, only stopping for a moment to move out of my way. They knew I was a reaper, and it made them nervous. A reaper had brought each one of them over at some point.

The Three Fates used to recycle the souls on their own, but it made for tiresome and constant work. Some time ago, they discovered a way to keep a small fraction of souls in Limbo and persuaded them to work at the factory in exchange for a grander entrance back into the human realm. I can tell every time I harvest a soul from America. More and more celebrities are sprouting up all over the place.

I passed the Muses Union House and Bank of Eternity before reaching Purgatory Lounge. Gabriel's musical voice spilled out as I opened the door.

"I haven't had this much fun since I told Joseph his fiancée was knocked up by God!" the angel slurred. He sat at a booth with two nephilim, fallen angel half-breeds.

"Gabriel! What do you think you're doing?" I plucked a feather from one of his wings, and he fluttered them in protest.

"Owww! What was that for?" he whined.

His drinking buddies eyed me suspiciously. Their wings were smaller, but their bodies larger. They weren't as attractive as real angels, but they were close.

"The ship is sailing with or without you, Gabriel. If you don't leave here with me now, you'll have to find a ride over later. I don't think Peter will be very pleased with you," I scolded him.

"Peter's halo's gotten a little fat these days. I tried to take him on vacation with me, but he doesn't seem to think anyone else is fit to man the gate," Gabriel laughed.

"I can't imagine why when archangels keep coming home drunk."

"Give it a rest, Lana. Josie must be rubbing off on you. You used to be fun. What happened?" He hiccupped and slid an arm around my waist to pull me down in the booth with him. The nephilim across from me gave a sheepish smile.

Gabriel was getting careless with his reputation lately. If another heavenly host spotted him mingling with the offspring of the fallen, he'd never hear the end of it from Peter. He'd be stuck with cherub tasks for a decade.

"I was just telling Bob here," Gabriel slobbered, "how I can do whatever I want, because when people get to Heaven, who do they wanna see? Me! Right after Jesus and Mary, but still. I'm not gonna lose my job. I've been busting my halo for thousands of years. Thousands! I think I deserve a little fun now and then. Don't I Lala?" His head rolled onto my shoulder.

Lala wasn't exactly a nickname. Gabriel only used it when he was tanked, which was about half the time.

I sighed. "Gabriel, Josie will leave us both here and take my commission if we don't go now."

"Fine, party-pooper. See you boys later."

The half-breeds nodded and went back to their drinks.

Gabriel left his arm around my waist as we made our way back to the ship. I didn't stop him because I didn't think he could walk upright otherwise. We got plenty of strange looks. A reaper and an archangel walked out of a bar. I almost had to laugh.

"About time!" Josie shouted at us from the deck where she untied the ropes holding our ship to the dock.

It was quieter now. Most of the reaper ferries had already departed for the afterlives. Gabriel spread his wings and flew up ahead of me. Feathers rained down as he ran into a mast and fluttered like a spooked chicken to catch himself.

"Don't fly on my ship while you're drunk!" Josie was still in a sour mood. She turned her hostile glare to me.

I grinned at her. "Told you I'd make it back in time."

"With the state he's in, I wish you hadn't." She turned away to pull up one of the sails. "A little help would be nice."

I stomped over to the next mast and untangled a web of ropes.

Once we were out of the harbor and the noise faded behind us, I went to check on Lial. He was curled up on a couch next to James, who looked relieved to see me.

"Miss Lana, I don't know if I have enough time to prepare him," he said, nervously tugging the cuffs of his robe.

I nodded. "Just do your best. I'll take care of it when we get there."

I hadn't told James that I had a coin, and obviously Lial hadn't mentioned it to him either. It wouldn't have done much good, seeing as neither of them knew how our coin worked.

Our coin wasn't just used as currency to make purchases. It held a doorway to the other realms. It would have been nice to just transport the souls to their afterlives with a coin, but if we did that, our boss would take it out of our commission. So we sailed the Sea of Eternity.

"I'm the king of the world!" Gabriel shouted at the head of the boat, nearly falling overboard. Only the flutter of his wings saved him.

"Gabriel!" Josie growled.

"He's already paid, so let's just get this over with," I said as she shot me another nasty look.

"Next time, we're charging more. I like order on my ship—"

"Our ship," I corrected her.

We were both possessive of O'Malley's boat. It's not every day that you come by a legendary female pirate's ship.

The sails were open and gently tugged us along toward our first stop, Summerland, my favorite of the afterlives. Not too crowded. Lots of nature to take in. It was a nice break from the bustling city life in Limbo. The pagans were friendly and didn't seem to mind the occasional reaper on vacation.

"You wanna go out for a beer when we get home?" I tried to smooth things over with Josie. Her scrunched up face lightened a little and then flushed.

"I can't."

"Look, I'm sorry for messing up your schedule."

"It's not that. I have a date," she whispered so Gabriel wouldn't overhear.

"Oh, really? With who?"

"It's not a big deal." She toyed with the ropes of the nearest sail.

"Come on, who?"

She blushed and leaned over the railing. "Horus."

"Josie." It was my turn to lecture her. "You know he's just going to try to bribe you into sneaking more souls into Duat."

Duat was the Egyptian underworld, but its flow of souls has been steadily decreasing for some time.

"No he won't. They get enough to keep them happy," she argued.

"When's the last time we made a delivery there?"

"He doesn't care about more souls. Osiris is watching over Duat, and Horus has been vacationing for almost a decade now."

"Just be careful."

It wasn't like Josie to go after one of the old gods. The laws were more lenient these days, but most of society still frowned on reapers dating outside the corporation.

"Hate to interrupt ladies, but we have company," Gabriel sang out to us.

"What now?" Josie stormed off to the front of the ship

with me close behind. We were an hour from Summerland, with three more stops to go. We didn't need trouble this early.

"Shit." I frowned at the horizon.

A ship approached us from the north. Clusters of dog-faced demons scaled the masts and sides of the black boat, and a dark-winged man stood on the main deck, holding a leash attached to a soul.

"Caim, that bastard. He's snatched a clairvoyant soul." I squeezed my eyes shut. The day just kept getting better.

Caim was enjoying his exile from Hell a little too much, especially since he left with two legions of demons. After his impeachment, he had gone underground for half a century. Now he was out stalking reaper ferries to loot souls.

"I'll get my bow. You better go find your scythe." Josie took off for our cabin.

My scythe lay next to the hatch where I had left it the last time I had to terrorize a group of Hell-bound souls down in the hold. There were thirty of them that day. Grim had given me an extra miserable lot after he found out I had snuck a boy, destined for the sea, into Summerland. The Hell-bounds were plotting an escape until my scythe flashed before them.

I grabbed my weapon and headed back to the front of the ship with Josie, who now carried her bow. She had a scythe too but rarely used it. The bow was a gift from Artemis for delivering a message to her twin brother, Apollo. Artemis set up an archery shop after she saw what a hit Athena's Boutique was, but her brother still resided on Mount Olympus in Summerland.

"We should really get that soul back." I sighed over Gabriel's shoulder.

"I wasn't planning on getting that close." Josie's eyes widened with concern as her fingers twitched over the arrows in her quiver.

"You wouldn't have to," Gabriel offered. "Distract him, and I'll go over and get the soul."

"Do you really think you should be flying under the influence?"

"I'm an archangel. Give me some credit here."

Josie frowned and lifted her bow. "Fine. You ready Lana?"

"Ready and armed."

I couldn't use my scythe long range, but as soon as she let loose an arrow, the demons that could fly would be on us. I could see Caim's cocky grin now and the sullen expression of the female soul he had captured.

"Go Gabriel!" Josie shouted as she unleashed an arrow.

It was a perfect shot through Caim's wing. He twisted in agony and dropped the leash. Josie strung another arrow as I lashed out at two demons hovering above us. I didn't want them to land on our deck. We'd just had it washed. Demon guts were acidic and would burn holes in our ship if they weren't cleaned up right away.

Three more of the creatures appeared in mid-air, snapping and snarling. I swung to behead them, only missing one. It landed on the deck and scrambled toward Josie as she pumped Caim full of arrows. I lashed out, catching the creature's underside with my blade, and flung it overboard with a shriek. Sticky demon pieces splattered my leather pants.

"Lana! They're coming over the side!" Josie backed into me.

Four more demons clawed up the side of the ship and circled us. They were smaller than the others. Three sets of leathery wings scaled down their boney spines. One inched closer, dragging its talons along the deck with a squeal that rivaled a dozen chalkboards.

Josie cringed. "Now that's uncalled for." She lifted her bow and popped an arrow through the little devil's head.

The rest of the litter rushed us. Josie nodded to me, and

we attacked together. She darted one with an arrow while I gutted another, splashing the deck with steaming gore. The last demon latched onto my boot just as Josie put an arrow through its head, pinning the toe of my boot to the deck floor in the process.

I sucked in a breath, anticipating a sharp pain that thankfully didn't follow. The arrow had wedged itself between my toes.

"Nice shot." I rolled my eyes and reached down to jerk the arrow free.

"Please, you've had those boots for nearly a century. It's time you invest in a new pair anyway." Josie took the arrow from me and stuffed it back in her quiver. "We're going to have to file a report now."

"I'll do it," I groaned. "I have an evaluation with Grim in the morning anyway."

Attacks on reaper ferries had tripled in the past week. Where Limbo City was the ultimate free world, the Sea of Eternity was an aged battlefield, just as hostile as Limbo was neutral. The attacks were the big news of the week, headlining on the covers of Limbo Weekly and the Daily Reaper Report. Channel nine, Council Street Live, had even issued a cautionary warning to sea travelers and transporters.

Gabriel landed on the deck behind us. The captive soul trembled in his arms. I wondered if she could smell the alcohol on his breath. She stared at us, as though trying to decide if we were any better than the creep we'd just rescued her from.

At a more comfortable distance away, Caim was busy yanking arrows out of his bloodied wings.

"Jerk," I muttered and wiped my hands off on my pants. They were ruined.

"So, where do we take you?" Josie cooed at the soul. The woman pulled away from Gabriel and looked up at him.

"It's okay," he said. "They'll get you where you need to be."

She turned back to us and smiled. "Do you travel to Summerland?"

Enjoyed Chapter 1 of *Graveyard Shift*? You can find and purchase the book at your favorite retailer.

ACKNOWLEDGMENTS

Once upon a time in college, I would waste a great deal of time writing about a girl who died for a living. There were a group of fantastic ladies in my life then, affectionately called "The Pod" and I will thank each in turn, in no particular order of importance.

First, thanks to Kathy "Zcat" Zlabek for the following reasons. Foremost, like any good friend, you never ratted me out. When I was called on in class and would look up desperately from my secret scribblings, and say the first thing that fell out of my head, you never called me out, or contradicted our teacher when they (erroneously) mistook my bullshit for "profound observation." Thank you further still for always meeting me at the gym when I asked you to, yet amazingly, would also leave the gym BEFORE having worked out at the merest suggestion that a pint of organic ice cream might IN FACT be better for our health. Lastly, thank you for meeting me in Paris, keeping your promise and coming all that way to see me, even after your bus blew up. I'm very sorry about your grandmother's jewelry, but infinitely happy you're still around.

Meghann Meeusen! What wonderful and amazing things can be said about Meghann Meeusen. The fact that you named your dog Frodo should be a clue to your epicness. To me, your dinner parties are some of my fondest memories—and I'm not even the one who drank all the wine! Thank you for being such a wonderful listener and friend in those days. Thank you for telling me I looked like Audrey Hepburn when I cut off my haircut and then cried about it. Thank you for the "jelly bellies" and the "good news" and all the evenings in the movie theater watching very bad movies, yet somehow having a tremendously good time. Thank you for letting me and Melinda climb onto your broom and bounce circles around your kitchen table, singing....what? What were we singing again? But even more importantly, thank you for the encouragement you never withheld, being one of the first to tell me to hitch my wagon to a star. I relied on you more than you know.

To Melinda Moustakis—see broom comment above. Also for helping me discover the algorithm for a hit song during that roadtrip to see Meghann. Should I ever decide to write one, I won't forget to spell something and repeat myself at least four times. I'll title it "Real Men Call Back". Thanks also for all those lazy days on the lake. Keep being your awesome successful self and should I ever need a guide through the Alaskan wild, I know who to call.

To Kate Dernacoeur—one of the most inspirational people I know. If I can be half as accomplished as you are when I'm your age, I'll be pretty pleased with myself. You train rescue dogs, you're a firefighter/paramedic, globetrotter, you hike mountains and all before I can get up in the morning (9 a.m. isn't that late!). I'm so glad we connected in Prague and that you were there when I was pickpocketed in Barcelona. And I'll never forget your very kind and wise words over dinner in Marseille. Be the moose!

Hilary Selznick—you're a saint for putting up with me all those years! I'm honestly not sure how you did it. You were a wonderful work buddy, sitting with me for hours at the Waterstreet coffeehouse where most of this book was first drafted. And when the drafting stalled your kindness and encouragement were essential to getting it back on track. Thank you for everything.

There were a few others that came along later in the process, that were also influential in shaping of the novel that would become *Dying for a Living*. Fellow horseman Katie Pendleton, and fellow Breadloafer Katherine Tighe both being essential in the later editing/developmental phases. Thanks for your amazing feedback ladies!

Thanks to John K. Addis for his help with the original covers and author photo. And thanks to Christian Bentulan for the latest rendition of the covers.

And last but certainly not least, thanks to Kim Benedicto, to whom this book is dedicated. Not only is she the great love of my life, but she is also a great reader, supporter, and friend. She's responsible for talking me down from many an imaginary ledge, and easing me back into the writing chair where the actual work gets done.

Needless to say, this book would not have been possible without them.

ALSO BY KORY M. SHRUM

Dying for a Living series

Dying for a Living

Dying by the Hour

Dying for Her: A Companion Novel

Dying Light

Worth Dying For

Dying Breath

Dying Day

Shadows in the Water: Lou Thorne Thrillers

Shadows in the Water

Under the Bones

Danse Macabre

Carnival

Devil's Luck

Design Your Destiny Castle Cove series

Welcome to Castle Cove

Night Tide

The City: the 2603 novels

The City Below

The City Within

Learn more about Kory's work at: www.korymshrum.com

ABOUT THE AUTHOR

Kory M. Shrum is author of the bestselling *Shadows in the Water* and *Dying for a Living* series, as well as several other novels. She has loved books and words all her life. She reads almost every genre you can think of, but when she writes, she writes science fiction, fantasy, and thrillers, or often something that's all of the above.

In 2020, she launched a true crime podcast "Who Killed My Mother?" sharing the true story of her mother's tragic death. You can listen for free on YouTube or your favorite podcast app.

When not writing or producing her show, she can usually be found under thick blankets with snacks. The kettle is almost always on. When she's not eating, reading, writing, or indulging in her true calling as a stay-at-home dog mom, she loves to plan her next adventure. (Travel.)

She lives in Michigan with her equally bookish wife, Kim, and their rescue pug, Charley.

She'd love to hear from you!
www.korymshrum.com

Made in United States
North Haven, CT
10 November 2023